DAVID HANSARD

ONE
MINUTE
GONE

D0180035

A PORTER HALL NOVEL

Dead Road Press
Capitol Crime Writers

Contact: Deadroadpress@gmail.com

Design by Typeflow

ISBN-13: 978-0615887975
ISBN-10: 061588797X

For my parents,
Dallas and Yvonne Hansard
and
IN MEMORY OF
Camden Silvia,
taken far too soon

1

SHE STEPPED OUT OF A SHADOW AT THE FAR END OF THE room and began the long walk to the front door.

The room, the lobby of a high-rise condominium, was almost a block long. On one side were high windows, and near the front, a concierge desk. In the view of the man behind the desk, as long as that lobby was, it wasn't nearly long enough. He watched her like she was a parade, like she was meant to be watched. In replay the scene had a dreamy, Felliniesque quality, time-marked by the steady click of her spike heels on the marble floor. The skewed color rendition of the video enhanced the mystique, like an old Kodachrome set too many years near a window.

She was earthtones that day, colors of the fall. Sun-streaked brown hair, wide brown eyes in an oval face set off by a brown suit that looked hand-tailored, but was off-the-rack Bergdorf.

The 1947 rack, that is. The skirt was snug against her thighs and the fitted jacket emphasized her figure. Not that emphasis was needed.

The concierge, who watched her every step, would attest to that. So would the two college girls in flip-flops though they rolled their eyes at her dated couture. Still, each would have swapped a year of Daddy's tuition money for her figure.

Jamie Trent was her name and her outfit came from the Spence-Chapin Thrift Shop on New York's Upper East Side, that area of town being to collectors of pre-owned clothing what Florence is to art lovers. While some combed the thrifts for almost-new designer castoffs that could be had for a fraction of their boutique prices, Jamie sought the discards of society's *grande dames* of the Thirties, Forties and Fifties, whose closets passed to the charity shops when they passed on.

At the concierge desk, she stopped abruptly.

"Oh, hello, Miss Trent," the man said, as though noticing her for the first time.

"Orlando, I almost forgot. Put these in the lockbox. They're for 9H." She stepped over and handed him a set of keys with a tag on them.

"One of Mr. Hall's units. Yes, ma'am."

"I should leave him a note." She reached into her calfskin bag, a Chanel 2.55 from the late Fifties, and removed a small leather folio that held monogrammed notepaper and envelopes. She uncapped a fountain pen, a Parker 453, and wrote

Dear Porter,
  I need to talk to you, seriously. I regret this didn't work for us although I really tried. It would have been wonderful, but

as we both know, some things are meant to be, others are not.
See you at lunch. Ask for Babie, Baby.
   Love,
   Jamie

She glanced at her watch.

"This is silly. He'll be on his way to meet me when he gets this." She recapped her 1943 pen, supposedly like one Hemingway used, and stuck it in her purse.

She wadded the notepaper. Orlando extended a hand to take it, but Jamie tossed it over his shoulder. It banked off the wall and landed in a wastebasket. She winked at him.

"Two," he said, and smiled.

"If you see Porter, please tell him I'm at the restaurant."

She half-turned, stopped, and looked back at Orlando, who had started toward the room where the lockbox was kept. "Wait. I'm going to keep those. I've got a meeting with…" She looked briefly toward the front door, her deep concern visible even in the mediocre resolution of the security camera. "I'll drop them later."

He handed the keys back. She slipped them in the side pocket of her jacket and walked out the revolving door into the calm October light of East Twenty-second Street. Camera Three, an exterior camera, showed her heading west toward Fifth Avenue. She looked as good from the back as she did from the front. That was at 11:17 a.m.

Later, the shot from an interior camera would show another man exiting the curtained door behind the concierge desk. He reached into the wastebasket, removed the wadded notepaper, opened it, and read it. He said something to the concierge, which was unclear because the two college girls were passing by and their chatter muddled the sound.

The man re-crumpled the paper, dropped it back into the wastebasket, and followed them. He removed a cell phone from his pocket, punched a button, held it to his ear, and fell in behind the young women, his eyes affixed to their rear ends as though he were assigned to count the stitches on their jeans.

ON THE OTHER side of Broadway, Jamie used a pay phone. She was the only real estate agent in Manhattan who didn't own a cell phone, maybe the only one in the universe. She checked in with her office, told them she had a two o'clock meeting, she didn't say with whom, and asked her assistant to confirm a three o'clock showing at a condo in Chelsea.

She reached the restaurant at 11:35, where she was greeted with kisses on both cheeks by Tall Kate, a pretty, mocha-skinned African-American woman who was one of the owners. Kate told her that her table, in the back room against the Hepburn wall, would be ready in a few minutes.

The restaurant, Kates, was owned by Tall Kate Masters, who wasn't all that tall except when compared to her co-owner, Just Kate O'Meara. "Short Kate" was a more obvious nickname, but the five-two O'Meara disliked it.

The décor was all "Kates," floor-to-ceiling with photos and memorabilia of the famous: Kate Hepburn, Kate (Katherine) the Great, k.d. lang, Katie Couric, Kate Winslett, Cate Blanchett, others.

But it was Kate Hepburn that Jamie Trent worshipped, having once seen her on Third Avenue as the icon pushed heavy snow into the gutter in front of her townhouse. Jamie stared for a few moments until Hepburn looked at her. Her head had a slight tremor, but her eyes were clear, steady, piercing. Hepburn smiled. Jamie smiled back, flushed, and started across the street, almost stepping into the path of an oncoming taxi.

The actress once dubbed "The Most Powerful Woman in Hollywood" returned to clearing her walk.

Jamie thanked Tall Kate and took a seat at the bar. She removed a book, *Ship of Fools*, from her bag and began to read. Just Kate was behind the massive oak front bar, which, along with the mirrored back bar, had been extracted from her grandfather's defunct Irish pub in Red Hook, Brooklyn. She looked at the cover. "Oh, my. Another Kate."

"I hadn't thought of that," said Jamie, looking at Katherine Ann Porter's name across the top.

"We should make a place for her," said Tall Kate.

By 12:15, Porter still wasn't there. Jamie went outside and stood for a moment, looking toward Fifth Avenue, the direction from which he would likely come. She went back inside to a pay phone near the restrooms. At 12:19, the records would show, she placed a call to his home, and a minute later to his cell phone. She left messages both places saying she was at Kates, and leaving the number.

By 12:30, Jamie was growing more concerned. Porter might be ten minutes late, but beyond that he would call. She had known him for ten years, and dated him for one, long ago. He would call. Something bad had happened. She was sure of it. A waitress working the sidewalk tables came in and said a man outside was asking for her, saying Porter Hall wanted to see her. Jamie slid off the stool, took two steps toward the door, went back and grabbed her purse. She left her second Perrier, her book, and the unpaid tab.

At one o'clock, Just Kate noticed Jamie's book, check, and Perrier still on the bar. She picked them up and headed to the back room to take them to her. Two other women were at the table. She found Tall Kate and asked if she had seen Jamie.

"I guess something came up."

Kate O'Meara shook her head. "She left these."

"So?"

"In the book."

Tall Kate opened the book and saw the unpaid check for two small bottles of Perrier. "Oh, my God," she said, her face going a shade paler. "We better call."

They went to their tight windowless office, where Just Kate picked up the phone, called the Thirteenth Precinct on East Twenty-first Street, and explained the situation to a sergeant.

"Some chick walked a six dollar check? Hold on. I'll put out a BOLO, an APB, an Amber Alert. Want a SWAT team, maybe National Guard, too?"

"You don't get it, officer. Jamie wouldn't walk a six-*cent* check and we don't care about that anyway, and she wouldn't leave her book. She's the most…"

"No, you don't get it, lady. I got a stack of files on my desk, domestic violence, sexual assault, grand theft auto, breaking and entering, two murders, you name it, and you want me to go after some gal who beat a six buck check a half hour ago? Keep the damn book and call it even."

Just Kate's freckled Irish face turned a brilliant red and she screamed at the phone. "Not *go* after her, *find* her. And it's not the money. She stayed until four in the morning helping us clean up after a broken pipe and wouldn't even let us give her lunch the next day. If you…"

"Well, la-ti-da, call me heartless, call me lazy, call me in two days and file a report." said the officer, "If she don't show up."

Her head dropped and tears burned her eyes. She looked at Tall Kate. "They don't know. They don't care." Her hands were trembling.

"What can we do?"

How could they explain that the pope was more likely to rob a bank than Jamie Trent was to walk a check? Her ethics were as stubborn and old fashioned as her wardrobe, and to Jamie right was right, wrong was wrong, and things were just that simple.

The inescapable conclusion is that had Porter Hall left his place at the Medora condominium when he was supposed to, Jamie Trent would not have disappeared. But he got caught up in some crisis of his own, and it wasn't until the three-story clock on the Met Life tower outside his window began to gong noon that he realized the time. He grabbed his jacket and cell phone, found his sunglasses, which had mysteriously made their way to his daughter's vanity, hurried to the elevators, and pushed the call button. It came in thirty seconds and stopped five times on the way down.

When he reached the lobby, he checked the time: 12:04. He stepped out of the elevator and almost bumped into Marvin Plockman, the management company rep. Plockman was on his phone.

He said, "Marvin, hey. I need to talk to you."

Plockman raised a finger, nodded over his shoulder, and kept walking. He went through a metal door marked STAFF ONLY, which led to a service corridor.

"Marvin, it's important," Porter called. The door thunked shut behind him.

Porter shrugged. "Yeah, call me later. That's fine."

Just then Orlando, the concierge, appeared carrying a Styrofoam cup and a paper bag with the logo of a neighborhood sandwich shop. He was on his way to the break room, accessed by the same door Marvin Plockman had disappeared into.

"Oh, Mr. Hall. Miss Trent said to tell you she's waiting at the restaurant. She still has the keys to 9H. That's the only back-up set."

"Thanks. And if you see Plockman back there, tell him to call me."

Porter turned into the long lobby, a faux-1890s concoction with oak-paneled walls, period furniture, imitation Bierstadt, Eakins and Durant nature scenes, and copper compact-fluorescent fixtures made to look like the gas sconces you might find in a turn-of-the-century theater.

At that moment two men in bad suits entered the front door. Two minutes earlier, even one minute earlier, and Porter would have missed them. He would have been gone, out the glass doors, walking briskly toward Kates, where he would have arrived at 12:10. He would have gone to Jamie at the bar, put his hand on her shoulder, kissed her cheek, and said, "Hi, Babie." They would have walked to the table that awaited them beneath framed original posters of *Bringing Up Baby*, *Adam's Rib*, and *The Philadelphia Story*.

But that Wednesday, Porter Hall wasn't a minute earlier, so Jamie was gone. By 12:30, when she really needed him to be there, he was blocks away, cuffed to a metal bench in the local precinct. His eyes were closed, and a song about *a candy-colored clown* was playing in his head.

Jamie Trent is gone and Porter Hall is the reason. He failed her. It's just that simple.

He believes that.

I believe that.

I'm Porter Hall.

2

WITH ITS EASY-TO-CLEAN GLAZED-BLOCK WALLS AND CLUT-tered bulletin boards, the ground floor of the Thirteenth Precinct looked like an elementary school. The fluorescent tubes above me were snow bright and humming like a power line. As annoying as that was, it wasn't my real problem. My real problem was the clock on the wall. It said 3:23. In twenty-two minutes, a small yellow bus would stop in front of my apartment, and my tired, cranky six-year-olds would get off. Assuming I was there to meet them. If I wasn't, if no one was, I didn't know what would happen. I closed my eyes.

A moment later someone tapped my leg. It was Sergeant Diaz. Again. She was pretty and didn't smell like a cop. She had checked on me twice before. In her palm was a small, rolled tube of dark plastic. She pulled and it unfurled into a pair of disposable shades.

"I went to the eye doctor last week," she said, and nodded up toward the buzzing fixture. "I found these in my desk. Want them?"

"That'd be great." I reached. There was a loud clink as the handcuffs stopped my hand.

The sergeant laughed and gently placed the plastic over my face.

"Thank you."

She wiped her thumb across my cheek and walked away.

I closed my eyes and an old Wurlitzer that had been running in my head for a couple of days began to play an appropriate Merle Haggard song, one about a prisoner being led to his doom. A woman's voice interrupted. "How's it going?"

I opened my eyes. She was mid-twenties, petite, attractive. She wore jeans and running shoes and had shoulder-length dark hair pulled into a ponytail. Three hours ago when I was brought in, there'd been several reporters and photographers outside. She was one of them.

She said, "You're Porter Hall."

"Actually, I already knew that. Who are you?"

"Cat Marten, *New York Journal*."

"Cat." I smiled.

"What?"

"Good name. As in Stevens or Ballou?"

"Neither. Catalina Island."

"Bet there's a story there."

She shrugged, didn't offer to tell it.

"How'd you get in?"

"The officer on the desk knows me. He said not to talk to you, then he winked. So either it's okay, or he wants a date. Or both."

"Or neither."

She moved closer, studying my face. "Nice shades."

"Thanks. A present from Sergeant Diaz. That light gets annoying." I nodded at the fluorescent.

"Speaking of Diaz, she asked me to give you this."

She handed me a business card. With my free hand I pulled off the plastic shades so I could read. They snapped into their tube shape around my finger, and I slipped them into my shirt pocket.

The card had the NYPD logo, and under that it said Sergeant Samantha Diaz. It gave a main number and a direct line. On the other side was a 917 number in pencil.

"What's this for?"

"She thinks you're cute. That's her cell on the back."

"She's into criminals?"

"I get the feeling she doesn't think you're much of a criminal. I'm inclined to agree."

"About which?"

A quick flush came to her cheeks. "That you're not all that bad."

I stuck the card in my pocket.

"Why?"

"Do you know the last time someone in the City of New York was charged with 'inciting to riot'?"

"Vietnam era, maybe?"

She had delicate hands, a turquoise and silver ring on her right hand, no jewelry on her left.

"Actually, there was a case in Harlem recently, but before that it was twenty years. You must be special. What else did they charge you with?"

"Nothing. When they picked me up they said they were going to charge me with starting a riot and assault with a deadly weapon. But they haven't booked me, charged me, anything. I've just been sitting for three hours."

She frowned. "What was the weapon?"

"A gavel."

"Like judges use? That wasn't nice."

"I know. I'm the one who got hit." I turned my head so she could see my left ear. The two-day-old bruise was mauve and purple and pink, the colors of a western sunset.

"Then why are you the one in custody?"

"The guy who hit me claims I broke his nose."

The clock said 3:37: eight minutes until the small yellow bus with its dreadlocked driver released my mismatched twins. Assuming I was there to meet them. If I ran, I could make it in three, but there was that bench to deal with.

She said, "Did you call a lawyer?"

"They said getting lawyered up makes you look bad."

"You bought that?"

"Of course not. I called but he was in a meeting, a long one, I guess, because he's still not here. I asked for another call. They said later, maybe."

"And you've been on this bench the whole time? That doesn't make sense. There's got to be a story."

"And whatever it is, it's yours. An exclusive." I glanced at the wall behind her.

"Sure," she said with half a smile, "but there's a catch."

"How'd you know?"

"I've been down this road. And you can't keep your eyes off the damn clock. Let's hear it."

I told her.

She gave her head a quick shake and tilt, like she was trying to get water out of her ears. "Did you say pick up your children? You want me to babysit?" She looked toward the lobby and exhaled. "I'll give you this, Mr. Hall. It's original."

"Call me Porter. Will you do it?"

She looked at a Bulova on her right wrist. "You don't have a nanny?"

"Luisa, but she's off today."

Cat Marten stood, smoothed her pants. "A wife, maybe?"

"Not around."

She gave a slight nod. She wanted to ask more, but didn't. I told her what she needed to know and she wrote down the key points in a small spiral.

"Don't forget the code, or they won't go with you."

"Slimey toads?" she lifted an eyebrow.

"No, slithey toves."

"Brilliant?"

"No, brillig."

"What's 'brillig'?"

The thing about Ginger's shoe."

Then they'll say, 'What time is it?' And you say…"

"Humpty Dumpty says it's four o'clock."

She put the pen and notebook in her pocket, looked at the cop on the desk and then me. "A quote from Humpty Dumpty. Editor's going to love this one." She started away, stopped, looked back. "Are you sure you trust me to get your kids?"

The cops knew her, she worked for a major newspaper, and she passed the eye-ball test. Not that those things mattered. I could have mentioned I didn't have much of a choice.

Instead: "If you can't trust the press, who can you trust?"

She thought about it. "That's' a very good question."

"Can you be there in four minutes?"

She looked at the Nikes on her feet. "I was supposed to be off today." Her eyes narrowed. "Are you crying?"

"No." I pressed my eyes tight, and tears fell down my cheeks. "It's the lights." She reached into my pocket, pulled out the curled plastic shades, opened them and set them on my face. She glanced at her wrist and walked away.

3

A FEW MINUTES LATER, A UNIFORMED OFFICER WHO DIDN'T smell or look as good as Sergeant Diaz removed the cuffs and escorted me to a cluttered room on the second floor. He directed me to a chair and pushed a desk phone in front of me. Again, I called Dennis Fenton, my divorce attorney, the only attorney I had a working relationship with at the time. He answered.

I said, "Why didn't you come?"

"I don't do criminals."

"That's all you do. Besides, I'm not a criminal, just misunderstood. Come get me out." Forty minutes later he showed up with a short, solid man named Webster, who was once with the DA, Fenton said, and the only one in their office who knew anything about criminals. Webster went away and eventually returned with Detective Arnold Kurch, the one who arrested me. Kurch was short, puffy, and disheveled, and he had a black pencil-mark mustache like an old-time matinee idol.

"You're free to go," he said, running a finger above his lip. He handed me a bag with the things they took from me when I came in. Phone, sunglasses, belt, wallet, money.

"You're letting me go? Seriously? You keep me three, no, four hours, and let me walk?"

"Get outta here. You got trouble with your ears?" He looked at my left one, grinned. "Guess you do."

Webster said, "Detective."

Kurch spoke to the floor. "The department wishes to extend its apologies for any inconvenience you have experienced. This was the result of a misunderstanding." The words had the sincerity of numerals stamped on a license plate.

I leaned into his face. "Kurch. Explain."

He put his fingers on my chest and pushed me back. "Hey, I said I'm sorry. OK, I'm *very* sorry. How's that? Or maybe you wanna stay?"

"No, I want to know who's behind this dimwit stunt, you denotative ass..."

Webster yanked my arm and shoved me toward the door. Over my shoulder I said, "You've heard of harassment, Kurch, false arrest, lawsuit? Know any two-syllable words?"

Webster guided me down the stairs and out the front doors where Fenton was waiting on the sidewalk. Webster pushed me against the brick and held me. "One arrest a day isn't enough, Hall?"

"I just want to know..."

He held up a palm. "They said they got a call from the commissioner's office to pick you up. Later, they got another one from the commissioner's office and were told to let you go."

"The police commissioner? That commissioner?" Webster nodded, and Fenton looked as surprised as I was. "You can't be serious."

His eyes turned toward an ambulance with its siren pulsing as it rushed down Second Avenue. "It's highly unusual. I'll grant you that."

I took a step back toward the station. "Something's going on and I want…"

Webster grabbed one arm, Fenton the other, and they guided me to the curb. They stopped a cab and put me in. Fenton told the driver my address and Webster leaned into my face. "Go home, get some rest. Don't make this worse. Go home, Porter. Home." He slammed the door.

I started to tell him that wasn't feasible. Home was two thousand miles away.

4

AT TWENTY-THIRD STREET THE DRIVER HEADED WEST, TO-
ward my apartment. I owned it, it was where I lived, where I
had lived for ten years, but it wasn't home. Home had mountains, not hills that tried to pass as mountains, snakes that could
kill you, animals that would eat you, and winters so hard you
could freeze to death on a mild day. Home had endless plains
and distant purple peaks from the tops of which you would
swear you could see right through eternity. However, as great
as home was, the canyons of Manhattan, with their hard-edged,
plumb-straight walls of glass and brick and mortar, had one
thing weathered Western arroyos didn't: cell service. I took out
my phone and checked messages. There was one, from Jamie
Trent.

"Porter? Are you okay? It's 12:20, and I'm starting to worry.
Call if you need me. I showed 9H, and I'll tell you about that,

but I really need to talk to you about something else. I'm at Kates." She left the number.

Obviously she wouldn't still be at the restaurant so I tried her office. Her assistant said she wasn't in. I left a message and tried her home, got her machine, left another message.

When I walked into my lobby the doorman said, "Something wrong, sir?"

He'd been on duty when the police came. "No. Everything's fine," I said. "I like getting arrested. You should try it sometime."

He glanced sideways, said softly, "I have. Sucks."

"Are the kids upstairs?"

"A young woman brought them in. Luisa's back, too."

INSIDE MY APARTMENT I found Luisa, our live-in, sitting on the sofa between my kids. B.J., my son, was on her right, and Cici, my daughter, on her left. Luisa was sobbing while Cici, also crying, was trying to comfort her in Spanish.

Cat Marten was in an armchair looking miserable. She raised her eyes. "Porter, you're home."

B.J. said, "Dad, Luisa wants to know who will take care of her and us if you're in jail. She also asked if we'll go live with Grandmother and Granddad and if she should pack."

"Luisa, I'm not going to jail." She looked up and the sobs began to wind down. I got the feeling she was disappointed she wouldn't be moving to a mansion in New Jersey anytime soon.

I turned to the kids. "Hey, gang."

B.J. hugged me and Cici glared from the sofa, arms crossed, tears streaking her face.

"Were you in jail?" she said.

"I was at the police station, but we just talked."

She came over. I picked her up and she clamped her arms around my neck. "Can you go play a game or watch TV? I need to talk to Ms. Marten."

"You mean Aunt Mary Ann?" said B.J. "Did you and the Professor find Ginger's shoe?" Our emergency code, the one required for them to go with a stranger without prior notice, was all nonsense, made up on a rainy day to kill time. I was sure it would never be used. "And tell her it's 'slithey toves,' not 'sliding totes.' Cici almost didn't go."

Luisa took the kids to the playroom and I went to Cat, who had moved to a window that overlooked Madison Square Park. To the right was the Metropolitan Life clock tower, and beyond it, to the north, New York Life and the skyscrapers of Midtown: Empire State, Chrysler, Citibank.

Cat Marten said, "Where did they learn Spanish?"

"Same place they learned French, German, and a little Swedish, from nannies. It's staggering how fast kids can pick up a new language."

She looked around the room. "Nice place."

It had clean-lined, neutral-colored furniture, glass-topped tables, and no clutter. The artwork was simple and non-representational, nothing fussy. My wife couldn't tolerate it. It made her ill, literally.

"You must love living here."

"It's fine, for a box in a high-rise."

"Some box. Your living room is bigger than my apartment."

"Would you like something to drink? Coffee, tea, Yoohoo?"

"Yoohoo?" She wrinkled her nose. "Coffee's fine.."

When it was ready, I gave her the Snow White mug, took Mickey as the Sorcerer's Apprentice for myself, put milk in mine, and watched her add two teaspoons of sugar to hers. We sat at the kitchen table. She stirred and sipped.

"That's bad for your teeth."

"Thanks, Dad, I'll be sure to brush. What's this so-called *exclusive* you promised me?" She waggled her eyebrows. "Remember?"

"Do you read the *Post*?"

"I only look at the pictures."

"So you saw me yesterday." She shook her head. I went to the den, got the paper, showed her page six.

"How'd they get pictures?"

"A guy in the building is a photo stringer for the tabloids. He was at the meeting Monday night."

"Why was he there with his camera?"

"Coincidence, I guess."

"Let me get this straight. The riot you started was at a home-owners' meeting? I've heard of people going to their apartments and coming back with guns and bats. If they started arresting people for that, Riker's couldn't hold them all."

My phone buzzed. The caller ID indicated Jamie Trent's office. I said, "Excuse me, but this is important." I hit the button. "Jamie, I am really sorry I missed lunch, but the strangest thing happened. Did you get my message?"

A man's voice, obviously not Jamie, said, "Porter, it's Herb Schneider." Herb was her boss.

"Is everything okay? Where's Jamie?"

"I was hoping she was with you. So, no, it's not. She missed her appointments this afternoon and hasn't called in. Jamie doesn't miss appointments."

"What can I do?"

"Nothing I know of. We've called the police, friends, every clinic and hospital in Manhattan. Not a trace."

"Are the police helping?"

"They said she's probably off with a boyfriend, happens all the time. File a report in two days if she doesn't show up."

"She has a boyfriend?"

"Not that I know of." Herb paused, cleared his throat. "I'll let you know if we hear anything."

"That sounded serious," Cat said.

"It's…I don't know, it might be. I was on my to meet a friend for lunch when they arrested me. She was at the restaurant for a while, but hasn't been seen since."

Cat nodded, sipped her coffee. "Speaking of odd, there was this man on the elevator when I brought the kids up. He got off on your floor. I thought maybe he was following us."

"What'd he look like?"

"Short, odd face, and very, I don't know, meticulous. He had an umbrella and a bowler hat. He looked like he was on his way to some high society party a hundred years ago."

"28A, across the hall. Did he say anything, bother you?"

"No. I just got a weird vibe, like he was dissecting me."

"You want me to go hit him or something?"

"Maybe later."

My coffee was too bitter to drink. I got up and dumped it in the sink. "Would you like some wine?"

She checked the big clock on the Met Life building. "Sure."

I poured us each a glass. We went to the living room, sat down and clinked glasses. We didn't say what we were clinking to. We didn't know.

"Your story," she said.

"Okay, but first a question. Why were you at the precinct this afternoon? Was something big going down?"

She gave me a perplexed look. "Uh, yeah. Obviously."

"What?"

"You."

"Seriously? I was the story? What'd they tell you?"

"Just that someone who was a member of an important family was about to be arrested."

"That's it?"

"I don't mean to insult your capacity for criminal mischief, Porter, but so far this exclusive is a dud. You may have to pay me for the babysitting. Tell me the rest of it, from the beginning."

"What do you mean?"

"Where you're from, where you went to school, why you're in New York, all about your prominent family, how you wound up in custody. We call it background."

I took a sip of my wine. It tasted bitter too. "Born in Texas, grew up in Wyoming, undergrad at UW, then the University of Texas at Austin for a Ph.D. program. Got a job, went to Dallas for a while, ended up in New York." I set my wine down. "That's the long version. Sorry if I bored you."

She patted her hand over her open mouth, as though stifling a yawn. "Sorry if I dozed off in the middle. You do love to talk about yourself. So you're Dr. Hall?"

"I didn't finish my dissertation. I taught a couple of sections of macro to undergrads while I was supposed to be writing, but I didn't finish it."

"My father's an English professor. He gets highly annoyed when that happens. What stopped you?"

"My topic was co-relatives in population aggregation and income levels, and monetary velocity as related to the growth of markets. I came up with an algorithm."

She gasped and thumped her palm on her chest. "Oh, Porter. That makes me want to tear my clothes off right here."

"I know. Stay calm. You'll be fine in a few minutes. That's why I never wrote it. If I mentioned my topic at a party, women would start screaming and throwing underwear at me."

"Seriously, why didn't you finish?"

"I delivered a paper at a conference in Dallas. A big developer was in the audience, understood what I was talking about, and offered me a job. The algorithm allows you to plug in variables and get a reasonably accurate prediction of the success of retail centers in specific locations. When you're investing between half a billion and two billion a pop to build a project, you want all the help you can get. My starting salary was double what the head of the econ department was making.

"I spent a couple of years in Dallas and then moved to the New York office. They asked me to manage it, and I quit. I don't like managing. I started investing on my own and consulting on the side."

Outside my window the scene had passed from daylight to dusk. Tears ran down my cheeks. I blinked like I had a lash.

Cat leaned toward me. "Are you crying? Again?"

5

"No." I wiped my eyes. "It's allergies."

"Of course it is," she said. "And your colorful ear. When did you get that?"

"Monday night, at the homeowners' meeting. I was presiding and had a gavel. It was your usual dull event until a little old Chinese man named Jackson Wu stood up and accused me of taking kickbacks from my brother-in-law in the carpet business."

"Are you?"

"I don't take kickbacks, because I don't do things like that, and I don't have a brother-in-law — have never had a brother-in-law — in any business. After that Mr. Wu called everyone on the board a bunch of 'big *thiefs*.'"

"Why?"

"No idea. His daughter kept trying to get him to sit down, but the guy on his other side would say something and he'd start up again."

"Who was the guy egging him on?"

"By an odd coincidence, it was your elevator companion, 28A."

"How'd you get hit with your own gavel?"

"People started yelling and I started banging the gavel to get the meeting back to order. The head broke off, a guy picked it up, came over and started yelling at me. I walked away and he slammed me with it. I took a blind swing backwards and broke his nose. Or so I'm told."

"That's your assault charge."

"Apparently."

She picked up her wine, sipped it, and looked out at the scattered lights as they glowed and glistened in the charcoal night. After a moment she furrowed her brow. "Can I ask something that may be a little personal?"

"Sure."

"Where is your children's mother?"

"New Jersey, with her parents."

"Are you divorced?" She held up a hand. "Sorry. If that's intrusive…"

"It's fine. By coincidence, Monday morning I got a call from my divorce attorney saying my terms had been accepted."

"So that's good, right? It'll be over with."

"Mostly it's weird. The terms have been on the table for three years. There's been only one point of contention ever. Custody."

"She didn't want to give you joint?"

"They would have been thrilled with joint. I insisted on sole."

"You didn't want their mother to share custody?"

"She has issues."

"What kind?"

"She…" I paused. "She's been known to have a tenuous relationship with reality. She used to get confused about certain things."

"Such as?"

"Who I was, who she was, who the two kids in the playroom were. When my attorney told me he accepted my terms it didn't make sense. He could have had the same deal three years ago."

"*He*? Is your wife a man?"

"No, but her father is, and he's the one who wanted the divorce, and he's the one who was adamant about joint custody. Then, by a strange coincidence, an hour after the call from my attorney, my mother-in-law called and said she wants the kids to still come out this weekend, but Laurie won't be there. She's moving to her own place."

"Like an apartment, alone?"

"A *facility*." Finger quotes.

She raised an eyebrow. "Was there a connection?"

"Between what?"

"The same morning you agree on a settlement, your wife moves into a *facility*." She waggled her eyebrows.

"I…" I put my feet on the table and leaned my head back. Tears spilled from my eyes and I wiped them away. "No. At least I can't imagine one." I waited for Cat to mention the tears but she didn't.

"How's your relationship with your in-laws?"

"Good, or at least it used to be. My father-in-law can be difficult. He's opinionated."

"You're not?"

I opened my eyes wide. "*Moi?* Certainly not. We used to argue a lot, and we're both a little competitive. We played golf several times a month, fished, skied, went to football games.

Before Laurie moved out I managed most of his real estate dealings. He's got quite a bit of money."

"So that's the prominent family they were talking about."

"I guess."

"Were you the son he never had?"

"With Laurie he didn't need a son. She's an amazing athlete, marksman, horsewoman, you name it."

Cat wrote in her notebook. I said, "Jamie called, too."

"Who?"

"Jamie Trent. the one I was supposed to meet for lunch, the one who's missing."

"Why is that important? Another coincidence?"

"What do you mean?"

"You're using the word about once a minute," she said. "Why is it important that Jamie called two days ago?"

"It's not. It's just happened to remember that, and now no one's seen her in a while."

Cat looked at the clock. "Six hours isn't that long. She's an adult."

"No, but it's out of character."

"Maybe her battery's dead, or she lost her phone."

"She doesn't have a cell phone."

"A real estate agent without a cell phone. Is that legal? Is she a Luddite?"

"No, just stubborn as hell. She thinks phones are fine if they have rotary dials. And at this point being unwired is her signature."

I started to take another drink, felt nauseated, and set my glass down.

"Porter, what's the matter?"

"Nothing. I'm a little woozy. I haven't eaten since breakfast. Maybe I shouldn't be drinking."

She leaned toward me, extended a hand, and with the tips of her fingers pressed hard behind my left ear. I winced.

"What was that for?"

"There's a lump." She wiped her thumbs under my eyes and spread the dampness. "Did you cry when you got married?"

"No."

"When your kids were born?"

"No."

"Do you cry in movies?"

"*It's a Wonderful Life, Imitation of Life, Born Free.* And *Bambi*, right after the fire."

"If you don't cry in those, you're probably a psychopath. I covered football in college so I've seen this. You're weepy, disoriented, dizzy, and sensitive to light. That's why you were using Diaz's disposable shades."

"No, that was because I wanted to look cool."

"Right. How does that wine taste?"

"Bitter."

"Actually, it's a little sweet. You should see a doctor. And don't drink any more alcohol. You've got symptoms of a concussion."

She leaned back and crossed her arms. "Did you do anything yesterday?"

I squinted. "Tuesday?"

"Yeah, that yesterday."

I stood. "Let me show you something." I led her to my dining room where my nine-foot-long trestle table was covered with stacks of papers.

"What's this?" she said.

"Financial reports. After the meeting I quit as board president and got appointed board treasurer. The old treasurer sent me these."

"Why is this interesting?"

"It's not. It's boring as hell. But it's what made me late to meet Jamie. I started going through back statements and it looks like a lot of money is unaccounted for. There may be a good explanation."

Although I couldn't imagine what that might be. I had found double billings and double payments, all of them big-ticket items. Withholding taxes, fuel oil, water and waste water, insurance, electricity, some as high as forty thousand. It appeared that at least half a million dollars was missing. That could explain why Marvin Plockman, our management rep, was avoiding me, even though I suspected he was more incompetent than crooked. When I needed something done, or when the board needed something done, it was Marvin who did it. I had to tell him five or six times and threaten to fire him, but eventually things got done, some of the time, anyway. I was anxious to hear his explanation.

Cat's phone buzzed and she looked. "My editor wants me at the office ten minutes ago. Can we talk tomorrow?"

6

Thursday morning, after B.J. and Cici left for school in the small yellow bus with its Rasta driver, seriously cool in his dreads and Wayfarers, I went around the corner for coffee and a bagel. I didn't order, didn't need to, because the counter girl with red hair got it for me anyway, same order as always, same smile as always. I took it across the street to the park, sat on a bench, and called Jamie's apartment. There was no answer so I tried her office. A raspy voice I didn't know said, "May I help you?" I said, "Herb Schneider, please."

"Porter, this is Herb."

"Sorry, it didn't sound like you."

"I haven't slept. I haven't even been home. We're still looking for Jamie."

"Are the police helping?"

"Now they won't even take my calls." I waited for my eyes to get damp, but they didn't. That was a good sign. I said I'd get back to him and called Cat.

"Porter," she said, but her tone was formal. Her business voice, I guessed.

I told her Jamie was still missing and the police weren't helping, asked if she'd give them a call. "Sometimes they're more responsive to the press, I think."

"And sometimes they're not. I'll see what I can do."

A few minutes later she called back, said she'd spoken to someone at the Thirteenth who got huffy when asked why they wouldn't look for Jamie. She said if that didn't help to let her know.

BACK IN MY apartment, I went to the dining room and retrieved the pages that showed the double billings, along with previous year's consolidated summary, and the last six monthly summaries. I took those to my office and scanned them into my computer. While that was going on, I called the management office again. A man said, "This is Mr. Plockman."

I said, "Good morning, Marvin. Can you..."

"Oh, hey, buddy. I heard about all that junk yesterday. Are you okay? Can I do anything?"

"I'm fine, and you can do something. Tell me why we're making double payments for insurance, FICA, elec...?"

"We're not." He was emphatic enough to let me know the discussion was over. I love quick, decisive answers uncluttered by fact. "Porter, what is it? Give it to me straight."

"That's what I'm doing. I'm emailing you a list of bills I have questions about. Check them out and give me an explanation." The scan was finished and I forwarded the PDF to Marvin.

"Porter," there was a long pause. I could hear him breathing heavily and shuffling papers. There were some clicks, suggesting he was looking at the pages I'd sent. "Porter, now listen to me, Porter. I always take care of you, and you know it. Let me know exactly what you need, exactly, and I'll take care of it this time too. But please be reasonable."

"I just told you what I need, Marvin, and this is as reasonable as it gets."

I hung up, and my phone rang. Herb Schneider said, "Whatever you did, thanks. The police are coming today to go through Jamie's files and talk to people in the office."

"That wasn't a favor, Herb. I want her back too."

I HAD JUST returned the documents I downloaded to the dining room when I heard three knocks on my door that sounded like they were made by a wrecking ball. I rushed to open it before there were three more that would have buckled the metal and ripped it from the frame. In the hallway was Bobby, my six-four, two-hundred-seventy-pound street-find with an IQ about the same as the Wyoming speed limit. He had short hair and small eyes set in a big head. He whuffed, "Porter they're doing it again what you told them not to do they're doing it again."

Bobby, who lived in a rent-controlled apartment with his mother a few blocks away, used to sit for hours in front of our building on the brick planter box, an out-sized, soft-faced gargoyle, watching people go in and out. After I fired the night porter, the fourth in three months, this time for a technical infraction of building rules, i.e., a prohibition against selling angel dust and crack out the service door during your shift, I offered Bobby the position.

The building superintendent at that time, a cousin of the recently fired night man, who probably had another cousin already lined up for the job, glanced at me, at Bobby, and put his face back in his paper. I told him Bobby was taking the position. He said, "I ain't hiring no retard. I'll quit."

I said, "Call me if you need a reference."

Bobby started that night.

"What are you talking about, Bobby?"

"They're putting my boxes away Porter. The jugs are mine and the rolled-up things are theirs but they've been emptying my boxes that's not fair you said so remember."

"Wait. You want them to take the supplies they put away off the shelves so you can put them away?"

"It's my stuff my job you said so they can't have my job."

"Of course not. I'll check on it." He stood waiting, like a dog that wants to be taken out, his head slowly moving up and down. I was thinking about how I was going to explain to the others they were doing too much work. "Later, Bobby."

"Promise Porter."

"I promise." Bobby ambled toward the elevator. After he was gone I went down to the lobby where Jorgé, one of our concierges, was reviewing a list, probably having to do with Christmas tips.

"Jorgé."

He looked up, tilted his head back. "*Mr.* Hall." He always italicized *mister* to let me know the esteem in which he held me.

"Keys to the basement, please."

He didn't move.

"Jorgé."

"I'm sorry, sir, but Mr. Plockman said no one was to have building keys without prior written authorization from him. Would you like a request form?"

"And Mr. Plockman reports to the board, of which I am a member. Is that right?" He nodded. "Did Mr. Plockman also explain how to file for unemployment? I hear you can do it on-line now."

Jorgé stood there long enough to show me he wasn't intimidated, walked into the backroom, returned with a large ring that held about twenty keys, and dropped it on the counter. As I walked away he picked up the phone.

The typical basement in a New York City residential building is a cold, dank dungeon full of small wild things, but without the charm. It is littered with brooms, mops, boxes, and the detritus of the humans who live above. It smells like mildew and heartbreak. Not ours. Ours is clean, dry, well lit, recently painted beige, and the doors and closets are better labeled than some museum exhibits. It is immaculate and smells like artificial strawberries.

In the supply room I found a shelf full of five-gallon plastic jugs labeled as cleaning solvent. I took one down, removed the lid, and sniffed. There wasn't much of a scent. The color was about right, but a good whiff of our regular cleaning solution would reduce your IQ by twenty points. I checked another bottle, and then several more. Every one was full of colored water. That explained why the other porters were doing Bobby's work. If one of the jugs happened to come open, even Bobby could tell the difference between hydrochloric acid and green Kool Aid.

I heard something behind me, and started to turn. That's when the curtain came down on that scene.

7

"PORTER ARE YOU OKAY YOU'RE BLEEDING POR-
TER YOUR HEAD."

Bobby loomed above me. It took me a few seconds to figure out where I was and why Bobby was there. "I'm okay. Help
me up." I extended my hand. Bobby ignored it, squatted like
a weightlifter going for five hundred in the clean-and-jerk, and
lifted me with no more effort than it takes me to lift B.J. or
Cici.

"Take you to the hospital Porter."

Had I agreed, he would have carried me to St. Vincent's on
West Eleventh Street or New York Presbyterian on Two-hun-
dred twentieth.

"Just my apartment. I can walk."

He let me down, turned to close the door, and noticed the
shelves. "Porter my jugs my jugs they're gone Porter."

He was right. The plastic bottles with the fake solvent had all been removed.

"It's called evidence, Bobby."

"They're my jugs Porter."

When I got upstairs, I used the spray nozzle in the kitchen to wash the blood from my hair. I went to the medicine cabinet, dressed the wound, went to the den and sat down. Half an hour later I woke with a serious headache. I knew I should stay awake and upright, and was trying to think of something to engage me. I remembered my other headache, the thousands of sheets of looming fraud issues laid out on my dining table.

I made my way on wobbly legs to the dining room. What I saw almost gave me another concussion. The room, except for the furniture, was bare. Between the time I left my apartment to go to the basement and the time Bobby brought me back, 25,000 sheets of paper had disappeared. I checked cabinets, closets, other rooms. Not that there was anyone to move them, or any place to put them, but I checked anyway. There was nothing. I thought about calling the police, but if they weren't interested in looking for a missing woman, I was pretty sure they weren't going to look for paper.

I went back to the living room, sat down, and tried to stay awake. I kept drifting into groggy memories of conversations that never happened with friends I never had. The buzzer of the building intercom woke me. I got up slowly, went to the front door, and picked up the handset.

"Miss Marten is here," the doorman said. I told him to send her up. I leaned against the wall and waited until a gong sounded. I opened the door.

Cat was wearing a brown leather jacket, tan slacks, and a silk blouse. She smelled good. She was also wearing a smile I hadn't seen before. When she noticed my head, she took her smile back and put it away.

"You look nice," I said. I started to help her out of her jacket, but she pushed my hand away.

"You don't. Go sit down."

I went and sat on the sofa and she stood over me. She tilted my head toward her, looked at the wound, and ripped the bandage off.

"Ouch. What are you doing?"

"Where are your first aid supplies?"

"Hall bath, on the left."

She took me by the wrist, led me to the bathroom and told me to sit on the edge of the tub. She found bandages, Neosporin, and scissors, and trimmed the hair around the wound. She put on disinfectant and a butterfly bandage.

"You had hair in the cut and it was going to get infected."

She lifted my chin and looked at my face.

"You look nice," I said.

She put her fingers on my cheek and then my forehead. Her eyes were sad. "Thanks," she said. "But you already said that."

She leaned close and looked in my eyes. "Do you have a thermometer?"

I pointed at the cabinet. She found it, turned it on, and when it was reset put in my mouth. When it beeped, she took it out and looked. "Ninety-eight point two. That's not good."

"It means I don't have a fever, right?"

She didn't answer.

I could feel tears gushing down my cheeks. She dabbed my face with a tissue, walked me to the living room and went to the kitchen. She came back with a glass of water that was warm, a Ziploc bag with crushed ice in it, and a dishtowel. She told me to take a drink. I could see from the water in the glass that my hand was trembling. She told me to lean my head back. She put the ice pack on it and fixed the towel to hold the baggie in place.

"You're probably in shock. The knot on the outside is huge and I can only imagine what's inside. Sit while I find the closest ER. But don't lie down."

"Bellevue."

"That's where you want to go?"

"That's the closest. I'm not going there. They killed Andy Warhol."

"They'll want to know what happened."

"Some kind of infection is what the papers said."

"Not to Warhol. To you."

I gave her a brief synopsis of the phony inventory, losing consciousness, Bobby finding me, and the missing jugs. "And one other thing. Go look in the dining room." She was back in less than a minute. "When did this happen?"

"While I was downstairs."

"Who has keys to your apartment?"

"The front desk has everyone's. And I may not have locked it anyway."

"Who would do this, and why?"

"No idea." I shrugged. "The documents were copies and I can get another set so I don't even know what the point was."

"Like you didn't know the point of your arrest. That was strange too."

"Because I didn't do anything, or because the order came from the police commissioner?"

"The *what?*"

"Yeah. That's where the order to pick me up came from. Same with the order to release me."

"That's more than strange, Porter. I was going to say it was strange because they didn't follow procedure. They didn't put you in lock-up, they held you but didn't process you, and they let you go not long after it was too late to meet your kids. Remember?"

"Coincidence."

"There's that word again." She furrowed her brow. "I had a journalism professor, lousy teacher, real bitch, but the one thing I got from her was this. If you want to be a good reporter you learn to look at what's there, not what you think is there, or what you think is supposed to be there."

"So what's there that I don't see?"

"They didn't charge you. Maybe they never intended to. They picked you up and held you incommunicado for four hours, which made you miss your kids' bus and your lunch with Jamie, who's now missing. And your attorney wouldn't take the one call they let you make."

"Those sound like coincidences."

She shook her head. "We've got to get you to a doctor. Your brain isn't working very well."

Before I could respond the intercom buzzed and Cat went to answer. I closed my eyes and drifted in semi-twilight down an empty street to that dim café where dream and reality sit at the same small table, drink from the same bottle, and tell each other lies. In the doorway of my dream, or my living room, it was hard to tell one from the other, a man appeared. A man in a bad suit.

8

THE WORLD FELT VAGUE AS A WISHFUL THEORY, DISTANT AS A bitter lover, hollow as a polite kiss. Cat was above me. I reached, but it was like trying to touch a hologram.

She said, "Are you awake?"

"I don't know." I pulled my hand back. "Are you real?"

"Depends. What's my name?"

"Cat. Don't you know?"

"The last time you woke up you called me Barbara Ann and G-L-O-R-I-A."

My internal Wurlitzer must have hit a patch of girl-name songs.

"One question," I said.

"Sure."

"Why am I in a hospital?"

"Does the term 'concussion' ring any bells?"

"Which one?"

"Concussion or hospital?" she said.

"Hospital."

"St. Vincent's." She touched my face. I started to sit up but she pressed me gently down. My head felt like it was full of wet cement and I wanted to cry. I felt tears on my cheeks.

Cat said, "Do you remember talking to Kurch?" I shook my head. "He came by your apartment to ask some questions, like if you killed Jamie because she broke up with you."

"What did I say?"

"Nothing much. You faded away and he left. But he'll try again, I'm sure."

"The concussion?"

"The doctor said you were lucky. Something must have cushioned your fall, maybe whoever who hit you, because dropping straight onto concrete would have cracked your skull, maybe killed you."

I started to lift a finger, but there was a clamp on one and a plastic tube ran up my arm.

"That was today, not yesterday."

"This is Friday, Porter. You've been out for twenty-four hours. They've been monitoring the pressure in your skull."

"What time is it?"

"Three-thirty."

"The kids?"

"Luisa's with them, or will be when they get home."

"Jamie?"

"The FBI is involved. The story is she waited for you at the restaurant, disappeared, and the owners tried to report her missing. Kurch insists she left with you."

"I was never there. He knows that. I was with him."

"According to him you were there before he picked you up."

"That doesn't even make sense. When can I get out of here?"

"Two or three days."

"I've got to leave. I don't know what's going on, but it's out of control."

"They want you here for observation. Plus..." She nodded toward my arm then touched my thigh near my crotch.

There was an IV drip from a plastic bag on a hanger that fed into my arm, and a plastic tube running from beneath the sheet to another plastic bag clipped to the side of the bed. A catheter.

"Your doctor should be by soon. You can talk to him."

At the door of my room a face appeared, as cold as tundra, and beyond it another, older, fleshy, familiar. Kurch glanced over his shoulder at his partner, a man named Bakey, and stepped into my room. Bakey moved toward Cat.

Kurch said, "Outta here, miss. We're havin' a little chat with Mr. Hall."

I said to Kurch, "Don't call her 'miss,' pea brain, and you," I said to Bakey, "get away from her." Bakey stopped cold and Kurch's face flushed.

"Kurch, I need you to do something."

After a couple of heavy breaths he said, "Yeah, what?"

I spoke slowly. "Go find the sewer where your mother lives and help her catch her lunch."

Kurch took a giant step toward me, Cat stepped into his path, and they both fell onto my bed. Bakey stood there for a moment then stumbled forward, dropping onto his knees. Behind him was an angular man in a doctor's coat who looked seven feet tall. He stepped past Bakey, went to Kurch, and wrapped an arm around his neck. He told a large, brown nurse behind him to call security. She yelled into the hallway.

Kurch was flailing at the doctor's arm. Bakey, still on his knees, said, "We're police officers and you're under arrest."

The tall man, who was my doctor and was, in fact, only six-five, pinched Kurch's neck just above the collarbone. Kurch yelped and quit struggling. The doctor said, "I don't care if you're Florence Nightingale. I'm in charge here."

Moments later two men in suits entered my room, stopped abruptly, and looked around.

The doctor said, "Security?"

"Something like that," one of the men said, showing a badge. "FBI."

The nurse raised her eyes. "Sweet Jesus."

The other agent said, "What's going on?"

The doctor said, "This man tried to attack my patient."

The first said, "I'll take it from here." He walked to Kurch, felt under his jacket, and removed his badge and wallet and then his gun. He looked at the ID. "Detective Kurch, come with me."

Kurch held back. "You got no jurisdiction here, Agent Who-ever-You-Are."

"Wrong, detective. We're investigating a possible federal crime, and you're interfering." Kurch glared back at me as the agent started him toward the door.

The other agent took Bakey by the arm, helped him stand, and led him away. The agent with Kurch said, "Doctor, we're working a missing persons case and we need to talk to Mr. Hall ASAP."

"It's up to him." I nodded it was okay. "Give us twenty minutes," the doctor said.

Cat left and the nurse checked my vitals while the doctor, named Hecht, looked at my head. The nurse removed my tubes. When she pulled the catheter out, it felt like a burning sparkler moving through my urethra. The doctor crossed his arms and looked down.

"Mr. Hall…"

"Porter."

"You know your name. That's progress." He sighed. "You've had three concussions this week. Another one anytime soon could lead to permanent impairment, even death."

"Fine. I won't get any more. When can I go?"

"In a few days, after the bruising subsides and we can be sure there's no clotting or fluid accumulation." He tilted toward my face. "And after you quit crying like the mother of the bride every time anyone says anything about anything."

"But…"

"This is not a negotiation." He handed me a couple of tissues and walked out.

Cat returned and sat on the edge of my bed. I put my hand over hers. "Why are you being so nice to me?"

"It's my story, an exclusive. Remember?"

"That's it?"

She looked into my face and smiled, the same smile as before.

The FBI agents reappeared. Hermann and Torino were their names, and Hermann did the talking.

"We're trying to find a missing person. At this point that's all she is. We want to locate Jamie Trent."

"Why are you involved?"

"There was a potential sighting of Ms. Trent in New Jersey. It's not confirmed, but that's why we're here."

I told them everything I knew and anything I thought might help. They didn't say what happened with Kurch and Bakey, and I didn't ask. As he left, Hermann said, "If you think of anything else…" He handed Cat his card.

When he was gone, she said, "I'm going outside to call my office. Need anything?"

"Could you get someone to run Plockman through your database?"

"Full name?"

"Marvin G. Plockman is all I know. He's the account rep for the building management company."

"Did you ever talk to him about the financial reports?"

"I did."

"What did he say?"

"I have no idea because it made no sense."

WHEN I WOKE, Cat was in an armchair a few feet away. "What time is it?"

"Four-fifteen."

"Would you call Luisa? I want to talk to the kids."

She stood and walked to the window where the reception was better. "Luisa, it's Cat Marten. Could you put the kids on?" She listened. "What do you mean?" She listened some more. "Slowly, Luisa. *Despacio, por favor.*" More silence. "I'll call you back." She looked at her phone for a moment and turned toward me. What little color she normally had had been drained.

"What's the matter?"

She turned to me and said, "They aren't with Luisa, Porter."

"What does that mean? Then where the hell are they?"

"She thinks they're with you."

9

I SAT UP AND THE ROOM BEGAN TO LIST. I GRABBED A FISTFUL
of sheet to steady it.

"What are you talking about?"

"Another kid who lives in the building got off the bus but B.J.
and Cici didn't. The driver told her you sent someone to pick
them up from school."

"Where's my phone?"

Cat reached into her bag, fumbled a few seconds, and
handed it to me. I hit the button for Roger, the bus driver. It
rang five times and his voicemail picked up. In my contact list
I found the number for Herky's Citywide Transport Company.
I got a woman with a Hispanic accent and asked to speak to
Roger Dupree. She asked, "Why?"

"He lost my children."

She said, "Oh, my God," and went to get him.

It didn't take long.

"This is Roger (ro-JAY)," he said, Caribbean accent gliding over the words like clear water over river stones.

"It's Porter Hall, Roger, and I want to know where my kids are."

"Should be with you, Porter (por-TAY). One of your lady friends got them."

"I didn't send anyone. I don't know who that was."

"Hold there, mon. What you saying to me? I do something wrong?" The rolling lyric of his voice turned jagged. "It was like last time, just like the last time. Lady I don't know says things that make no sense and your kids go with her. Not my fault…"

"Roger, I'm not blaming you. I just want to find them. Tell me everything you remember."

A tall woman with dark hair and a thin face came onto the bus just after he had loaded the kids from Coldfield Academie, my children's school. She said I sent her to pick them up, that she was going to take them to see me, and repeated the code verbatim, the same one Cat had used.

Before he got off the bus B.J. had whispered to Roger that something didn't seem right. "Why would Daddy get us off the bus? He could have called the school?" Roger told him he didn't have to go if he didn't want to, but Cici was already in the back of a black Town Car. The woman told B.J. to hurry, his father was waiting.

The driver of the car was Asian, but Roger could tell me no more. "And one other thing, Porter. The woman that other day I would have gone with my own self. She was hot. This one was not."

To Cat I said, "I need clothes."

She went to a white Formica cabinet near the TV, opened it, and brought me a sealed brown bag that held my things. I went into the bathroom and dressed while she wrote a note for my nurse. It said Porter Hall had business to take care of and they shouldn't worry. She left it on the pillow.

It would have taken hours to formally check out of the hospital, but it took only a few minutes for me to wobble out the Seventh Avenue doors leaning on Cat. No one paid any attention.

We turned right and walked up to Twelfth Street, where we caught a cab going east. I told the driver to take us uptown.

"What's happening?" I said. It was a lament, not a question, but Cat answered anyway.

"I covered one of these in Chicago and it's usually one of two things. Molestation is unlikely because they were both taken. It's probably ransom." She paused. "I don't meant to pry, but do you have that kind of money?"

"My in-laws do."

"Should you call them?"

"If they got a ransom demand, they'd call me. I'm sure of it."

"Would they pay it?"

"Not if it were more than half a billion dollars. That's all they've got."

She said, "Billion? With a 'b'?" I nodded. "That is a prominent family."

"Other possible motives?"

"Custody or revenge."

"Does either seem likely?"

I tried to take deep breaths, but they felt shallow, unsatisfying. "No. Custody," I shook my head.

"What about their mother? Could she have taken them?"

"No."

"We need to call the police." She took out my cell and hit 911, gave the operator some basics and handed the phone to me.

"Are you Porter Hall?"

"Yes."

"When did this incident occur?"

"An hour and a half ago."

"Where do you live?"

I told her East Twenty-second but added that that was not where the abduction took place. She said that didn't matter, my local precinct would take the report.

"That doesn't make sense." I didn't need to go another round with Detective Kurch.

"Sir, don't waste time arguing with me. By now those children could be anywhere."

Tears were streaming. I handed the phone to Cat, who dialed the Thirteenth Precinct.

I opened the door and threw up. The wind closed it for me. The cab was moving faster.

"Hi, Mike," Cat said. "Please put me through." She handed me the phone.

I put it to my ear and waited. A voice came on that was as bouncy as a flat tire. "This is Detective Kurch."

I said, "My lucky day."

"Hall? That you? What the hell you want?"

"Someone who can help. I've got a real problem."

"No one else here, just me and Bakey. We shoulda gone home but there's a buncha paperwork when you get escorted back to your precinct by the FBI. You believe that? We have to fill out a goddamn incident report like it was a crime. So how can I help you, Mr. Hall, *sir?*"

"My children are missing."

"You jerking me off? You got some nerve."

"If you're not going to help, say so."

I looked at Cat and killed the call. She grabbed my wrist. "Did you hang up on him?"

"It's a federal crime."

"Only if they were taken across a state line. But we don't know that."

"Or that they weren't. The woman on the phone said they could be anywhere. I'm going with that. What was the name of the FBI agent?"

"Kurch already hates you, Porter. You take him out of the loop and you've got an enemy."

"I've got one anyway. He takes a report, maybe he makes some calls. If they don't show up, eventually he calls the FBI to help. I'm just giving them a heads up."

She stared at me for a second, then reached into her bag, took out a leather cardholder and removed the front one.

The driver said, "Where are we going?" He was an African-American man with a closely trimmed Van Dyke who looked like he should have been playing tenor sax in a West Village jazz club. Maybe the Coltrane that was coming through the radio had something to do with that feeling. I closed my eyes and started to drift with the crisp, sweet notes. Cat poked me.

"I don't know. Where should we go?" I looked at the driver's eyes in the mirror.

He looked over his shoulder. "Mister, all I can do is take you there."

"Let's go to the school, look around." I told the driver Eighty-eighth and Madison.

Cat punched in Special Agent Hermann's number. She got a switchboard and was put on hold. While she was waiting my phone rang, a 646 prefix, a New York City cell phone. I answered, my heart beating so hard it felt like it might crack a rib.

A voice, bitter and slow as crude on a winter day, said, "Porter Hall." Telling, not asking. It sounded like an African-American woman, with remnants of a southern accent worn flat by years up north.

"Who is this?" There was chatter in the background, muddled horns, a siren. Cat had Agent Hermann on the line. I shook my head. She told him she would call him back.

"Do you know where your children are, Mr. Hall?"

"What do you want?"

"Do you know where your children are?"

"No. Do you?"

"Come to Starbucks, Eighty-seventh and Lex."

"Are they there?"

"Immediately." The phone went dead.

I told the driver to take us to Union Square East and Fifteenth Street.

Cat said, "The subway?"

"We'll take the express to Eighty-sixth."

She shook her head. "I'll take it, you stay in the cab. You don't need to go up and down stairs, and if there's a problem with the train, you'll still get there."

10

By the time we reached Fifty-ninth Street I'd offered God more deals than a Wall Street banker sees in a decade. Cat called and said she was off the subway and would call from Starbucks. Seven minutes later, as I got out of the taxi, I still hadn't heard from her. Through the window I saw why. Cat was standing, fists on hips, nose-to-nose with a large black woman.

Actually, it was more like nose-to-chest because the woman, a light-skinned African-American, was a solid six-one. As I approached, the woman's eyes went above Cat's head to me. *She recognized me. How?*

The narrow store was jammed with students and commuters. Cat turned and gave a slight nod to her left toward a cluster of teenagers from a nearby private school. Cici shrieked as she ran through knees and skirt hems. A young man's legs were stretched across her path and she cleared them in a *grande jeté*.

I caught her in mid-flight and hugged her a little too tightly, a little too long. B.J. got there a moment later.

Cici said, "You're out of the hospital, Daddy."

"Are you okay?" I said with forced calm. Never let dogs or kids sense your fear.

"We're fine," said Cici, "but we need to get home or we'll miss Full House." She whispered, "You're crying."

"Sorry."

"It's okay. I cry sometimes."

I said, "Who's Cat talking to?"

"Doris. She stayed with us till you got here. We've been playing checkers. She got us different colored sugar packages and that table has a board painted on it. B.J.'s brown sugar and I'm Equal."

"Get your things. After I talk to Doris we'll leave."

Cici went back to the table, but B.J. took me by the hand and led me to the woman. He said, "This is my Daddy."

I said, "Porter Hall," and extended my hand.

"Doris Hebert," she said, giving Hebert the French pronunciation, *A-BEAR*. She shook my hand indifferently. Her shoulder-length hair was coppery chocolate, sort of latte with cinnamon, and had a loose curl. Her nose was high-bridged and distinct, her eyes black, and thistled as briars. She wore a loose fitting striped dress suggestive of African tribal influence and a beige outer-coat that reached her ankles.

We looked at each other. She seemed to be expecting something, an apology, a thank you, money. I wasn't sure. But something wasn't making sense.

"Thanks for watching my kids. How did you happen to be here?"

"I'm a social worker for the city. Child welfare, abandoned children, those things. I stopped here on my way home and saw them unattended. I notice things like that. I asked who they were with and they said they were waiting for their father. They gave me your number and I called."

"Not to seem ungrateful, Ms. Hebert, but why wouldn't you tell me they were with you when you called?"

Her thick brows pushed together. "Would you rather I called the police?"

"What time did you get here, just out of curiosity?"

"You're interrogating me? I care for your children and you question me." She was talking loudly and we were starting to get stares. "I don't think so, mister." She grabbed a large handbag from a table, started toward the door, stopped. "Next time I'll just call the cops straight off."

"Good plan."

"You will be hearing from child services."

"Fine."

"On second thought, my office tomorrow, nine o'clock. I'm opening a file." She reached in her bag and removed a business card. She held it in front of her face and waited for me to reach for it. I stood there until she extended it to me.

I studied the card. "Tomorrow is Saturday."

"That's not a problem for me, Mr. Hall. I suggest it not be a problem for you."

She turned abruptly toward the door, bumping a petite, sweet-looking Asian girl in a school uniform. The girl almost dropped a cup from Jamba Juice across the street. As Hebert brushed past, the girl, maybe fifteen, unleashed a streak of profanity that could have scoured gum off the sidewalk.

"What did you talk to her about?" I asked Cat.

"I started out nice. I told her I was a friend of yours, thanked her, said she could go if she wanted, you would be here soon. The kids hugged me so she knew I knew them."

"Then…"

"She said, 'Like hell I'm going to turn these children over to some little white girl who tells me to get lost.' After that it went down hill." Cat's cheeks turned red. "She called me 'little.' I should have called her a bitch."

I put my arm around her. "Yeah, that would have helped."

Cici pointed to a paper cup that sat on a shelf with insulated mugs and other coffee-junkie gadgets for sale. "She left her drink," she said. Next to it was a receipt. I went over, picked up the cup, and shook it. Half empty. The receipt, which displayed the last four digits of her credit card number, was for a vente skim frappucino and a piece of marble pound cake. I guess the skim milk offset the pound cake. There was one other interesting bit of data. The time stamp said 15:09. One minute before my kids got out of school. I stuck the receipt in my pocket and dropped the cup in the garbage.

Outside I was about to hail a cab, stopped. "Come on," I said. B.J. and Cici looked perplexed, along with Cat, but they followed me around the corner to a wireless store where I added two more lines to my plan, one for each of the kids. The kids picked out top-of-the-line devices that would do everything except make their beds, but settled for the basic model when I played the it's-this-or-nothing card.

On the way home I said, "No more codes. If there's a change of plan, I'll call one of your phones and leave a message. Or you can call me or Luisa or your grandparents or someone you know." Cat looked down. I added, "Like Cat." She looked up and smiled. "Otherwise, no changes. Stay where you are until someone you know comes for you, even if it means going back to school on the bus."

WHEN WE WALKED into our building, the doorman handed me a FedEx envelope. Sender: Dennis Fenton.

If I signed the papers inside, my marriage would be finished. I decided I should think about it over the weekend, but after two steps I turned, went back to the front desk and asked the doorman to call Mildred Duffy, a fellow board member, who was an attorney and notary. If three years weren't long enough to think about it, another two days wouldn't help.

Cat took the kids and I went to Mildred's, sat at her kitchen table, and rechecked the only item that meant anything to me. I asked her to read it and tell me if it said what I thought it said, that I would get sole custody. She said it did. I signed away my marriage.

I took the envelope back down to the doorman and told him to call a messenger.

11

THE KIDS HAD SETTLED IN THE PLAYROOM, BUT I CALLED them in for debriefing. They asked if they could watch the last ten minutes of their show first.

"But you missed the first twenty."

"That's okay. We've seen it lots of times."

Cat called St. Vincent's and explained my absence to a sympathetic woman in administration who had three children of her own. She said I needed to speak with my doctor and come by so they could check me out officially rather than AMA, against medical advice. Otherwise my insurance wouldn't pay.

Cat's eyes were on me, but her mind was not. A moment later she said, "What was the very first thing you thought when you found out your kids were missing?"

"Ransom. I was waiting for the instructions. When Doris Hebert called, I thought that was it."

"If they knew enough to kidnap your children, they had to know their grandfather has money. But they didn't ask for it."

I said, "That doesn't make sense. Or does it?"

She looked past me toward the sound of small footsteps. "It does if money wasn't what they wanted."

The kids walked in and sat on the coffee table facing us.

I said, "What happened today?"

They looked at each other, then me. "What do you mean? We got new cell phones, but you know that," said B.J.

We eventually got an account of the abduction, but didn't learn much that Roger hadn't told us. A lady they didn't know had picked them up in a black Town Car, which took them into Central park, drove the loop twice, and then took them to the Starbucks where Doris Hebert was waiting.

Doris told me she saw the kids unattended when she stopped for coffee, but the kids confirmed what the receipt said. She was already there when they arrived. She watched them but pretended not to, they said.

"How do you know that's what she was doing?"

Cici rolled her eyes and B.J. said, "Because it's the same thing you do, Dad."

"I see. But how could the woman who took you off the bus have gotten the code? Did you tell anyone?"

The kids looked at each other. "No," said Cici, a sarcastic elongation to the word, "it's secret. Maybe Cat did."

"Of course not," Cat said. "It's secret."

"Besides, Cat didn't say it right," B.J. said.

"And the lady did?"

They both nodded.

The kids raced back to the playroom.

I said, "How did they get the code? It sounds like the woman had it down perfectly, and no one should have known it except you and the kids. Roger heard it wrong because you said it wrong, but the woman from the Town Car got it right. But what's the point of taking them and then dropping them six blocks away a few minutes later?"

Cat looked at me, tilted her head, shifted her jaw out of line, incredulous. "Porter, we may need to see if we can get you into some sort of program for the logically impaired. You really don't know?"

My head hurt. "No."

"It was a message. Someone wants you to know they can get to your children any time they want."

"But why, who?"

"I don't know." She shrugged. "Who doesn't like you?"

"I'll tell you who does. That won't take as long."

12

When I woke, the Met Life clock outside my window said it was 3:31. It was a dark twilight, which is as dark as the city gets except in a blackout. For the first time in days my thoughts were crisp and clear. I went to the kitchen, started coffee, showered, and dressed in sweats. By four I was on line looking for the woman called Doris Hebert.

Her business card read Special Advisor, Administration for Child Services, so I pulled up the web site for New York City ACS. Other than a couple of high-level people, there were no names. I Googled her and got a single hit, a one-paragraph article in the *Post* detailing a series of minor mayoral appointments from three years ago. Doris Hebert had twenty years' service specializing in abused children cases and was appointed special liaison between the mayor's office and the child welfare system. This happened as the result of several particularly heinous examples of oversight that resulted in a number of dead children and a lot of headlines. So Ms. Hebert was a social worker-turned-bureaucrat who just happened to live in the vicinity of the subway stop at Eighty-sixth Street and Lexington Avenue. Or so she said.

I looked for her address on line and got nothing. I checked my study and found a four-year-old Nynex white pages. There were about twenty Heberts in Manhattan, and one D. Hebert. I blocked my own number and called a D. Hebert on East 104th Street. If I woke someone else, I would apologize. If I woke her, that was fine.

A recorded voice directed me to leave a message, but didn't give a name. I didn't need one. The voice was like thick, dismal syrup. Doris Hebert.

I hung up and called someone I knew would be awake, Fred Althorn, my skip-tracer. Fred was always home, it seemed, always on line and always available, except for a few hours either side of noon when he slept. The rest of the time he was navigating cyberspace the way bats fly through underground caverns, but with clicks instead of squeaks. "Porter. What do you need?"

"To get to know a woman."

"Who doesn't?"

"Well, this one is yours if you want her."

"Tell me."

I told him her name, home address, and the information on her business card.

"Anything else? A social, a DL, a credit card?"

I found the receipt from Starbucks. "Will the last four digits of a credit card help?"

"Of course. But it's going to be a while. The pretexter I use for black women screams if I call her before five-thirty."

"Her credit card company knows Doris Hebert is African-American?"

"You're joking, right?"

Fred Althorn was the most frightening person I'd ever met, though at five-nine and two-twenty with a lumberjack flannel shirt under a Jimmy Carter cardigan, untied Chuck Taylors, and black-framed glasses that rode the end of his nose, he didn't look too scary. I was referred to him when I needed to track down a tenant who moved in with a single suitcase and moved out with all my furniture and appliances. It took Fred two hours to find him.

Fred gets about forty percent of his information from the Internet. The other sixty comes from the telephone, most of it through what is known as "pretexting." Some would call that lying, although Hondo Crouch, the late mayor of Luckenbach, Texas, had a better term. "Play-liking," he called it. Fred or one of his associates calls, let's say, a bank, gets the accounting department, asks for something they won't have, and gets transferred to another department. That makes the call looks like it's internal. He then "confirms" everything the institution knows about you. He takes that data, things only you could know, and some you don't, to the next institution and the game is on.

Privacy? That bird was plucked and eaten a long time ago. How to stop that from happening to you? Don't give anyone a reason to look into your life.

While Fred was doing his thing, I worked the angles I could. I checked for coffee bars in her neighborhood and found three within a block of her home. For her to go to Eighty-seventh and Lex for a frappuccino would have been like driving from Manhattan to Jersey City to buy a hot dog from a street vendor.

At six-thirty, my phone rang. Fred said, "Check your email. It's all there. I'll hold."

I touched my mouse, the screen lit, and I opened the document and read it. "How did you find this stuff?"

"On the Internet, plain sight, most of it."

"Why couldn't I find it?"

"How to put this? You played baseball in college, right, even got drafted." I'd never told him that, but of course he knew. "How come you never made the majors and hit three hundred?"

"I wasn't good enough."

"There you go."

I READ THE report, ate breakfast, and left a note for Luisa telling her to get the kids ready to go to the country for the weekend. I got my Rover from the garage and headed north to Harlem on Third Avenue. I reached 104th Street at 7:45 a.m. and parked in front of Doris Hebert's building.

At five till eight, an African-American man dressed in khakis and a light jacket entered the building with a key. At eight, dressed in a uniform, he reappeared, unlocked the front door and positioned himself behind a small desk. A daytime doorman. I went in.

The lobby had terrazzo floors and no furniture except for the doorman's station, suggesting late eighties, subsidized housing. His nametag said Charles. He said, "Good morning, sir."

"I'm here for Doris Hebert. Has she left?"

"I don't think so, sir. Saturdays, if she goes in, she leaves eight-thirty. Shall I call up?" Doormen still know more than the Internet. "No, I'll wait. I'm going around the corner for coffee. Can I get you something?" He leaned toward me and said quietly, "A large regular." That was New York vernacular for coffee with a lot of milk and sugar, a necessity for the bitter stuff that New Yorkers drank before the coffee bars invaded Manhattan.

While waiting for the barista, I thought of something that should have occurred to me sooner. I called home, got Luisa, and told her to put one of the kids on. "Did Doris ask you for my cell phone number?"

B.J. said, "Yes. Why?"

"I wondered how she got it."

"We didn't give it to her. I told her we weren't authorized to release that information."

Which is how B.J. would have put it. Cici would have said, "None of your beeswax, lady."

That removed the last shadow of a doubt. When I returned with the coffee, Charles thanked me and slipped his under the desk. He looked at a panel on the desktop and said, "An elevator just went to her floor. She should be right down. You won't mention the coffee, will you, sir?" I shook my head. "She's president of the tenants' association and she's, you know…"

"A stickler."

"That, too."

I waited in the center of the lobby in the path between the elevators and the front doors. After a few moments a gong sounded, a door slid open, and Doris Hebert stepped into the vestibule looking into a large brocade bag that swallowed her arm up to her elbow. As she came toward me she removed a cell phone, looked at the screen, looked up.

Saw me.

Stopped.

Her eyes were pointed in my direction, but there was no tell, as though she were looking through a ghost. Her face, as much Indian as African, was dead as an old mask carved of wood.

I offered the cup. "You forgot your drink yesterday. I brought you another."

Her lip flinched into a quick sneer that promised I was going to regret the day I met her. I was about to make the arrangement reciprocal.

13

"Explain your presence at my home, Mr. Hall. Or shall I call the police?"

"Yes," I said.

"Which?"

"Both. While I explain, you call."

"This better be good, mister, because you're digging yourself a hole. A deep one." She glanced at Charles, who was fiddling with the phone cord on the desktop.

I said, "You know about self-dug holes, I guess."

With her head she motioned toward the door. Charles stepped to it, quickly opened it, and she and I walked out onto the small plaza with its uneven pavers arranged in a swirl pattern for the purpose of some design statement.

"What are you saying?" she said.

"I'm saying you were an accessory to the kidnapping of a minor. That's a felony, two, actually, since there were two victims, and accessory carries the same penalty as the primary. It's got to be twenty-to-life or so on each count. Although you can always ask for concurrent."

"I had nothing to do with that."

"*That*? So you knew what was going on?"

"No," she said, "the children told me."

"No, they didn't, because they didn't know, and they didn't give you my cell number. Where did you get it?"

She took a breath and flared her nostrils. "You should be thanking me, not harassing me. I just happened to be there."

"Like I just happen to be here now. Let's go."

She pulled her head back. "Where?"

"To your office. We have an appointment."

"Cancelled. Call my assistant and reschedule."

I said, "Really? So where are you headed? I'll give you a ride."

"Hell you will. Now go away, you. You have no idea who you're dealing with."

"Sure I do. Doris Leone Hebert, honors graduate in social sciences, Marshall University. Grew up in Selma, Alabama, high school valedictorian, ran track, hurdles and the two hundred relay, second in state, played basketball. Part Cherokee, African-American, and maybe Cajun, but that's a guess from your looks, your name, and where you were born."

"You're a good guesser, Mr. Hall, but I wasn't talking about me. Now get away from my home."

I turned toward the street, stopped. "You had the good sense not to use your cell phone for any of this, I hope. That's another felony or two."

She abruptly turned and headed toward Adam Clayton Powell Boulevard, her big bag pressed to her side. I looked at the cup in my hand and yelled, "Your frappuccino."

She turned and faced me. She was standing in a hard slat of light from the rising sun that cut through a gap between tall buildings beyond her. The sunlight created a red-tinted penumbra around her wild raves of hair. Backlit, her shape was mammoth and stark. She stood motionless for several moments, then said in a steady, stinging voice, "If I were you, Porter Hall, I would remember the words of the prophet. 'That thing which has happened once can happen again.'"

She turned with a swirl of hair and garments, a spinning mahogany shadow in the cold golden light, and was gone.

I stood for a moment with her drink in my hand then went back inside and gave it to Charles. He smiled with considerable kindness, and said, "I believe today will be a fine and blessed day, sir." He grinned and showed a set of large and perfect teeth, took a sip of the milky drink. "But then I believe that almost every day. My wife reckons me to be some sort of fool."

I STARTED MY Rover and coaxed it toward the corner watching for Doris Hebert. I didn't see her. I wished I had so I could have told her that in all the time I spent in church as a kid I never once heard of any prophet who had made any such assertion.

That thing which has happened once can happen again.

It sounded more like a venal threat from a devil woman than prophecy.

I TOOK THE West Side Highway downtown, went to St. Vincent's, and officially checked out. My doctor had put a note in the file reluctantly agreeing to it. When I finished, it was 9:30, and if the kids were ready we could be at our country place by noon. I called Luisa and asked if they were packed.

"Oh, Mr. Porter, no," she said. "Miss Cici very sick. She in bed, look very bad."

"Does she have a fever?"

"Yes, very much fever."

"Let me talk to B.J."

There was a pause. "B.J. not here, Mr. Porter."

"Where is he?"

"Other room."

"Go get him, please."

She yelled and in a few moments B.J. was on the line.

"What's the matter with Cici?"

"I'm not sure."

"Make a guess."

"Luisa made bacon and eggs for breakfast but Cici wouldn't eat them. She hid under her bed until Luisa gave her what she wanted."

"Which was…?"

"Cheetos and strawberry ice cream. And she had some gummy bears hidden from the last time we went to the movies."

I got sick thinking about it. We wouldn't be leaving for a while since Cici was prone to carsickness anyway.

I HAD JUST crossed Fourteenth Street, heading north on Sixth. I was planning to turn right on Twenty-second, changed my mind, cut in front of a bus, and turned onto Eighteenth. I found a spot across the street from Kates.

The sign on the door said closed. I took out my phone and called my voicemail. I quit breathing for a moment when I heard Jamie speak. I replayed her message from Wednesday, and called the number she left for Kates. Inside a phone rang.

Kate O'Meara answered. I told her I was outside. A moment later she came running to the door.

She fumbled with the lock, pulled it open and looked at me, eyes wide, lips parted, trembling. "What, Porter? What is it? What's happened?"

"Nothing."

She seemed to wilt and age in front of me. She turned and walked to a small marble-topped table and sat. "I'm sorry. Come in. I thought maybe...I don't know."

Tears were spilling from her eyes. Mine, too.

"I wish I did," I said. "I came by to talk to you, maybe ask some of your employees a few questions. I know the police were here."

She looked toward the bar where a young man was setting up. "Marcus, find Eva." He walked out. "She's the only one they really talked to."

Marcus returned a minute later with an innately attractive young woman who had done about everything she could to make herself unattractive. Nose ring, tattoos, multi-colored hair. Or maybe I was just old.

She looked at Kate, at me. I'd seen her a couple of times, but she'd never waited on me.

"Hi," she said, revealing a tongue with a silver stud.

"Tell Porter about your talk with the cops." Kate motioned her to an empty chair and she sat down.

"They came in Friday. I had four tables, two orders up, so I was a little distracted." Her voice was soft, pleasant, articulate, and completely without attitude. She sounded like the daughter everyone wanted. She looked like the daughter everyone feared they would wind up with.

"They asked me to step outside and showed me a picture of you. They described you and asked if I knew who you were. I said I did, and they wanted to know if you were here Wednes-day. I said not that I remembered. They said they knew you were and met Jamie Trent. I said I didn't remember seeing you, but that someone outside did tell me Porter Hall wanted to see Jamie. I gave Jamie the message. She jumped off the stool, started out, stopped, went back and grabbed her purse. I told them that.

"The cops said, 'So Hall was outside waiting for her.' I said I didn't see you, but there was a short, dark man, Hispanic, prob-ably, who gave me the message. They kept telling me I saw you, and that it was before noon when I did. I said I didn't, because I didn't start my shift until twelve that day. The older one says close enough, and wrote down '11:45.' They had their minds made up. It didn't matter what I said."

Kate said, "I tried to tell them they had it wrong. But Kurch, I've dealt with that asshole before, he just gave me this patroniz-ing look and said he'd call me if he needed anything else. I even showed him the receipt. Her second Perrier was time stamped 12:13. He said that didn't mean anything, maybe that receipt wasn't even hers."

If they had accepted that it was Jamie's receipt, they'd have had to admit I wasn't there since they took me into custody at 12:05. I've been accused of a lot, but never of being in two places at the same time.

Tall Kate walked out of the dining room, saw us, and came and sat. Just Kate reached over and squeezed her hand. Most of their patrons probably assumed they were a lesbian couple, which, in New York City, added a certain cachet. In fact, Kate O'Meara was married with three kids, and Kate Masters was di-vorced with a six-year-old son and dating a personal trainer.

"Porter, I don't know what we'll do without her. We almost went under in the first six months. She brought clients here to eat, she got her office to rent the back room for parties. Then she helped us renegotiate the lease to percentage with a low minimum."

Every hour Jamie was gone the less likely it was she'd return unharmed. If there was something I could do, I had to do it immediately.

14

THANKS TO A HARD SELL BY MARVIN PLOCKMAN, WHO'D pushed the purchase like it was the only thing that could save his grandmother from living in a cardboard box under a bridge, the Medora had installed a three hundred thousand dollar state-of-the-art security system that had more bells and whistles than an arcade. It had one server behind the concierge desk and a backup locked in a secure room on the second floor. There were fourteen security cameras, three with audio. Maybe Marvin's toy could tell me something.

Orlando was the concierge on duty, which I was glad to see, since he was mine. I hired him. Large New York City residential buildings operate like feudal fiefdoms with warring lords and loyal, or disloyal, serfs. Of the four concierges, I only had problems with Jorgé. Jorgé's resume wouldn't have gotten him a job at McDonalds. It was summer, however, and two days after his interview I went away for a month with my kids. When I got back I learned that Marvin had hired him anyway. Under the building's contract with the union, once someone has been hired, you have thirty days to terminate without cause. Thereafter, unless you want a prolonged, ugly, expensive fight, to get rid of a doorman or porter you better have video footage of him beating a resident with a baseball bat in the lobby.

I was livid that Plockman had hired Jorgé, but it got him what he wanted: a loyal inside man. But Orlando, like Bobby, the porter, was one of mine.

I said, "I want to watch the security videos for this week. Can you help me?"

"Yes, sir. I'll show you how to use the system. It's quite user-friendly. He took me into the back room, had me sit at the console in front of the control panel, and explained what to do. He set a spindle of blank DVDs on the desktop. "Use these if you want to copy anything."

WATCHING PAINT DRY is exciting compared to scanning security videos. I started with Monday, just to be sure I didn't miss something of significance, and worked to Wednesday. I had the screen split into four images: three interior, and the exterior view west. I kept falling asleep. Until I saw Jamie walk into the building at eleven on Wednesday. That woke me like an I-V full of espresso.

The time stamp read 11:03. She said hello to the doorman and went to Orlando to get keys. They talked a minute, then she went to a waiting area and sat. At 11:06, a man in a gray suit, no tie, came in, spoke to the doorman, and walked to

Jamie. They went to the elevator vestibule and got in one of the cabs.

At 11:09, a tall bald man dressed in a suit and tie came in, spoke to no one, walked back to the elevator vestibule and out the service door. Marvin Plockman.

At 11:11, the man Jamie had taken upstairs stepped off the elevator and walked brusquely through the lobby.

A minute later two college-age girls, one carrying a canvas book bag with an NYU logo, a purple and white flame, came from the elevators and plopped into two of the wing chairs near the concierge desk. Thirty seconds later Plockman reemerged from behind the desk. As he passed the girls in the chairs his walk slowed and he gave them a long look and a smile. The two girls turned to each other, locked eyes, and became stone-faced. Plockman walked past the concierge desk and into the package room. When he was gone, the girls burst into giggles, one of them doing a decent facsimile of his leer.

At 11:14, Jamie got off the elevator and walked toward the front. She looked regal. She walked that long space alone, and all the attention in the room belonged to her.

The girls were watching and the concierge was watching, but Jamie's eyes were straight ahead as she walked. That walk. She was naturally sensual, more so because she didn't try to be. Orlando watched as though he were in a trance. She stopped and looked at him. The resolution wasn't good enough to pick up his blush. He quickly looked down. I turned up the audio.

Three times I watched it through the point where Marvin came out of the package room behind Orlando, picked up the note from the wastebasket, and dropped it back in, but I was never able to decipher the conversation between Plockman and Orlando.

What did they say to each other? What did that note say? That was four days ago. Was it still around somewhere? Probably not. But that was midday Wednesday, and the building's weekly trash collection is early Wednesday morning. If I could see which porter emptied it, there was a possibility I could find it if I didn't mind digging through bags and bags of garbage. I started scanning at 8x waiting for someone to empty the trash basket. At 12:55, Orlando returned from his break. At 1:09, with no one in the lobby except for him and the doorman, who was gazing outside, Orlando glanced around, walked over and took the note out of the basket. He went back to the counter, opened it and smoothed it flat. He studied it until 26F, easily the most annoying resident in the building, stopped to pick up her dry cleaning. He folded the note and slipped it into the drawer in front of him. He got her dry cleaning and gave it to her, but she stayed there talking to him until a man came for a package. After he finished with the man, Orlando went into the back for a few minutes. Just before three o'clock, when he was to go off duty, he opened the drawer and reached in. Then he bent over and looked in, stuck his hand in, and felt around. He made a similar check of other drawers with the same result. No one else had been near that drawer. He couldn't know that. But I did.

Orlando wasn't around when I left the video room. I went to the doorman's station and asked Ramon, the porter, where he was.

"His daughter has a soccer game. Someone is supposed to come in for him but he's not here yet."

I went behind the desk and opened the drawer. There were notepads, pens, paper clips, a stapler, but not Jamie's note. I reached to the back but didn't find it. As I closed the drawer I heard a soft scratching. I pushed the drawer back-and-forth and it scratched both directions. I depressed the plastic locking clips on the sides of the slides and pulled the drawer out completely. Crumpled at the back was a folded piece of wrinkled paper. I took it out. It started:

Dear Porter,

I read it, folded it, and put it in my pocket. I had several dozen notes from Jamie upstairs that she had left me over the years, and each was special, each an expression of Jamie, not a mere functional communication like an email. In each there was a bit of Jamie's heart.

My phone rang.

Luisa said Cici had recovered from the 'flu' and the kids were packed and ready to go. Translation: *I'm ready to go to my sister's, come get them. Pronto.* I told her I was at the concierge desk, to send them down.

I went back to the monitor and watched the sequence of Jamie leaving the building one more time, but this time stayed with the exterior camera longer. She crossed Broadway to a bank of pay phones set at the base of the legendary Flatiron Building. It was Jamie's favorite. In 1902, it was the tallest habitable building in the world. Only the uninhabitable Eiffel Tower was taller.

The Flatiron once anchored the shopping district known as The Ladies' Mile. On Twenty-third Street, young men hung out to see the ankles of young women whose skirts were lifted by the perpetually swirling winds at the intersection of Fifth Avenue, Broadway and Twenty-third Street. Cops chased them away in what became known as "the old Twenty-three skidoo."

Jamie was on the phone for a few minutes. When she got off, she started in the direction of Kates. After a few steps she stopped and turned east, back toward the Medora, and seemed to be looking directly into the security camera, directly at me. It was as though she knew I would be watching. Something sharp and cold touched me. Would that be the last time I saw that face? Was that grainy image her final farewell?

She turned and went toward Kates to wait for me. I never came.

15

I INSERTED A BLANK DISC INTO THE TRAY AND CLICKED COPY. The first saved through Tuesday. I put in a second and recorded Wednesday and part of Thursday. The disc was about ninety percent done, according to the progress icon, when the door opened. I looked up and saw Jorgé.

He said, "What the hell are you doing in here?"

There was no fake respect, no italicized *mister*.

I looked at him for a moment and turned back to the screen as the words, TRANSFER COMPLETE flashed. I hit the eject button. "It has nothing to do with you."

"You're wrong. I am responsible for the security of this room."

I took the second out and put both in my jacket pocket.

"According to whom?"

"Mr. Plockman."

"We've been through this," I said. "It's called chain of command, and I'm at the top." I moved toward the door.

Jorgé blocked it. "Give me those or I will not let you leave this room."

"You're going to stop me? How?"

"Believe me," he said, as he poked a finger into my chest, "you don't want to know. Now, I will count to three, and if you haven't given them to me, I will take them. You've been formally warned."

Jorgé was two inches shorter than I was, but fifteen years younger, and much thicker. Paunchy, but muscular.

He said, "One..." and I hit him in the face. His head bounced off the sheetrock.

I probably should have warned him that I'd been through a Mommy and Me self-defense class a few months earlier, and that I also used to take martial arts classes with Laurie. She was so much better than I was it was embarrassing. In the Mommy and Me class, which was evenly divided between mothers and fathers, I was the best adult. Cici was the best of all.

I followed with a fist to Jorgé's gut, grabbed his wrist and bent his elbow backward to the point that ligaments were about to snap. I grabbed his collar and twisted until he gasped for air.

"What are you and Marvin up to?" I twisted tighter. "Spill it, Jorgé." His face was turning blue. After a few seconds he sank toward the floor. I released his collar so he could breathe, pulled him back up, and was about to knee him, when someone said, "Daddy?"

B.J. and Cici were behind me, their small monogrammed L.L. Bean duffels over their shoulders. I took a step back. "Hey, kids. I was just showing Jorgé something from our self-defense class." I let him go and he slid down the wall.

Cici's eyes were wide, her mouth half-open, waiting for my next move. B.J. turned red. "You're supposed to use your words, Dad." He turned and walked out.

I turned back to Jorgé and leaned down. "I'll show you the rest of the moves later. Marvin, too. Be sure to tell him."

I walked toward the door, but Cici didn't move.

"Cici, come on."

"Can I show him my roundhouse?"

"No."

"How about my knee drop or sidekick?"

"Let's go, Cici."

She looked at him like he was a chocolate chip cookie she wasn't allowed to eat. "No fair! I just want to show that mother…"

"Cici!"

16

OUR COUNTRY PLACE IN THE TOWNSHIP OF WOODSTOCK SITS in an oblong valley spackled with white pine, pin oak, maple, and a massive stand of birch. Through the meadow runs a stream that is wet most of the year, and there is an old stone wall that crosses the meadow into the trees.

The farmhouse, begun over a hundred-and-fifty years ago as a one-room cabin by German settlers, has two stories, four bedrooms, three baths, and an illogical floor plan. The day was what you expect of fall days in the Catskills. The richness of the colors is matched by the musky scent of late-blooming flowers, ripening fruit and vegetables, and damp, fallen leaves in decay, returning to the earth that bore them.

Sunday morning, while a fifteen-year-old girl from down the road fixed the kids breakfast, I rode my bicycle. Passing Lake Hill, near the end of my ride, I hit the stench of death, thick and hard as an invisible reef. It was a deer, most likely, run down by a car or shot out of season. Some people do that, just because they can, just to watch them die.

Monday I rode again. I took a breath and braced myself as I neared the spot, but the foul odor was gone.

On the way back to the city I took out my cell to check messages. There was one from Herb Schneider asking me to call, and one from Doris Hebert saying we needed to talk. There were also twenty-eight calls from Cat, though she only left four messages. She wanted to know where I was and wanted me to call her as soon as I could. As I listened to the last my phone rang.

Cat said, "Where are you? Why didn't you answer?"

"Hi. What's up?"

"Come get me."

"Where?"

"Rhinecliff."

"The train station? How'd you get there?"

"Submarine, how do you think? Come get me."

"I can't get there from here."

"Now, Porter. You're in so much trouble."

"I haven't done anything."

"Since when does that matter?"

TWENTY-FIVE MINUTES LATER, on the east side of the Hudson, I turned down the ramp into the lot of the old stone station. Cat was dressed in black boots, jeans, and a khaki vest over a white oxford cloth shirt. She had on a Cubs cap and was leaning against a No Parking sign. Beads of sweat made her face sparkle. Suddenly, a sharp spine of pain and nausea ran through me, as a memory returned, an image of Jamie. Ten years ago, when we were first dating, she came out for a weekend. When I got to the station to pick her up, she was standing where Cat was standing, except she was dressed like Coco Chanel starting out on a tour of Provence. Her face was shaded by a plum hat with a large brim, and beneath it she was smiling.

Cat got in, shut the door hard, started to say something, but stopped.

"What?" she said. I shook my head, pushed the old truck up the steep ramp and headed toward Route 9 south.

After a mile she said, "Why couldn't I reach you?"

"Cell service was out this weekend, and I don't have a land-line."

She was quiet for a few minutes as she watched the rolling farm lands of Dutchess County pass by the window. She said, "I found stuff on Plockman."

"Anything interesting?"

"He worked with a development group that was doing projects along the Jersey shore and was involved in a couple of lawsuits. Is that interesting?"

"Not terribly."

"Try this. He had his own firm, he ended up in bankruptcy, and was charged with misappropriation of funds, theft, wire fraud, forgery, and some EPA violations."

"Those are felonies. Did he do time?"

"He pleaded to a couple of things, plea bargained the others, and cooperated with the prosecution. He got a fine, community service and sixty days in county. The rest was suspended, contingent on his staying out of the real estate business for ten years."

"When did this happen?"

"Nine years, ten months, and two weeks ago."

"So another six weeks and he's home free."

"Right. Or he would have been if you hadn't started asking questions."

A sleepy voice said, "Where are we?"

In the rearview mirror there was a head on the left then a head on the right. B.J. looked into the front seat. "Cat?"

Cici's seat belt latch clicked, she stood, and looked over the seat. "Where'd you come from?" She reached around the seat, hugged Cat, and started to get in her lap.

"Seat belt, Cici." She moved back to her seat. "We picked her up at the train station when you were asleep."

B.J. said, "I'm hungry."

I said to Cat, "Have you eaten?"

"I have. I think it was yesterday, or maybe the day before."

"We're close to the kids' favorite restaurant. We'll stop."

"Is it fancy?" she said, glancing at her clothes.

"Does a life-size talking moose head make it fancy?"

"Does to me."

WHEN WE GOT back on the road, the kids reverted to their handheld video games and Cat stared out the window. We made small talk because every time Cat tried talking about Marvin the kids put their gadgets down and started listening. Just before we reached the city they both fell asleep. At the Third Avenue Bridge, Cat said, "There's a problem with Marvin."

"More than what you told me?"

She nodded.

"Bad?"

"He turned himself in Saturday."

"Why?"

"To beat the rush would be my guess. Not only is he looking at new charges, but he could end up doing the suspended time from the earlier charges. He decided to deal."

"It worked before."

"Exactly. And whoever turns first gets the best deal."

"He's owning up. Why is that bad?"

"He's not owning up. He says if he did anything wrong, it was because someone else forced him to."

"That's absurd. There is no one else. Who does he blame?"

She glanced into the back seat to make sure the kids weren't tuned in. "You. He says you're behind everything."

I almost drove over a Porsche in the next lane. "That's ridiculous. Who's going to believe it?"

"The federal prosecutor, for one. He issued an arrest warrant for you. What are you going to do?"

"The Giants are on Monday Night Football. Tomorrow I'll surrender. I wasn't busy anyway."

17

When I turned onto Twenty-second Street, my first thought was that there was a street fair, except there were no falafel and shish-ka-bob stands. Then I thought maybe it was a TV or movie shoot, which tourists love and New Yorkers hate because it messes up alternate side of the street parking. As I neared the entrance to our underground garage, a uniformed cop stepped in front of me and held up his hand. I stopped and he came to my window.

"Step out, sir," he said, hand on his weapon, "and keep your hands where I can see them."

"Can I park first?"

"Out of the car now. Hands where I can see them."

I turned to the back seat. The kids were awake and wide-eyed. "Cat, take them inside, please."

I stepped out and Cat got the kids out and went to the sidewalk. She tried to move them toward the building but Cici stopped at the curb.

The officer said, "Hands on your vehicle, feet apart."

He frisked me, cuffed me, and started me toward a gray sedan a few feet away. A man, late fifties, gray suit and hunched shoulders, approached us and stopped in front of me. He showed me an NYPD badge, said, "Lieutenant Marsh." A tow truck on the far side of the street started backing toward my Rover.

I said to Marsh, "What are you doing here? They're federal charges, from the federal prosecutor." He squinted, as though he had no idea what I was talking about. "I'll surrender tomorrow."

"Federal? I don't think so."

His hair was white with flecks of black and his face had deep lines, like canyons dug by ancient rivers—chain-smoker wrinkles. But unlike the other cops I had dealt with, his eyes had a flicker of intelligence.

"There'd better be a good explanation for this, detective, or you'll be retiring very soon."

"That would break my heart." He studied my face. "How's this for an explanation? Porter Hall, you're under arrest for the kidnapping and murder of Jamie Lynn Trent."

Only the strength of the two officers beside me kept me from dropping to the pavement.

18

MARSH MIRANDIZED ME, PUT ME IN THE BACK OF A SQUAD car, and cuffed me to a chain run through a D-ring on the floor. Out the window I watched Cat. She was about to enter the building with the kids when a hand grabbed her shoulder. She turned and looked up into the briar-black eyes of Doris Hebert.

Cat slapped the hand away and Doris Hebert made a move like she was about to hit her, but didn't. Cat was saying something and Doris Hebert was talking too. A wailing noise stopped their conversation.

Two men and a woman, all in blue suits, emerged from the doors. Between them, hands in cuffs, face distorted in agony, was Luisa. The men escorted her to a van, and the woman looked around as though trying to spot a friend. She saw me, grinned, came to the car, and across the roof said something to the lieutenant. He came around and opened my door. The woman leaned in, smiled and said, pleasantly, "Mr. Hall,

Deborah Winter, INS. We believe Luisa Saenz, who is in your employ, is in this country illegally and is involved in criminal activities." She stuck a business card in my breast pocket and tapped the knuckle of her index finger against it. "Call me when you get a chance."

"Happy to. But it may be a while."

THE DISTINGUISHED, TIRED Lt. Marsh, sat in the passenger seat and a uniform drove. As he ran a red light, I said, "Sarge, I need to make a call."

The lieutenant looked around, raised an eyebrow. "Maybe you don't know how this works, Mr. Hall. We get you downtown, process you, and then you get a call."

"Officer," I said as we turned north onto Park, "maybe you don't know how this works. If you stop me from taking care of my children, you're contributing to endangering the welfare of minors, and the Channel Four investigative reporter will be in your office before you finish your next cup of peas. And please call me Porter."

He didn't answer. The driver turned on the siren as we crossed East 23rd Street to FDR and turned south toward downtown. It took us ten minutes to reach the brick box with hundreds of square windows known as One Police Plaza. I was taken to an interrogation room and the cuffs were removed.

"A phone call, Lieutenant."

He raised an eyebrow. "Lieutenant? I'm a lieutenant again? Do I get a raise, more vacation?"

"Please."

"Polite. This must be serious." He nodded and the uniform led me to a small room with a table, two chairs, and a phone. "Five minutes."

I called Cat's cell. She answered on the first ring.

I said, "Where are you? I saw you swing at Doris and was afraid you'd be in jail by now."

"That almost happened, and she almost took the kids."

"How'd you get out of it?"

"My trump card. My *Journal* ID. I asked her if she wanted page one or three of tomorrow's Metro. What do you want me to do?"

"Call my in-laws. Tell them they need to come into the city and keep the kids. Next, call Dennis Fenton and tell him what happened."

"I already did. I found his number on your desk."

"Did you tell him about Luisa?"

"He said he'd take care of her, but they won't be able to send someone to you until in the morning."

"I'll survive. Let me talk to the kids."

Cici sobbed for a few seconds and handed the phone to B.J.

"Daddy, what's happening?"

You want to be strong for your children, reassuring, and you also want to be honest. Sometimes those two things won't fit in the same box.

"I don't know, B.J. I wish I did."

MORNING TOOK ITS time getting there. When it finally did, I was escorted to an interrogation room and left alone. A few minutes later Lieutenant Marsh walked in, sat down, and greeted me pleasantly.

He said, "How were the accommodations?"

"Not the best. I requested an upgrade to a king on a high floor. Didn't get it."

He rubbed one eye. "Those you have to book in advance."

I told him I did like the interrogation room, however, that it looked good, like the real thing, like you saw on *Law and Order*. I asked who their decorator was. He said he was glad I liked it, and shook his head slowly, tiredly. "They said that about you."

"What?"

"Smartass."

"Who said that?" He shrugged.

When I first saw him, I thought it was the heaviness of life, the long years on the force that had dulled his edges and weighted his soul, or maybe he'd just had a hard night. But I was beginning to think he had been born tired. It was his way. I had an aunt like that.

A uniform cop brought him a file, left. He opened it and flipped through a few pages. He stopped on one. "You were a ballplayer in college."

"That's in there? I'm impressed."

"Drafted, twenty-third round, by the Reds. Says you were versatile, a decent contact hitter, below average arm, average speed, slow first step, and I quote..." He looked at me. "'Best hands I've ever seen. Major league hands.'" He looked down, shook his head, continued reading. "'Too bad the rest of him is minor league.'" He closed the file.

I said, "Did you play?"

"Shortstop, high school and in the service." He coughed into his fist, started to speak, and coughed again, harder. "Sorry." He wiped his mouth with a handkerchief.

I tapped the table. "Now that I've softened you up with a personal connection, lieutenant, let's talk."

"That's my line," he said.

"Tell me about Jamie Trent."

He looked at the reflective glass on one wall, at me again. "This is backwards. You know that, right?"

"What's backwards is you charging me with her murder, if in fact she's dead. If she is, and I pray she's not, I certainly didn't kill her. Your next line is, 'Nobody we bring in is guilty.' Go ahead, say it."

"Consider it said. Keep going."

"No, that's it until you tell me what's going on. The FBI agent I talked to Friday said she was missing. Fill me in and maybe I'll talk some more."

He leaned onto his elbows, put his hands together. "Where were you Wednesday afternoon?"

"That's a joke, right?"

"Am I laughing? Where were you?"

"Cuffed to a bench in the Thirteenth Precinct from 12:15 until four."

His eyes widened like a snake had just slithered across the table. He looked at the glass again.

I said, "Go ahead. You can laugh now."

He didn't laugh, but he did get up and walk out.

19

A FEW MINUTES LATER HE RETURNED WITH TWO MEN AND A woman. One man was African-American, fifties, and the other white with black hair, in his thirties. The woman was tall and stunning with almost blond hair, a black suit with a knee-length skirt, and heels. Her white silk blouse had a banded collar and was buttoned up to her neck. She sat where Marsh had been, the younger man on her left. Marsh and the other man stood against the wall.

She looked at me, but didn't say anything for what seemed like minutes. She wasn't staring me down. It was more like I was some contraption that needed assembly and the instructions didn't match the object. At one point the man beside her started to say something, but she lifted the pinky on her left hand and he stopped.

When she was ready to talk, she said, "I'm Elizabeth Winslow, this is Andrew Carmelo." She nodded toward the younger man next to her. "And Lieutenant Erskine." He was standing next to Marsh. "Mr. Carmelo and I are with the district attorney."

"Nice to meet you all." I nodded to each of them. "Now, I want you to listen, carefully. All of you are already in pretty serious trouble so I suggest everyone be as pleasant as possible. Then, when you're sitting where I'm sitting, I'll try to make things go a little easier for you. Deal?"

Winslow looked at Carmelo, who gave a slight shrug, then at Marsh. "Is he always like this?"

"Since the day I met him."

"Mr. Hall…"

"Call me Porter." Since there was an observation window, I figured they were all in the room for show. "Honestly, ma'am, I'm honored you think you need four people to intimidate me, but I intimidate pretty easily. Two or three would have been plenty, and a lot more cost effective."

"Mr. Hall, you are not even close to being the first suspect to threaten us, but you are the first to offer us a deal. We attempt to treat everyone with respect although I can't promise we'll be pleasant."

"No you don't, Liz, Lizzie, Beth?" She didn't respond. "You don't treat anyone with respect. Elizabeth, look around. Tell me what you see."

"What are you talking about?"

"How many people are on my side of the table?"

"One."

"Exactly. But at some point my attorney is going to walk through that door, tell me not to say anything, and berate you for questioning me without counsel. Does that sound right?" She gave her hair a flip sideways. "Tell me what you know, and I'll talk to you until he gets here. The only indication I have that Jamie is dead is that I've been arrested for her murder. I'm not convinced. I haven't seen any evidence."

Without taking her eyes from me, she put her hand into her valise and kept it there for several seconds. She withdrew a file, pulled out several photos, held them where I couldn't see, and looked through them. She chose two, and, finally, one, which she slid to me.

It was a picture of a small riverbed with rocky banks bordered by mountain laurel and holly. Beyond the bushes were stands of hemlock and birch. The bed was dry, and lined with rounded stones covered with leaves of brown and gold and red. It lacked only a Thoreau quote to be a poster stuck with push pins to the walls of thousands of dorm rooms. I wasn't sure what I was supposed to see.

Winslow saw my confusion, reached into the file and pulled out a small, sealed cellophane bag. She slid it toward me. Inside was a cheap chrome key ring with two Medeco keys and a white tag with the number "611." It was a lockbox tag like they used at the Medora, and 611 was the log number for apartment 9H. There was only one set of keys to that apartment, as Orlando, the concierge, had reminded me. I knew who'd had them last.

I looked again at the photo and then, like one of those psychologist's drawings that demonstrates figure-ground reversal, it popped. I saw it. A human shape, clothed in brown, partly covered with leaves. Face down, legs and arms akimbo. A few feet away was a brown Chanel bag, a 2.55.

My face was as numb as if it had frostbite. The hope I'd been holding onto had been flicked away like lint off a lapel. I looked at the photo for a few more seconds, put my fingers on it, and started to push it toward Winslow. I stopped, pulled it back and looked again. Not only did I recognize Jamie, I recognized the place. It was along the Saw Kill by Route 212, and not just anywhere. It was adjacent to my property.

A moment later something else hit me. I gagged, took one deep breath, then another, clenched my teeth. I leaned to my left and threw up on the floor.

20

Carmelo put a hand over his face and turned away. Erskine went to the door, said something, and a uniform came for me. He escorted me to a restroom and waited outside. There was no window to escape through and I guess he wasn't worried about me hanging myself. I hung my head over a toilet but after a couple of minutes I knew I wouldn't get sick again. I went to the sink, rinsed my mouth and washed my face and dried my face with paper towels. I threw them away and looked in the mirror.

One thing the scouting report omitted was that I was a good two-strike hitter. Dig in, don't back down. Make the pitcher get you out. Don't do his job for him.

Later, I could give way to sorrow, and later I would do everything I could to find out who killed Jamie and who set me up, but in that moment, as I stood in front of a mirror that was gauzy with fine scratches from decades of cleaning, I knew had

to be on my game. I owed it to Jamie, my children, and now
Cat, who had signed onto my losing team for reasons I didn't
understand.

I stepped out of the restroom. The officer looked me up and
down. I said, "Let's go."

IT WAS ALL the same people, but thankfully a different room.

I was different, though, and as I looked across the table at
Elizabeth Winslow, she seemed different. Carmelo wasn't. He
had the same tough guy expression, the swaggering body language of a bad actor in a bad movie.

Winslow said, "Where were we?"

"In another room. I was throwing up."

"Of course you were. Now, what can you tell us, Mr. Hall?"

"Porter, please. I'm going to tell you where she was found,
and approximately when."

She and Carmelo looked at each other.

"Told you," Carmelo said, smug. He looked back at me. "Get
it off your chest, Hall, admit what you did. You owe it to her.
You'll feel better. I promise you."

I looked at him, and Winslow did, too. I laughed out loud,
and Winslow twisted her mouth and looked down.

"Why, Carmelo? Because you always feel better when you
confess to a murder you didn't commit?"

We stayed that way until Carmelo cleared his throat and
fumbled with some papers. I turned back to Winslow.

"I didn't kill her. But I know where, and maybe when, she
was found. Do you have a Woodstock map?"

Winslow reached into her portfolio, withdrew a map and
unfolded it on the table. It was a U.S. Geological Survey map
with topographic markings. Features like hills, valleys, streams,

and game trails were marked. I found Route 212 and pointed to a place just past Lake Hill, on a creek called the Saw Kill.

"Right there, sometime before Monday morning."

She nodded, said, "You may be off by four or five feet. Some kids found her Sunday around noon. How did you know?"

"I rode past there Sunday about ten. There was a horrible smell, much worse than the usual dead animal. It was…"

I swallowed hard to avoid being sick again. "It had to be Jamie. Monday it was gone."

I swallowed again. "If I had looked in that direction…" I closed my eyes and took several long breaths. "There were vultures circling. Did they…?" I looked at Winslow. I was begging.

"No, I don't think they got to her."

"That stream cuts across the corner of my property. You know that. Maybe you should hire me to assist your investigation rather than prosecuting me for something I didn't do."

Winslow looked to Marsh. "Lieutenant, got an application on you?"

Marsh shrugged. "Sorry. They're all in my desk."

"Please, continue," Winslow cleared her throat, "Porter."

"You've got a couple of holes in your case you could lose a horse in. From the time I was supposed to have lunch with Jamie until you arrested me you can't isolate me for more than two hours, and most of the time I've got multiple alibis. Since I drove my kids out Saturday, unless I took her body with us, I would have had to take her out before the weekend. There's no time I could have done that."

Elizabeth was about to speak, but I held up a hand.

"Did I have an accomplice? I've killed a close friend and former lover for no apparent reason, and now I'm going to get someone else involved, which increases exponentially my chances of getting caught. I could have taken her to

Connecticut, New Jersey, the East River, but I get someone else
to take her body and dump it no more than a sand wedge from
the back of my own property. Why?

"I hear juries like the simplest explanation that fits the facts.
Yours doesn't, and any theory that has me as the killer is ridiculously complicated. You need help? Would you like me as co-
prosecutor?"

"Excuse me."

"I have a right to defend myself, shouldn't I have a right to
prosecute myself?"

Marsh lowered his head and cleared his throat, trying to re-
press a laugh.

"To make it worse, you don't have a motive. I had no reason
to kill Jamie. I loved her."

Winslow said, "Then that proves your innocence since no
one in the history of the world has ever killed someone they
loved." She held up a finger. "You know what I just remembered? People are most often killed by someone they loved
at some point. But that motive issue bothered me." Winslow
pulled a plastic sleeve from her valise and slid it to me. Inside
was Jamie's note. "Until I saw this."

"I want that back."

"It's evidence in a homicide investigation. This looks like a
motive for murder. I've gotten convictions on less."

"How do you get motive out of that?"

"Would you read it for us, Mr. Hall? Out loud."

Keeping my eyes on Elizabeth's, not bothering to look at the
note, I said,

Dear Porter,

*I need to talk to you, seriously. I regret this didn't work for
us although I really tried. It would have been wonderful, but*

*as we both know so well, some things are meant to be, others
are not. See you at lunch. Ask for Babie, Baby.*
   Love,
   Jamie

"Thank you," said Elizabeth taking the note back. "If that's not a Dear John note, then I've never read one."

"Then, Elizabeth, you've never read one. Although you've probably written a few."

She looked at her hands, rotated the bracelet on her wrist. The men in the room had turned to stone, intimidated not by me, but by her.

"So it's coincidence that the body of a close friend of yours, whose last known meeting was supposed to be with you, was found near your property?"

"No, the one thing it is not is coincidence. She was left there for a reason. But I don't know the reason, and it wasn't me who put her there. Plus, all the Medora's exits have security cameras. How did I get out without being seen?"

"I'll bet there's a way, isn't there? And you're on the board so you would know it."

Actually, there was, and I did. That reminded me of the DVDs from the security system. I touched the left pocket of my jacket where I'd put them along with Jamie's note. They weren't there. I remembered I'd stuck them in the door pocket of the Rover.

"Add to that," said Winslow, "a waitress at Kates gave her a message that you wanted to see her. She left the bar and that was the last time she was seen. We know you were already being held at the Thirteenth by then, so it had to be an accomplice."

"A half-dozen people knew we were having lunch. That tells you nothing."

"In that case, would you care to give us another explanation," she smiled, "Porter?"

"Sure. And it's a great story."

"You're in luck," she said. "I love great stories."

21

"Last Monday, Jamie called, scheduled a showing of one of my apartments, and asked if we could have lunch Wednesday, because there was something she needed my advice on. I asked what, but she didn't want to discuss it on the phone.

"'I'm sorry things didn't work out' means the client she showed my apartment to didn't take it. Our 'special place' is Kates."

"I've been there," Winslow said. "What's with the 'baby-babie' stuff, and 'Love, Jamie'?"

"That's how she signed things. The 'baby/babie' thing is a play on Pinky with a 'y' and Pinkie with an i-e from…" I looked at Marsh on a hunch.

He grinned. "*Adam's Rib*. Tracy and Hepburn play a married couple who are attorneys and are opposing each other in a trial."

"Exactly," I said. "We watched it one day at a vintage house in the Village, on a double bill with…" I looked back to Marsh.

"*Bringing Up Baby*. That's with Cary Grant and Baby's a pet leopard," he said, his face looking less tired than usual. "That scene on the golf course is the funniest thing I've ever seen, except maybe for the one in the dining room…"

Winslow gave him a look and he got tired again.

"Were you lovers?" said Elizabeth.

"A long time ago."

"How about last summer?"

I shrugged. She took out several photos and fanned them in front of me.

"Where did you get these?"

"I got them. That's all that matters."

They were grainy and flat, the result of compressed depth of field, meaning they were taken with a long lens. Jamie and I were on the porch at my house in Woodstock. We were kissing. And we didn't have many clothes on.

"She was in Woodstock," I said.

"June Twenty-first. You went to dinner at the Bear Café."

"Yes. Then we went back to my place."

"And undressed on the porch," she said. "You were lovers, she broke it off, you got angry, killed her."

"No."

"And you've got a hair-trigger temper and you almost beat a man to death at a Yankees game."

"Jamie was with me. A guy spilled beer on her, I said something to him, he took a swing at me and hit her in the face."

"It took four men to get you off."

"Three."

"He needed five hours of reconstructive surgery."

I'd been told seven, but five was close enough.

"Why was she in Woodstock?"

"She'd been in Connecticut visiting her mother and decided to hit a couple of vintage shops on the way back. I was on my bike, saw her, and invited her to my house."

She said, "What did you talk about?"

"A lot of things, including my marriage. She wanted to know if it was really over. I said it was. I found out she and Laurie, my wife, were friends. I didn't even know they knew each other."

Winslow looked down her nose at me. "How is it possible you didn't know something like that?"

"At that point, with two small kids, I saw Jamie maybe once or twice a month, and then just to give her keys or sign a lease. Laurie had mentioned a friend called J.T. several times, but I didn't think anything of it. Jamie came by once to pick up keys, I wasn't home, Laurie gave them to her and they started talking. They got to be friends, but I didn't know about it. Laurie could be a little, I don't know, oblique. I guess you'd have to know her."

Winslow said, "Actually…" and stopped short. "Go on."

I tilted my head and we looked at each other. *She did know Laurie.*

"And that's when you resumed your affair with Jamie." She clicked a nail twice on the table.

"No, that's when I *didn't* resume it. After that night it went back to pure business. Until my divorce was final it wasn't fair to Jamie to get involved with her."

"You were lovers," Winslow said, slapping the table. "I want details." I slapped the table, leaned forward, and smiled.

"You know, Elizabeth, I've got a better idea. Let's talk about your sex life. It's probably a lot more interesting than mine."

"I'm not the one on trial here."

"Neither am I."

"That's about to change."

"If it does, Elizabeth, and I'm saying this as your friend, it will be the biggest mistake you ever made, and you will regret it for the rest of your life."

She came out of her chair and leaned across the table, her jacket hanging loose. The sudden movement caused the top three buttons of her blouse to come undone, revealing lovely, full breasts in a white lacy bra. My eyes went there like metal pips to an industrial-strength magnet.

Elizabeth waited a moment and said barely loud enough for me to hear, "My eyes are up here."

I said just as softly, "I know where your eyes are," and kept them on her chest. Something else had caught my attention.

Elizabeth glanced down. Her cheeks turned pink. She knew what I was looking at.

Carmelo caught that part and made a sniggering sound. I had a barely repressible urge to reach across the table, punch him in the face, and knock several teeth down his throat. I was pretty sure no one in the room would try to stop me.

Elizabeth sat down and crossed her arms tightly over her chest. There was a look in her eyes that was close to panic, not because her breasts had been bared momentarily, but because of what I had seen. Her chest was pocked with bruises. A lot of them. Some were fresh, some fading. I wondered if anyone besides the two of us, and the one who had done it, knew this beautiful, educated prosecutor was a battered woman.

22

Elizabeth covered her embarrassment with anger.

"Two things, Mr. Hall. My life is going just fine without your advice. And you are not, and never will be, my friend."

"Elizabeth, you don't mean that. Let's have dinner, talk, maybe go away for the weekend."

She relaxed and smiled with soft irony. "I'd love to get away for a weekend with you, Porter, up in the Catskills, near Ossining. It's such a pretty town. I'll find a cute B&B. You won't be able to join me since you'll be on death row, but I'll take pictures. I'll show them to you just before I press the button that starts the drip. I do hope they let me. I've heard it feels cold when it hits your veins."

"That's strange."

"What?"

"A button. I thought it'd be a like a lever or a knob. I guess everything's gone digital."

Before she could respond, the door opened and a short, solid man in a good suit walked in. "I'm representing Porter Hall, and he has nothing else to say." Don Webster was addressing the room in general. He looked at me, then Winslow. He said, "Elizabeth?"

She straightened up, looked around. "Uncle…uh…Mr. Webster. Why are you here? Miss the Midtown exit? I'm not holding any of the corporate crooks you represent."

He walked toward her, kissed her on the cheek. She embraced him, reluctantly. It struck me, first, as unprofessional, and, second, as clever strategy.

"I'm representing Mr. Hall, my dear. What a coincidence. Now you'll want to recuse yourself."

"Au contraire. This will be the most fun I've had since law school."

"In that case, I will turn lawyerly and say I hope you haven't done anything improper or you will have already lost your case, or you would have if you had one, but you don't, so maybe it doesn't matter. Have you broken any rules?"

She looked at me. "I haven't, but you may want to speak with your client about the proper deportment for someone facing a capital murder charge."

"What did he do?"

"Let's see. First he offered us a deal. Then he offered to help us solve the case, and next he offered to help us prosecute him because he thought we were going to have problems." They both looked at me. I felt like I was the catch of the day being weighed and filleted. "Then he insulted me, threatened my career, and asked me for a date."

Webster gave me a look. "Has he been charged?"

"Not yet, but Russell is all over this one."

"Let's talk," Webster said.

THEY ALL LEFT and Webster returned in half an hour.

"You're in serious trouble."

"I'm innocent."

"With you, that's irrelevant. It looks like someone wants you to go down in flames and has the clout to make it happen. That's why Elizabeth was here. Russell Lewsky, the DA, put her on your case and told her she didn't have a choice. Would you mind telling me who you pissed off?"

"I wish I knew. I'd apologize, bake them a cake, send flowers. She's your niece?"

"My goddaughter. Her father and I roomed together in law school."

"A thirty-five-year-old dishwater blonde is supposed to put fear in my heart."

"She's thirty-three, and yes, she should. The last case she handled, a Gambino captain, is now on death row. How much cash can you get together?"

"Twenty thousand immediately, although I can sell stock."

"Assets?"

"A couple of million, maybe more, mostly real estate equity."

He let out a sigh. "That should be enough."

Webster started to stand and I pulled him back down.

"Tell me about Winslow."

He cocked his head. "Why?"

"Just curious."

"Undergrad at Stanford, Yale Law, father's a major M&A attorney. She worked with him for six months right out of law school, was bored to death, became a prosecutor. And I know you're newly divorced and even assuming you don't wind up in Attica, don't get any ideas about her. Her husband runs a REIT and played hockey at Columbia. Bigger than you. Nice guy, but with a mean streak in the rink. Fairytale marriage."

Webster left. As he walked out the door I saw Elizabeth outside waiting for him. She and I looked at each other until the door closed between us.

A fairytale marriage. A mean streak in the rink. And out, apparently.

Fairytales are dark and terrifying and, at their core, is evil in a pure form. What is often forgotten is that when the happy ending comes, if it comes, someone has paid for it.

23

THE NEXT MORNING I WAS TAKEN BEFORE A JUDGE GOLDFARB, a severe woman with dark straight hair and bangs. She said to Winslow, "What charges will the people bring?"

Winslow hesitated, looked at me for a moment, and said, "Kidnapping and murder in the second degree."

The judge looked at Webster, said, "And how does…" She stopped and looked back at the prosecutor. "Excuse me. Did you say 'second degree'? And that was kidnapping, not aggravated kidnapping?"

"Yes, your honor."

Goldfarb seemed surprised and annoyed. "Fine." To Webster: "and how does your client plead?"

"Not guilty."

Webster asked for recognizance, and Winslow asked for bail of two million. The judge nodded, slammed her gavel, and said, "$10 million, cash." Webster protested and almost got contempt.

Winslow was stunned, looked at me as though she wanted me to explain it to her.

As I was I being cuffed, Webster stopped the corrections officer and took me aside. "I'm withdrawing as your attorney."

"You can't."

"I can, and trust me, it's in your interest. You need a real criminal attorney, not someone who handles corporate contracts. Elizabeth did you a huge favor just now."

"It didn't sound like a favor."

"She charged you with kidnapping and second degree murder, as opposed to aggravated kidnapping and first degree, which is capital. You can't bail out on capital."

"I can't bail out on ten million, all cash, either. But thank her for me."

He squinted for a moment, shook his head, and squeezed my arm. Then he walked arm-in-arm out of the courtroom with my prosecutor.

Ten million dollars. Who did I know with ten million dollars?

THERE WAS ONE person, of course, who could post my bail with a single phone call though I would rather have cut off my head with a plastic knife than asked. As I thought about it, having two kids in a private school in Manhattan, I probably knew another fifty who could post my bail if they wanted to. If I'd had a school directory and my cell phone, I'd have given it a shot.

An hour later, when I got to make a call, my father-in-law-for-the-time-being answered: "What now?"

I gave him a summary.

"Ten million. Not bad, Hall. Let me make a few calls, see if we can't get it up to twenty, or at least fifteen."

They let me make another call. It was almost as bad.

"Hi, Cat. Ready for the latest?"

"No, but tell me anyway."

"They're charging me with murder, kidnapping, and some lesser charges, in case they screw up the big ones. Bail is ten million, my attorney quit, something strange is going on with the prosecutor, and I'm going to be arraigned later on federal charges related to the missing condo funds."

"Business as usual, in other words. Do you want me to do something, like try to find you a new attorney?"

"They'll provide me a public defender. I'll use that for the time being. However, if you've got ten million you don't need for a while…"

"Dammit. I just bought that new yacht. I wish I'd known."

LOWER MANHATTAN IS home to the finance and justice industries. The world's leading financial institutions are there, along with the Federal Reserve Bank of New York and the New York Stock Exchange. A few blocks north of Wall Street sits One Police Plaza, and a couple of blocks from that is the County of New York District Attorney. Around it are a proliferation of federal, state, and county courts. Very convenient, that, having financial services and legal institutions all together. Like glove and hand, love and marriage, and it cuts down on transportation costs.

The next morning I was driven a short distance to the Daniel Patrick Moynihan United States Courthouse from One Police Plaza. As we pulled into a back entrance reserved for special people like me, I said, "We should have walked. You boys could use the exercise." The two U.S. Marshals made like they hadn't heard. I'd been told that feds never laugh. It's as though that's part of their pre-employment tox screen: ten panels, plus humor.

The marshals escorted me to a room where a man said, "Porter Hall, you're under arrest for extortion, wire fraud, bank fraud, and racketeering. You have the right to remain silent…" I did, until the part about how an attorney would be provided for me if I couldn't afford one.

I said, "I'll take it."

He looked perplexed. "What?"

"The free attorney."

He looked at me for a moment, turned, and walked away.

THE FEDERAL JAIL was newer and cleaner than the city's, and the food was edible. Or maybe I was so hungry that food poisoning had more appeal than starvation.

I spent the night there and the next morning I was in another courtroom, a nice one, almost empty. The judge was there, along with a bailiff, a court reporter, and a couple of lawyers, a man and a woman. Neither belonged to me. If this judge were as kindly as the last, my bail would be near the national debt. She said, "Where is your attorney, Mr. Hall? Is he late?"

"I don't have one, your honor."

"You don't? You should have counsel."

"I agree. I had counsel, but we broke up yesterday." The prosecutors looked at me.

"Why wasn't I told this?" said the judge.

"We didn't know," said the woman. "We understood Mr. Hall had representation."

"Mr. Hall, charges have been filed, but you will not be formally charged, and there will be no bail hearing until you have an attorney."

"As there is nothing else we can do," she aaid, reaching for her gavel, a door opened behind me. The prosecutors looked back, then at each other. The judge's eyes were the size of pocket watches.

A voice that resonated like a a two-inch steel plate dropped on pavement said, "Your honor, my name is Clancy Gerard Hamilton, and I will be representing Porter Hall in the matters before this court."

I twisted around. In the aisle stood a man with an old rucksack over his shoulder. He had wavy, reddish hair that reached his neck, and he wore a Western shirt, a fringed leather jacket, and dark denim slacks held at the waist by a tooled belt with a silver and turquoise buckle. In one hand he held an expensive, off-white Stetson Rancher.

Clancy Hamilton was the benchmark for American trial attorneys. Everyone in the legal business, and most people in America, knew that voice and that name. I expected Clarence Darrow before Clancy Hamilton. Apparently so did the judge. She fumbled with her papers. In a matter of seconds she'd gone from Queen of the Nile to handmaiden.

Hamilton, who was close to six-five in his crocodile Wellingtons, dressed to remind people of his humble Western roots. He had defended heads of state, drug dealers, white supremacists, para-militarists, and, reluctantly, a couple of celebrities. No mob or serial killers. He didn't do those, and he had declined to be a member of O.J Simpson's legal "dream team." When asked why by Larry King, he'd snorted, "Would Babe Ruth bat eighth?"

I had met Hamilton once before, though he wouldn't remember it, and no matter what he claimed, I was sure his being there had nothing to do with me. He came forward. "Your honor, what is the status of this hearing?"

"Mr. Hamilton, I was about to adjourn because of Mr. Hall's apparent lack of representation. I'm still inclined to follow that course so you may confer with your client."

"That won't be necessary. I move to dismiss all charges on the basis of lack of evidence. What little the state has is circumstantial, tainted, and insufficient even to bring charges, let alone go to trial."

The prosecutors looked ill. Hamilton was legendary for turning any procedure, an arraignment, a hearing, a chance meeting in the corridor, into an event bigger than most trials.

The judge turned to the prosecutors. "How do you respond?"

The young man stepped forward. "Your honor, the government has amassed substantial evidence, far beyond what is necessary to convict. We expect to put Porter Hall away for life."

Hamilton stared at him. "Is this true, Mr....?"

"Willis. George Willis. Absolutely." He allowed himself a smirk for having held his own against the legend.

Hamilton shrugged. "Fine, your honor. You heard the prosecution's assertion as to the strength and completeness of the government's case. We know when we're beat so we may as well get it over with. We waive arraignment and, asserting my client's constitutional right to a speedy trial, request a court date two weeks from Monday."

The female prosecutor blurted, "What?"

Willis turned red. He stammered, "But your honor, I didn't mean…"

"Mr. Willis, were you lying to the court just now?" Hamilton said.

"No, of course not, but…"

"Then the government should look forward to getting this menace locked away as soon as possible."

"The prelim?" said the judge.

"We waive it."

"Mr. Hamilton, I'm looking at the calendar," said the judge, "and the earliest I could possibly get you on the docket would be six weeks from now."

"Your honor, I made a check through my own sources and I believe three suitable judges will be available within a week. Due to the visibility of this case, and because Mr. Hall has sole custody of two young children, it should be moved to the top of the court's calendar. Without a speedy trial there is no possibility of justice and his children will suffer irreparable harm."

The judge glared. "You can prepare your defense within this time?"

"I can."

"Jury selection — I'm assuming you want a jury trial, Mr. Hamilton — will begin three weeks from Monday. As for bail, where does the state stand?"

"Your honor," said the woman, "the state believes bail should be denied as the defendant has access to substantial family resources and is a flight risk."

The judge looked at Hamilton.

He said, "My client is a father, a businessman, and a property owner with no priors of any kind, and there is no reason to keep him in custody. Furthermore, he has no *family* money, as you say. His estranged wife's family has substantial wealth, but he is in the third year of acrimonious divorce proceedings and has no access to it. The government is aware of this, I believe, or should be. We request recognizance."

The judge took a breath. "Bail is set at ten million dollars. All cash." My magic number.

Smiles came to the faces of the prosecutors and the judge waited for Hamilton to protest. Instead, he turned to me and said in a low but audible tone, "One thing we know, Mr. Hall. The fix is in."

Her gavel slammed.

"Questioning the integrity of this bench will not help your case, counselor. Another remark like that and you will be held in contempt."

"I wasn't aware there was anything to question, your honor. That was a private communication with my client." His words were even and unhurried. "That bail is outrageous, but you already knew that."

She squinted, perhaps pondering whether or not in Hamilton's precisely constructed phrase there was an insult. Or maybe a compliment. She said, "Petition."

"We will."

"Dismissed." She rustled her robes and left. An officer came forward with cuffs.

"I'll see you shortly," Hamilton said. He went out the door, his cell phone to his ear, and they took me to get my fingers done.

24

Two hours later they told me I was being released. I almost argued, almost brought up the cumulative twenty million all-cash bail issue, but let it go. This was New York City, after all, where occasionally a mass murderer in custody is left unattended and simply walks away.

After they returned my belongings, a detention officer escorted me to the lobby. In the middle of the room, as motionless as Michelangelo's David, and drawing just as much interest, was Clancy Hamilton.

We shook hands. "Mr. Hamilton."

"Call me Clancy." I followed him outside to a black Navigator waiting at the curb with a driver. As the car pulled into traffic, I said, "We'll be ready to go to trial in three weeks? Seriously?"

He grinned. "Not in a year, and that's if we were ever going to trial, which I'm pretty sure we're not. You always want to keep the other side on their heels, and, in my case, my reputation precedes me. They never know what I'll do."

"Why are you doing this, defending me?"

He reached over, lifted my chin, turned my head one way and then the other, focusing on my discolored ear. "Looks like you've had a rough week. Relax. We'll talk at the office."

I started to mention our previous encounter, but didn't. I put my head back and closed my eyes for a few minutes. When I opened them, we were passing a large brick apartment complex called Stuyvesant, and Hamilton was watching a girls' soccer game at a field on the bank of the East River. When he saw I was looking, he said, "How have you been?"

"Excuse me?"

"Since we last met. In Austin."

"You remember that?"

"Anyone who has anything to do with my children, I remember."

"Not bad, I guess, except the last few days. What's Mallory doing now?"

"Teaching math, coaching girls' basketball."

"She likes it?"

"She does. I don't. She finished her law degree. I wanted her to follow me. My sons, on the other hand, I didn't, but they did anyway. She could have been the best."

I chuckled. "The best?" He tilted his head. "Or the second best?"

He smiled almost imperceptibly. "The best. She could have been the best."

Mallory, Hamilton's youngest child, had been in a macroeconomics course I taught at the University of Texas. She'd stayed after class one day to talk about her difficulty in finding a term paper topic. When we emerged from the classroom, her father was waiting. Hamilton, whose stare was known to make witnesses crumble and opposing attorneys lose their train of thought, engaged in a stare-down with the one person on the planet who could do it as well as he could. After several tense moments, Mallory introduced me. He and I shook hands, and I walked away.

I said, "Did she ask you to do this?"

"No."

"Then I don't understand. I can't afford your services."

"Few people can."

"I've heard you take three kinds of cases. Those where there's a point to be made. Those where there's a lot of money to be made. And those where there is both a lot of money and a point to be made."

"And those are the ones I love." He laughed. "But you, Porter Hall, have a guardian angel."

"Who?"

"I can't tell you."

"Okay. Are you working for him or for me?"

"Did I say 'him'?" He raised an eyebrow. "Reasonable question. I'm working for you. Whoever hired me is paying all fees and expenses, but I only work for you."

"And my bail?"

"It's been posted, or you wouldn't be here. But I don't advise you to skip."

"This nameless entity can afford it?"

"Yes."

"I've just been provided the services of the finest American criminal defense attorney of the last thirty years…"

"Sixty."

"Hundred. Whatever. Anyway, logic would dictate I should be planning a victory party for my friends, if I still have any, and yet what I feel is foreboding. Why?"

"Because you're not as dumb as the tabloids make you out to be. By the way, you made all the papers today, again."

At Third Avenue and Fifty-third Street the car stopped in front of a pink granite-clad structure with an oval footprint, dubbed the Lipstick Building for its resemblance to a tube of lipstick. We got out and went inside.

THERE WAS NO name on the door of Hamilton's thirty-third floor office suite, just LAW OFFICE. His space was nice, but not opulent, thereby making an even more forceful statement. At the end of the hallway a door stood open to what would have been a corner office except that the building had no angles. He walked to the desk, set his rucksack down, pointed to a leather chair a few feet away, and said, "Relax for a few minutes. That one reclines. When was the last time you ate?"

"Yesterday, maybe." He walked out.

After he was gone I nudged the chair to its prone position and fell asleep. I dreamed I was four and riding on my grandfather's lap as he planted peanuts with his big Farmall tractor, four hoppers dropping seeds into the red dirt as it tumbled over the plow blades. In my dream I also fell asleep. One of my boots fell off and was turned under by the plow. When I woke, I looked at my feet.

A surge of nausea told me I'd forgotten something, that I should be somewhere. B.J. and Cici. With their grandparents, I remembered.

At the large Mission-style desk with a single reading lamp sat Hamilton, slate eyes intent behind gold half-frames. I pushed the footrest and came upright.

"Are you with us?" he said, looking up.

"How long was I out?"

"Hour and a half."

"You should have woken me."

"We need you coherent."

I WAS SHOWN to a washroom, directed to a coffee maker and then escorted to a conference room. I was introduced to Sue Dershon, short dark hair; Brian Tortolo, slick black hair; and Carol Flannery, wavy red hair. Jewish, Italian, Irish. New York law firm functional diversity. In the middle of the table was a tray with sandwiches, fruit, cheese and crackers, and bottles of still and sparkling water.

Hamilton leaned back. "When did things start to go wrong?"

"When I came home and found my wife had been staring out a window for five hours."

"When was that?"

"Three years ago."

He said, "Let's talk about the last couple of weeks."

I told them about the calls Monday: my mother-in-law saying the kids couldn't visit their mother, the call from Jamie, and the one from Fenton saying the terms of the divorce had been agreed to. I described the homeowners' meeting, the fight, taking over as treasurer, the first arrest, Jamie's disappearance, my concussions, the hospital, the kidnapping, and Doris Hebert.

When I finished, Hamilton said, "How about your wife?"

"What do you mean?"

"Is she incompetent?" Sue clarified.

"No," I snapped. "I'm sorry, but no, she just gets…confused sometimes."

"After she left did you try to contact her?" said Hamilton.

"I called, I wrote, I went to the house."

"What happened?"

"Her father had me arrested. The sheriff let me go after an hour. Two days later I was served with divorce papers."

Hamilton was looking at a paper that detailed my legal issues. "Inciting to riot, assault, murder, kidnapping, misappropriation of funds, wire fraud…" It took him two minutes to read the charges. "Are you guilty of any of these?"

"I punched the guy at the meeting. Everything else is bogus."

"Is your live-in legal?"

"She has major medical and a 401K. Yes, she's legal."

Hamilton dropped the list on the table, took a deep breath. "We're not fighting the law. We're fighting the devil. I hate that son-of-a-bitch."

25

THE NEXT MORNING I WAS UP EARLY. I PICKED UP THE PHONE and started to call my in-laws, or ex-in-laws, whatever they were, to check on the children. The Met Life clock reminded me it was not yet 5 a.m.

At six, I put on a light jacket and walked from Twenty-second Street to the MacNeils' apartment on Seventieth. I got there just after seven. I told the doorman, a Montenegran named Dino with no vowels in his last name, to tell them I was on the way up. He said, "Please wait, sir," as he picked up the handset to the intercom. I kept going and got on the elevator.

"Good morning, Andy. Sixteen."

Andy, Dino's cousin, who wore white cotton gloves and touched the elevator buttons so the residents didn't have to, looked uncertainly towards Dino. "Are they expecting you?"

I pushed the button myself and stepped between Andy and the panel so he couldn't reach it. "They will be."

He said, "Sir, I can get in trouble for this."

"Tell them you were elevator-jacked."

When I rang the bell, the door opened and I stood facing a Lithuanian, I thought, a woman, I was pretty sure, named Stella. She looked like a middle linebacker in a white dress. Dino and Andy hadn't been a problem, but getting past Stella would require more than a head fake.

Just then Katherine, elegant, fine-featured, and looking barely fifty, rather than over sixty, as she was, showed up and dismissed the housekeeper. It occurred to me I'd rather take a crack at five-nine, two hundred pound Stella than my five-six mother-in-law.

"Porter." Her arms were crossed and she wasn't smiling.

"Good morning. Where are the children?"

"You should have called."

"I didn't want to wake you. Why should I have called?"

"Because it might not have been convenient at this time."

"*Not convenient* is not an acceptable when I want to see my children. And who is it I might have been inconveniencing?"

"Me," said a voice with dry gravel in it. Jack MacNeil stepped into the vestibule with its lacquered, blood-colored walls and architectural prints.

"Hello, Jack."

He said, "And for the record I've been up since five."

I said, "Well, for the record, I've been up since four."

"Stop it, you two." Katherine jabbed each of us with her eyes.

Jack kept talking. "We did you a mighty big favor by taking your children when you were managing to get yourself thrown in jail and featured in every newspaper and on every channel in the tri-state, and then you just show up at 7 a.m. Like you own the damn place."

"Excuse me. Did you say, *my children*? Taking *my* children was a *big* favor, a *mighty big favor*? Fine, it won't happen again, and you won't see them again, and even Laurie won't see them again until there's a court order saying she will. Since there will never be a court order saying you can see them, given that grandparents have no standing in these matters, you can tell them good-bye. They'll go to an ASPCA shelter before I burden you with *my children* again. Get them, please."

Jack did his tight grin. Once, when I was negotiating a deal for him and he didn't like the way I was handling it, he gave me a vitriolic lecture about overplaying your hand. Now, under the critical gaze of Katherine, I had just gone all-in. Jack folded.

Katherine gave him a look that could have put a welt on his face. She could do more with her eyes than medieval jailers could do with a cat-o-nine. He left the way he came in.

"They're in the breakfast room," she said.

Both had waffles, bacon, and orange juice in front of them, and both ran to me and jumped. I caught one in each arm and stumbled backwards. They cried for a few minutes and started asking questions like whether I was going back to jail and where they would live. I told them I wasn't going back to jail, they were going to live with me, and they were also taking the day off from school. The tears stopped. A day off from school cures virtually anything when you're six.

"What are we going to do?" said B.J.

"Zoo, planetarium, IMAX, whatever you want."

"Really?" said Cici. She was waiting for the catch.

"Really. Finish your breakfast and we'll go."

B.J. finished his orange juice, Cici picked up a piece of bacon, and both headed toward the room Katherine had set up with bunk beds for their visits.

"They're not going to school?" Katherine said.

"No."

"Porter, I know this didn't start well this morning. We weren't expecting to see you so soon."

"If you have the kids, expect me. But I will try to call."

"Coffee?"

"Please."

She took two cups, filled them, and added the right amount of milk to mine.

"It's been a hard week for you and the children and if you want to keep them this weekend I understand. But Laurie wants to see them. If we could have them for a couple of hours tomorrow afternoon, and we'll pick them up, of course…"

"Not necessary. I'll drop them off this afternoon and they can stay the weekend."

"You don't mind?"

"I'll get them Sunday."

Her eyes asked why I would do this.

"The school did a seminar about dealing with trauma, and the best thing you can do is keep them in routine. But today I want them to see that I'm here to stay."

26

When we reached the street, we headed east to Madison to catch an uptown cab to take us to the Bronx Zoo. Coming toward us was a man in a hoodie, hood around his face, sunglasses, khakis, and running shoes. He almost brushed my arm as he passed because he was paying more attention to my children than to where he was going.

When he was a few feet past, I turned and said, "Mark?"

He kept walking. Louder I said, "Henberg."

He stopped and turned. "Hey, Porter."

He didn't come toward me. I walked over, extended my hand, and he took it.

I said, "What are you doing here?"

"Oh, you know, visiting a friend. She sent me out to Starbucks. Know where one is?"

"Really? Where does she live?"

"Madison and, uh, Sixty-ninth, I guess."

"Well, you've got a hike. You're a good half-mile from the closest."

"That far?"

"It's the Upper East Side."

"Oh, right. You're on Twenty-second. I'm on the West Side, myself. They're all over around there."

I wondered why he knew where I lived.

"There are several pastry shops that are close," I said. "I'd go to one of those."

"She wants Starbucks," he said with an odd grin. "She's picky, you know." He looked past me. "Those your kids?"

I stepped in front of him to block his view. "I'm babysitting for a friend. See you around."

As I started toward them, B.J. turned away, but Cici continued to stare. I reached her, took her hand and turned her around. I glanced back and Mark Henberg was still looking at us.

She said, "Who was that?"

"A guy I used to know."

"Why did you say we weren't your kids?"

"The fewer people who recognize you the safer you are."

B.J. said, "I've seen that man."

Henberg turned away. I walked the kids to the building and told Dino to keep them inside.

"Where are you going, Daddy?" Cici wanted to know.

I walked quickly toward Henberg, who started to cross Park Avenue against the light. He stopped on the esplanade because of northbound traffic. I caught up to him.

"What?" he said, and tried to back away. "What do you want, Porter?"

"Why were you looking at my kids?"

"Jesus, I'm sorry. Why did you say they weren't your kids?"

"How do you know where I live?"

"It was in the paper. And I think Jamie mentioned..."

"What did you do to her?" I grabbed his collar and pulled him toward me, twisting it tight around his neck.

"Nothing. I didn't have anything to do with that."

"With what?"

"With whatever happened. Get your hands off me."

I pushed him backward over a ledge into a bed of freshly tilled dirt. He landed hard, held up one arm to keep me at bay.

"Shit. What's the matter with you? I've got nothing to do with what happened to Jamie and nothing to do with your damn kids. I'm calling the cops." He reached into his jacket pocket and withdrew a cell phone. I put a foot on his wrist, bent over, took his phone and threw it into the street. I stepped out of the planter box and Henberg sat up, breathing hard. After a moment I went back to my kids.

Heading up Madison in a cab, I said to B.J., "Where did you see that man before?"

"I don't know if it was him," Cici said. "It might have been someone who looked like him."

THAT EVENING, AFTER rush hour, I took the Holland Tunnel into Jersey, dropped the kids at their grandparents' estate in Short Hills, and headed for the Thruway. As I went through the tolls at Exit 16 my phone buzzed. It was Cat.

She said, "I just did the rewrite on a story we're running on Jamie. There's nothing in it you don't know except that her funeral is tomorrow at 10 a.m., in Lakeville, Connecticut, the Reform Church. Burial is in the Lakeville cemetery. I thought you'd want to know."

"Should I go? Would her family want me there?"

"What would Jamie want?"

27

THAT NIGHT'S DREAMS WERE FROM HELL, OR REVELATIONS, which reads about the same. My soul was severed from my body and there were layers, as in a Shakespeare play, people watching people watching people, except it was me watching me watching me.

I went for an early ride up Overlook Mountain. The sun was just breaking the horizon when I rolled back into my drive. I showered, changed, and was in Lakeville by 9:30. I parked down the street, watched the church, and debated going in. I finally did.

INSIDE, AT THE front on the right, were two women, one with gray hair, Jamie's mother, and one with bleached hair, her sister, Jeanne. I took a seat near the back.

There was a man in the robes of a pastor seated near the lectern, but at ten minutes after the hour he was still just sitting, occasionally checking his watch, as the choir sang softly. The sanctuary was less than a quarter full. Jamie deserved more. It made me sad, and I couldn't imagine how it made her mother and sister feel.

A few minutes later there was noise at the back of the sanctuary and the pastor stood. All three sets of doors opened and people filed in. I recognized some as Jamie's co-workers, some as friends, and there were many I didn't know. The two Kates appeared, looked around, and saw me. They came and sat by me, a Kate on either side. Just Kate said, "Jamie's company brought two buses from the city. We were afraid we were going to miss the service altogether."

One of the last to come through the doors was an African-American woman in a royal blue coat and matching hat, its veil down. She was accompanied by a girl who looked to be ten or eleven. They walked slowly to the pew behind Jamie's mother and sat down. Jamie had an eclectic group of friends but I couldn't imagine how the woman in the blue coat fit in.

The preacher said, "I did not know Jamie Trent well, certainly not as well as I would have liked to." I felt a knot growing in my stomach. There are few things more insulting than a eulogy delivered by someone who didn't know the deceased. He added, "But I did know her, and that is why I'm not going to talk about her. You are going to do it yourselves. If you would like to say something, tell a story, recount a memory, please come forward, up the aisle to my right."

Many of the tributes were moving, many funny, and a lot were repetitive. From them emerged a picture of a woman who was kind, generous, warm, loving, ethical to a fault, stubborn as reinforced concrete, and relentless as a blizzard. Hearing their stories, I saw Jamie with a clarity I had never felt before.

I went to the cemetery because I wanted to be with her until the last. It was selfish. I stood away from the others, lost in sorrow and memories and guilt. The sound of my name brought me back.

A few feet away stood Jamie's mother and sister. Her sister held her mother's elbow, and her mother leaned on a chrome walker.

I said, "Mrs. Trent, Jeannie, I am sorry for your loss."

Her mother's face was ashen and her breathing labored and raspy. She said, "Why did you come?"

"Because I loved Jamie. And I did not do this to her. I would never hurt her. I...I'm sorry." I had said too much. I should have walked away.

They moved in the direction of a waiting black car, but after a few steps Mrs. Trent stopped and turned toward me.

"You would never hurt her." She turned her eyes back toward Jamie's grave where the laborers were preparing to finish the interment. Her eyes were desolate, caught between a past that couldn't bring her comfort, and a future in which every new day brought pain.

She struggled for each breath. "Never hurt her? Porter Hall, you broke her heart."

28

Monday morning Roger drove the small yellow bus away with my children inside. They waved. I waved.

I went upstairs, sat in the kitchen, and made a chronology of everything that had happened, every single event, and on another sheet a list of everyone who was involved, even tangentially. I looked at the lists for a while, went to the craft closet, found poster board and colored markers, and drew a large circle. In the middle, like a bull's eye, I drew a small circle. That was me. I put the events around the outer edge and the people inside circle. It looked something like a mandala. Or maybe my personal Wheel of Misfortune.

I drew lines in different colors connecting me and the people to each other and each person to the related events. When I had drawn all the connections I could think of, I took the poster board to the den, taped it to the TV screen, sat on the sofa and stared at it. Every few minutes I would walk over and draw another line or two.

I hadn't needed a diagram to show that I was the hub. The question was how did all of the others relate to each other outside of me. One thing that popped out in the visual representation was that there was a stronger connection between Plockman and Jamie than I had thought. And there were a lot of lines to my children. That was the hardest for me. I didn't want them to be part of it, and didn't know why they should be. It was true they were the centerpiece of my custody dispute with Jack, but that was settled. Wasn't it? Beyond that, they shouldn't have been involved. But according to my diagram, they were.

So who was capable of making all these things happen to me, of making such things happen to anyone? Who was responsible for Jamie's death? Was there a single party/person/entity, or were there multiple points of origin, meaning the situations were genuinely coincidental? Or perhaps only casually, not causally related?

The person I kept coming back to was Jack MacNeil. He was acquainted with players in the city and state, the governor, the mayor, and several council members, but that wasn't his venue. His playground was Washington D.C. He might have been involved with my federal issues, but there was absolutely no way Jack MacNeil would have approved kidnapping his own grandchildren, not even for a minute. They were what he lived for.

The idea that he was linked with what happened to Jamie was unthinkable. Jack would lie, cheat, play dirty, and manipulate. I'd seen him do it. But the murder of an innocent woman was far outside his boundaries. I was positive of that. I knew the man well. I'd played golf with him on three continents.

And, on the bright side, who was the angel who sent me
Clancy Hamilton? And where did the twenty million in bail
come from?

I needed to start at the beginning, and the real beginning
was Wednesday, between noon and one, when I got arrested
and Jamie went missing.

Looking at my big circle, with its web of lines and names,
suddenly I got it. I was basing all of my analysis on one massive
assumption. I had assumed that Jamie's going missing, and my
simultaneous arrest by Detective Kurch, were only the worst
possible of coincidences. I was late to meet Jamie and, therefore,
I wasn't there to prevent someone from taking her. Had I left a
few minutes earlier, I assumed, I would have been with her, the
abduction would not have occurred, and Jamie would be alive.

I'd been positive of that from the beginning, positive that
Jamie was dead because of one lost minute, that single minute
of delay cost Jamie her life. One minute. Gone. That was what
I had believed.

I was wrong. My brain buzzed and I could feel sparkles of
energy on my skin. Cat was right. Flip the lens, and look at it
from a different angle. If you viewed all of it as a carefully laid
plan, the gaps, the chasms, the leaps in logic needed to make
sense of it went away. There were still pieces missing, but I finally saw the picture.

Damn.

I suddenly realized if I'd left five or ten or thirty minutes
earlier, it wouldn't have mattered. Whoever was behind it had
seized on the fracas at the condo meeting as a means of setting
me up. Hell, they may have even started the fight at the meeting. *Inciting to riot?* Absurd. Kurch arrested me while Jamie was
being kidnapped to keep me out of the way. Then, as Cat suggested, he held me until it was too late to meet my children.

What if, as Cat suggested, my own attorney, Dennis Fenton, was in on it? On top of that, the order to pick me up had supposedly come from the Police Commissioner.

Unconnected, the events suggested a world in chaos. Seen as a conspiracy directed at me, the events suggested a world ticking like a Swiss watch. That left one question. Whose perfect machine was it?

Whose?

I yanked the diagram from the TV, took it back to the kitchen and started drawing more lines. Changing that one assumption increased the coherence of the image several fold. There were still gaps, and there was a gaping blank space, a single hole, into which would go the name of the one who was behind it all. Who could make it all happen? And why? In that egg-shaped opening I wrote, *Force majeure?*

I HAD LOOKED at myself, at my own role, until I had become invisible. Psychologists call it attenuation. There is something called *edge theory* that suggests our brain filters stimuli only down to what is different, what is essential, because otherwise we would be so bombarded with information our neuro-processing would shut down. I needed to look past me, and the most obvious direction was Jamie.

The seeds planted by those who spoke at her funeral had germinated and were beginning to grow. They had not told me anything I didn't know, because I knew her better than any of them. That was the problem. I was too close. When I thought of Jamie, I thought sweet, kind, loving, someone I would trust my life to, but most of the stories others told had to do with her fairness and her unending crusade against injustice and corruption wherever she found it. Being a crusader is like poking a beehive with a short stick. The corrupt and the unjust don't fight fair, any more than a swarm of bees.

Lunch. An invisible bucket dumped ice water over my head. The meeting with Jamie was critical to everything. Someone didn't want it to happen.

What did Jamie want my advice on? Was she kidnapped to stop her from talking to me? Why was her body left almost at my back door? There were limited ways to put these things together. In fact, there was only one, and once I got on the right track it would be a downhill run on an icy slope toward an inescapable conclusion, an inevitable ending.

Jamie couldn't tell me so I needed to look where she had looked if I wanted to find what was behind all of this. I called the one from whom I learned she was missing, Herb Schneider, and told him I needed to meet with him. I didn't want to be seen going to Jamie's office so I asked him to meet me at a furnished rental I owned at Thirty-eighth and Lex that was vacant at the moment. I told him what to bring.

On my way out Jorgé, the concierge, had just handed the little man from across the hall, 28A, a hat box from a store called Severio's. I noticed it because that was where I bought my own hats. As I approached the desk, Jorgé looked up and said, with no trace of animosity and in an overly clear voice, "Mr. Hall, so good to see you." It was the first time I'd seen him since our altercation in the security room. Something was going on. *Mister* wasn't italicized.

He smiled a Judas smile, glanced past me, and nodded. I turned around and a guy with too much cologne was in my face. "Porter T. Hall, damn good to see you again."

I looked him up and down. "Why?"

"To give you this." From his pocket he withdrew a folded document in blue cardstock. "You're served, Mr. Hall." He walked away, and an Aqua Velva trail lingered in his wake. Jorgé stood behind the desk grinning, as though someone had just given him an overly generous Christmas envelope. The process server probably had. The little man from 28A watched quietly, then headed toward the elevators with his hatbox.

29

THE DOCUMENT SAID THERE WAS TO BE HEARING ON CUS-
tody, which perplexed me because I thought that was settled.
Upstairs, I read it several times. The critical point was that I,
the one with custody, was on the defensive. I had to show why
I shouldn't lose my children, meaning there was somewhere a
prior assumption they should be taken from me. It said, "as
stipulated by the decree of divorcement…"

In a filing cabinet I found my copy of the final document,
which I assumed would soon be official, if it wasn't already.
From the bottom shelf of a bookcase I took a ten-inch stack
of drafts, from the very first, which dated to almost three years
ago, to the last. It took me ten minutes to find the relevant pas-
sage and another half hour to trace its history. I picked up the
phone and called the man who created the stack of documents,
Dennis Fenton.

A woman's voice said, "I'll see if Mr. Fenton is available." She put me on hold. The voice returned, "Mr. Fenton is not available. May I take a message?"

"I'll hold until he is."

"Mr. Fenton will be tied up all day."

"No, Mr. Fenton will be on the line in one minute. Tell him it's a matter of life and death." She put me on hold for a few seconds, came back, and asked whose life and whose death.

"My life, his death." She put me on hold again.

A moment later Fenton came on. "What's this about, Porter? Are you threatening me?"

"No, and I'm sorry if you got that impression."

"What's this about?"

"Well, I was just sitting here trying to jot down what I was going to say at your memorial service, trying to come up with some nice things. It's not as easy as you might think. How does this sound? 'He always had a big smile when he stabbed you in the back.' Is that okay?"

"I'm recording this, Porter, and it sounds like you're threatening me."

"For the last time, Dennis, I'm not threatening you. As far as I'm concerned, you're already dead."

After a silence he said, "I can't talk to you. Have your new attorney contact me and I'll speak with him."

"I will, but first I wanted to congratulate you."

"For what?"

"For changing a key provision in the settlement agreement so subtly I never noticed."

"What are you talking about?"

"The clause that says if I'm ever charged with one or more felonies, legal custody of my children will cede to my wife or her parents until one year after the final charge is dropped. Or, if I'm convicted, five years after I'm released from prison. That one."

He was silent for a moment. Then he said, "It's part of a morals clause they insisted on. You read it, you signed it. You're supposed to read things before you sign them."

"That's what I thought. But you know how in each draft you highlighted the changes from the previous draft so all I had to do was read the changes?"

"You still have those copies?"

"I keep everything, and that section wasn't marked as a change. You snuck it right past me."

"We thought it was a silly clause and a moot point and I knew you'd never agree. And they were adamant. We didn't want to drag this out for three more years. We were doing you a favor."

"You call it a favor, I call it malpractice. You're *my* lawyer. And making me sit for four hours handcuffed to a bench was worse than malpractice. By the way, who paid you off?"

"They didn't…" He caught himself. "You're crazy. You know that, right?"

"Thanks for admitting the setup, Dennis, and thanks for recording it. Make sure you don't lose the tape. It's evidence, you know."

"Whoops. Silly me. I forgot to hit the record button."

"That's okay. I'm recording too."

"That's illegal, Porter. You didn't advise me so you'd better erase it. You know what happened to Linda Tripp."

"This isn't Maryland. It's legal in New York to tape your own conversations, but you know that. One question: do you care whether I wear a tie to your service?"

"Porter…"

30

"Thanks for coming," I said. "I wasn't sure you'd see me."

Herb Schneider was waiting in the living room when I walked in. He used the key I'd given Jamie.

"You didn't do anything to Jamie."

"How do you know?"

"I doubted you had anything to do with it from the beginning, and the police sealed it."

"How?"

"The stuff you asked me to bring was stuff they didn't want."

"That doesn't make sense. They should have gone through it with tweezers and a magnifying glass."

"Should have but didn't. Because they were sure they had their killer, a little too sure. Just like a deal in real estate. Once you've got it, shut your damn mouth and get out. And if you've got your killer, you quit looking because you might find out that's not your killer."

"They never checked her customers, her business dealings, anything? They didn't ask if someone was stalking her, or if she were involved in any disputes?"

Herb shook his head. "That's when I knew you were being set up." He reached down and lifted a canvas tote onto the coffee table. "This is all I could find. I would have printed out everything from her computer, but this is Jamie we're talking about. She put computers in the same category as greasy food. She used them to search for properties and list her own, but that was it."

I took the bag to the dining table, and for the next hour we went through contracts, listing sheets, contact lists, and every sale or lease she'd handled in the past three years. Even if the police had taken the material, it's not likely they would have found anything because Herb and I didn't, and we had a much better idea what to look for.

One folder contained correspondence, letters, and cards from friends and people she'd done business with. Three were from me. The other two had a whiff of impropriety. In both cases she was being thanked for "gifts" that helped with a move or helped someone "get settled." Our hunch was Jamie had used part of her commission to subsidize a cash-strapped renter or purchaser. In New York, as in most states, giving money to a buyer is illegal because, in effect, it's paying a brokerage commission to someone who doesn't have a license. But, given Jamie's history of generosity, it would have been hard to prove those were anything but copacetic.

The last item was the most interesting. It was a pale green, oversized envelope that contained a Hallmark card with "Friendship" in gold embossed letters above a reproduction of a watercolored country scene. I looked on the back. 0395. $3.95. A note was written in blue ballpoint in an unsteady hand.

Dear Jamie

I cant expres what you have done for us means. If you hadn't stood up for us we would live on the street now and I would not have a job and my baby would not be in school. I cant ever repay you or thank you enough. I don't know what I would of done without you. The others feel the same too.

Love

Waneeta Perkins

Enclosed was a folded sheet of typing paper with a colored-pencil sketch of a bicycle being ridden by a brown-skinned girl with dark ringlets of hair. Behind her was a square, red building. A note at the bottom said, "This is me in front of our home. Momma says you saved it for us. I love you. Jaylene."

The return address was on West Thirty-first Street, near Eighth Avenue, and the postmark was three years old. I handed him the card and drawing. "Is this familiar?"

He looked at them and shook his head. "No. I don't remember the details of every transaction, but neither the address nor the name rings any bells."

"I'm going to take this." I stuck it in my pocket. "And I hate to ask just because, well, I would have never asked her, but it may be relevant. Was she seeing anybody?"

Herb stuffed some of the papers back in the bag. "Not as far as I know. It wasn't something she and I talked about."

As HERB AND I parted my phone rang. Clancy Hamilton said we were meeting with Marvin and his attorney in the morning.

"Why would they meet with us?"

"We offered to help them out. I told them it's not right for Marvin to take the fall for something that's not totally his responsibility, and in the interest of getting your financial case resolved, so we can focus on the murder case, we may be willing to take some of the heat off him if they open up to us."

"Gee. Clancy, that's clever. I confess to something I didn't do to get me off the hook for something else I didn't do. No wonder you were number one in your class at OU Law School."

"Stanford. Be here at nine."

TEN MINUTES LATER I got out of a cab in the Garment District, an area in the West Twenties and Thirties, near the Fashion Institute of Technology. The neighborhood is comprised mostly of old office buildings and warehouses that for decades were home to importers and manufacturers, some union shops, more sweatshops. In the Eighties and Nineties, as the tide of gentrification lifted property values throughout the city, the *garmentos'* rents were jacked up until manufacturing became infeasible. Some were converted to luxury lofts, some torn down to make room for new construction.

Waneeta Perkin's building was a plain eight-story structure that was built, gauging by its style and colors, in the mid-Nineties. A glass-encased tenant roster denoted Perkins, W. as living in 1B. I buzzed.

A sleepy voice said, "Who's there?"

Good question. *Porter Hall* was more likely to get the door slammed than opened. "Lawrence, I mean, Larry Taylor." After a crackle that sounded like an electric baby rattle, I pulled open the door and entered. There was no lobby, just a corridor with off-white speckled tile, three doors on each side, and a single elevator at the end. 1B was the second door on the right.

As I was about to knock, the door opened slowly and a solidly built African-American woman of medium height stood facing me. She was wearing an ankle-length, pink chenille robe and hot-pink terrycloth slippers. I couldn't tell her age. In a closet, somewhere, hung the blue coat and matching hat she'd worn to Jamie's funeral. The girl with her must have been her daughter, Jaylene.

"Larry Taylor." She looked me up and down. "That's funny. On TV you look like a six-foot-five black man. I got to get me a new television set."

"Different Larry Taylor."

"Guess so. Cause that Larry Taylor ain't named Porter Hall. And he's retired. Why you here?"

"To talk about Jamie Trent."

She crossed the small living room and sat on a floral print chair. I sat on the sofa. The inexpensive furniture was from a place on Fourteenth Street with "free financing." The payoff term almost always outlasted the furniture. A child's bicycle leaned against a wall.

The woman looked at me. A tear came, then another, falling from her face to her robe. She paid them no mind. She said, "It's about time somebody asked about that sweet girl."

"Mrs. Perkins, in spite of what you may have seen on TV or in the papers, I didn't kill Jamie."

"I know you didn't." Her face had become as hard as mahogany.

"How do you know that?"

She stared straight ahead for the better part of a minute, then looked at me. "Because I know who did."

31

I LEFT WANEETA PERKINS SITTING IN HER CHAIR WITH ITS not-quite-matching head and armrest protectors, as firm in her belief that Jamie's killer would never be caught or punished as if the Lord had told her directly. The conviction that rich white men can do anything and get away with it was, to her, as imbedded in the fabric of America as the textured roses in the fabric of her chair.

Outside I turned back and looked at the building. Did something that happened in that place get Jamie killed? Waneeta Perkins thought so. Was Mark Henberg, the man I saw outside my in-laws' apartment, who seemed to have an inordinate interest in my children, behind it? Waneeta Perkins was sure of it.

WHEN I WALKED into my kitchen, the Met Life clock said 3:40. The kids' bus would be downstairs in five minutes. I had time for one call. "Hey."

"Hey," Cat said, almost chipper.

"Meet me for pick-up. I've got some new information."

"Where are you?"

"The usual."

"Which? Jail or hospital?"

"In front of my apartment."

"Sorry, I thought you said the usual. I'm walking into Grand Central now. See you shortly."

I was sitting on the front planter box when I saw Cat coming west from Park. It was 3:52, and the bus was seven minutes late. Normally, that's not a cause for concern, but normal was a bridge that washed out of my life a while ago. I tried both the kids' cells and got nothing. As she approached, Cat saw the worry in my eyes and pointed past me. The small bus turned the corner. I was at the door as Roger opened it. B.J was in the front seat, but there was no Cici.

"Where's your sister?"

He pointed toward the rear. I found her slumped in the backseat by the window with a glum, blank look, and eyes that had been crying. Roger said, "Sorry we late, mon. Water main break on Lex. Traffic messed up everywhere."

I coaxed Cici off the bus and asked what the trouble was. She didn't answer. B.J. said, "She was playing with her cell phone during class and Mrs. Trindle took it away."

Cici looked up. "Am I in trouble?"

"What do you think?" She walked into the lobby. I turned to B.J. "Where's yours? Why didn't you answer?" He took it from his pocket and handed it to me.

"Dead battery. And Mrs. Trindle said give you this." He handed me Cici's, also with a dead battery.

Cat said, "Got any other strategies, Dad? How about implanting each kid with a GPS chip?"

Upstairs I took the kids into the kitchen and gave them the rules about cell phone use. During school it was to stay in their cubby, and if it didn't, they would forfeit it.

I found Cat in the living room looking out the window, not smiling. I said, "What's the matter?"

"New York is the matter. There was a skanky guy on the subway and he kept staring at me."

"There are skanky guys in every city."

"Not that skanky."

"Plus most guys are creeps," I assured her.

She jerked her head around. "Wow. Are you a girl inside?"

"No, just a misanthrope. I need you to do something."

"Will it get me arrested?"

"It's perfectly legal."

"That wasn't what I asked."

I handed her a slip of paper and said, "Call this number on your cell, please."

"Whose is it?"

"Elizabeth Winslow's."

"From the DA's office? If you need more trouble, Porter, why don't you just walk around the street naked, selling drugs and shooting people?"

"Later. Please call her and tell her you need to talk to her, here, that you have information relating to the murder of Jamie Trent."

She pursed her lips. "What's the max for aiding and abetting an *ex parte* contact?"

"Can't be more than five, I'd think."

She glared at me, reached into a pocket, took out her phone and called. She told the receptionist she was a reporter and was put through immediately. From Cat's end of the conversation, I could hear that Ms. Winslow was reluctant to meet her. I started mouthing things she should say but she waved me off. She segued into a mixture of charm and belligerence, but Elizabeth still hadn't agreed to come. Exasperated, Cat said, "Porter Hall wants to talk to you, now." She listened for a couple of more seconds and disconnected.

"Thanks for trying," I said.

"She'll be here in fifteen minutes."

"Really?"

"Hard to believe, but my first boss told me this. It's usually best to tell the truth."

"That's what my mother said."

"Not mine."

32

"HELLO, PORTER." ELIZABETH SMILED AND WALKED IN LOOK-
ing more like she'd come from lunch at Café des Artistes than
the DA's office. She was wearing a camel-colored wool skirt and
jacket over a cream-colored turtleneck, maybe cashmere.

She said, "Nice to see you."

"Really?"

"Yes, really. Is this our 'date'?" Cat walked up from behind
and stood next to me.

I introduced them. Cat gave Elizabeth something that would
have had a hard time passing as a smile, gave me a look that felt
like a cold headwind, and turned and marched to the living
room. We followed. Elizabeth took an armchair and I sat on
the sofa next to Cat.

"Why did you want to see me?" she said.

"Herb Schneider, Jamie's boss…"

"Yes, I know Herb."

For a city with eight million people it was odd how small the communities were, and within those, how everybody seemed to know everybody.

"Herb and I went through all of Jamie's work files."

Elizabeth furrowed her brow. "But the police had already done that, at least that's what the report said."

"They didn't go through anything. It probably didn't matter because there wasn't much there, except for this. Even if they'd done what they should have done I doubt they would have caught it." I handed her the envelope. "It's from a woman named Waneeta Perkins."

Elizabeth opened it, read the card, and looked at the drawing. She looked to me for an explanation.

"If you give Mrs. Perkins fifteen minutes with the person she thinks killed Jamie, you can skip voire dire."

"I'm listening."

"Do you remember the 421a abatement?"

"The first apartment I bought had one. Ten years, right?"

"There were some wrinkles to it, but basically."

Cat was next to me, her shoulder against my arm.

"How is that related to Jamie's death?" asked Elizabeth.

I gave them a brief history of the Reagan years, the near collapse of the United States financial system, and the decimation of the real estate industry brought about by flip-flopping tax laws. I told them how this was exacerbated in New York City by the expiration of the 421a tax abatement program. To beat the expiration of the program's windfall benefits, developers threw up an eight-year supply of product in eighteen months, just as financing was drying up and the national and local economies were in collapse.

"A modified 421a plan was passed was based on an 80/20 split between market rate and subsidized units."

"I sort of remember," Elizabeth said. "Did it fly?"

"Like a turtle in a lead shell. Visualize this. There are two hundred apartments in a building and one hundred and sixty go for an average of $6,000 per month, while forty go for $600 per month to applicants classified "the working poor," who are selected by a city bureaucracy. It was like telling first graders the first one to finish their cooked carrots would get another serving of broccoli.

"Waneeta Perkins lives in one of the few projects built under that version of the plan. Jamie was the leasing agent. Then, when the leases started coming up for renewal, the developer tried to get rid of all the low-income residents so he could bump those units to market rate. That would dramatically increase the building's value by pushing up the cap rate."

Cat said, "The what?"

"The capitalization rate. It's a multiple of net income that gives you a building's investment value. Raising subsidized rent to market rate can increase a building's potential selling price by several hundred thousand, even millions."

"How did they try to get the tenants out?"

"The usual. No heat or hot water, no garbage pick-up, noise in the middle of the night, rent checks lost, thugs in the building. Waneeta told Jamie and Jamie fought back. She got a Midtown law firm to represent the tenants pro bono."

"Who was the developer?"

"Mark Henberg."

Elizabeth's eyebrows went up.

"You know him?"

"Not well, fortunately. His father is a builder on Long Island and used to play golf with my father. His family's been there for generations, mostly working class and farmers, but when land values around the Hamptons started going through the roof, they were suddenly rich. Then his father got into real estate development, was good at it, and they got even richer. But Mark is a screw-up. Talks big, comes up with grand schemes that always crash, has couple of busts for possession and DWI on his record. A lot of family tension there."

I shrugged. "But what do you care? You've got your killer."

"You didn't do it."

"How do you know?"

"Where to start? The autopsy report came back." She looked at me and gave me a moment to be sure I wanted to hear it. I nodded. "There were a lot of defensive injuries, plus cuts, abrasions, and blunt-force trauma, but the COD was asphyxiation from strangulation. The pre-mortem bruising suggests whoever did it was left-handed, and you're right-handed. Then there's the Occam's razor issue, which you raised during interrogation. Any theory that posits you as the killer, given the time you were in police custody and the hospital, is ridiculously complicated. And then there's Russell Lewsky, my boss."

"The DA?"

"Yes, him." The shape of her mouth suggested she'd just bitten a lemon. "I've got a major trial starting next week but he said I had to take your case anyway. That doesn't make sense. Then there was the way he reacted after I interviewed you and told him under no circumstances would I prosecute."

"But you filed charges."

"If I hadn't, he would have gotten Carmelo or some other moron to do it. They would have filed first degree and you'd still be in jail. Judge Goldfarb was obviously in on it because she was expecting murder one. There's no way she should've known. When I told Russ I wouldn't handle it, I thought his eyes were going to explode."

Cat said, "He was angry?"

"And sick, like he was about to throw up. That means the order to prosecute Porter, as well as the order to put me on the case, came from above."

Cat looked at me and back to Elizabeth. She said, "He's the DA. He's elected. There is no *above*."

Elizabeth gave her a slightly condescending smile. "How long have you lived here, Cat?"

"A year and a half," she said, a little defensively.

"Then you're still practically a tourist. In this city there's always an *above*, and it doesn't matter if you're the DA or the mayor. Elected officials have to get elected, judges have to get appointed or elected, but without the so-called *above,* that doesn't happen. This city is a machine. It's like *the house* in Vegas. No one beats it for very long. But all the house takes is your money. The machine can take your life."

I RODE DOWN in the elevator with Elizabeth. As we stepped into the lobby she said, "By the way, do you know a woman named Doris Hebert?"

"Unfortunately. Do you?"

"She called to find out what was going on with the murder charge, said she had an open file on you for child endangerment, offered to help me, and wanted me to help her. I told her there wasn't a case. She called me a stupid, lazy bitch and hung up."

"You're lucky you caught her in a good mood."

We walked the length of the lobby and out onto the street. I said, Thank you for coming, but one question." Her face tensed and she got very still. "Who beats you, Elizabeth?"

"You have no business looking at my chest, and you certainly have no business asking me that."

"Non-responsive, as I think you would say."

"But I'm not on the witness stand. You have no right to ask."

"That's true. And I'll bet the battered women who come into your office tell you that all the time."

On the ground two pigeons squabbled over a scrap of hot-dog bun.

"I know it's hard to admit abuse for anyone, but especially you. You're educated, wealthy, socially prominent, and you're a prosecutor. It's beyond what I can imagine."

Her eyes were focused a mile away.

"Elizabeth." She looked at me. "Does anyone else know?"

"My sister, maybe. The frosting on the cake is that my family adores my husband."

"Leave him."

"He'd kill me." Her tone was flat, matter-of-fact. The statement was neither drama nor hyperbole.

"How long has this been going on?"

"Since we got married, two years next month."

"Interesting."

"What?"

"You've had one of the highest conviction rates in the DA's office for the last two years. Right?"

She nodded.

"You work until midnight and go back at 6 a.m."

"If I go home at all."

She resented my asking, I could tell. I could also tell she was relieved someone else knew, but she never could have told.

"If there's ever anything I can do, call me. Anytime."

"And what is it you think you could do, Porter?" She gave a soft and bitter chuckle. "Even if you didn't have plenty of your own troubles, trust me, mine aren't the ones you want to borrow."

There was a squawk. I looked down at the noisy birds where six were now in the fray. I wanted to hug her and tell her it would be okay. Somehow, it would be okay. But the city has eight million people and sixteen million eyes, and any assurance I could make that anything would ever be okay for anyone were as meaningful as last year's campaign promises. She smiled bleakly and walked away.

I watched her go toward the Flatiron, watched men watch her, and women too. There probably wasn't one woman in a thousand who wouldn't jump at the chance to trade places with Elizabeth Winslow, with her brains and beauty and success, not one who wouldn't love her jewelry and fine clothes, not one who could ever imagine that beneath the silk and cashmere and Egyptian cotton, her life was a hair shirt of shame.

WHEN I WALKED into my apartment, Cat was in the entry with her jacket over her arm. She slipped into it without my help and walked out the door.

33

THE MORNING SKY WAS SURLY WITH GRAY CUMULUS, LIKE IT had rolled in from a bad night in a rough part of town and intended to make the new day pay for its bad judgment. When I arrived at Clancy's office, he and his crew were in the conference room. Clancy said, "Meeting's off. But Zedloff sent this over."

Bernard Zedloff was one of those TV sound-bite hounds who was always in the middle of breaking news, defending people the system was out to get, specifically, anyone who would hire him. His current victim-of-the-day was Marvin Plockman.

"What happened?"

"Zedloff says something came up and Marvin couldn't make it. But he had no interest in rescheduling, which suggests to me he has no idea where his client is." Clancy pulled pages from the envelope and spread them on the table.

"What's this?"

"Apparently it's the basis for Marvin saying you were behind everything." He pointed to one page with a column in which $25,000 was listed six times, each followed by a date and a nine-digit number and a ten-digit number. "He says he transferred $150,000 to you in increments of twenty-five."

I laughed. "It's news to me. Why would he do that?"

He pointed to photocopy of another sheet that was hand-written and had lines, as though torn from a tablet. On it was a note that said, "I have already sent you the receipts. They to-taled over $300, but as the board only approved $250, please re-imburse that amount. I will absorb the difference." There was another handwritten follow-up note also demanding $250.00, indicating I would fire him if I didn't get it soon.

Brian said, "You threatened to fire him over two hundred and fifty dollars."

"If I had a buck for every time I threatened to fire Marvin, I could have posted my own bail. He's one of those people you need a four-by-eight just to get his attention."

Sue said, "So Marvin interpreted $250 as $25,000. Why?"

Clancy said, "Mindset. He was skimming, expecting to get caught, and thinks Porter's caught him. He ignores the decimal because he knows Porter doesn't care about a couple of hundred dollars. Where's the money now?"

"I have no idea."

Brian said, "I looked up the routing number. It's a bank called Western Jersey."

I said. "Western Jersey is a bank Jack uses, and Laurie had several accounts there. We had one joint account, too, but I never saw those statements."

Brian gave me the phone number for the bank and I called. The second woman I reached said she would be happy to help.

Three minutes later she came back on and said she couldn't. Clancy signaled for the phone.

He identified himself. "Yes, that Clancy Hamilton, and if we haven't received the information in ten minutes I will call back with the head of the state banking commission on the line." He hung up.

I said, "You know the head of the New Jersey State Banking Commission?"

He shook his head. "I don't even know if New Jersey has a banking commission."

Ten minutes later we were each handed a copy of a fax print-out of the account showing deposits and disbursements. We all stared. Sue said, "Wow. You're generous."

Brian said, "No, he's a philanthropist."

"This explains some things," I said.

"Like what?"

"Like why I get invited to some amazing events and why I always get seated with the star dancers at the ballet, and why two of them, one man, one woman, seem to be in love with me."

"So you didn't give the City Ballet a hundred thousand dollars?" said Clancy.

"Not to my knowledge, nor twenty to the Museum of Natural History, nor twenty to the Guggenheim, nor ten to the Met. But it explains why, even though I gave the ballet a thousand, I couldn't find my name under Donor in the program. I'm a Patron."

"How can we find out about this?" said Clancy.

"Only my wife and my father-in-law would know, and only one of them will tell us."

I got information on the office phone, got a number for Moorcliff Village, called, and waited to be put through.

"What I can deduce, based on what I learned from the con-do's statements before they were stolen, is there is someone over Marvin. Over half a million was missing. If I got one-fifty, that leaves three hundred fifty thousand missing. I can't believe Marvin ended up with all of that."

I pulled out the set of the documents I'd copied to my computer before all the reports were stolen from my dining room and handed them to Sue Dershon. I said, "These contain all the double billings I found. There may have been more. There are also reports and consolidations from the accountants that I haven't had a chance to look at."

Finally, a voice said, "I'm putting you through to Ms. Hall," and my heart tried to climb out my throat. I was about to speak to Laurie for only the second time in three years. And she still went by Laurie Hall.

I said, "Laurie?"

She said, "Hi, sweetie. Will you come see me right now?"

I was looking curveball down and away, and I got a high slider at my face. "I'm sorry. I can't, not right now. But sometime I will."

"Okay. Bye. I love you."

"Laurie, wait. Do you remember that account we had at Western Jersey?"

I hit the speaker button and put the handset in the cradle.

"Yes." She recited the account number along with the bank's routing number. "That one?"

I never failed to be amazed by Laurie's recall of certain details, especially facts and numbers, especially when paired with her occasional inability to remember my name, our children's, or what year it was.

"That's it. Did you make any transfers out?"

"Yes," she said, and recited the amounts, dates and payees as though reading from the list in front of me, except for the last $20,000 to the City Ballet. I asked about it.

"I didn't do that one." I circled that transaction.

"Why did you give all that money away?"

"You said it was okay."

"I did?"

"Yes. I told you Ms. Reiner from the bank called and said we had a lot of money in that account, did we want to do anything with it, put it in stocks or CDs, or transfer it. I asked you and you said to do whatever made me happy. So I did."

I had a vague memory of such a conversation. Her father set up that account and, if there was money in it, I assumed it came from Jack, or from Laurie's trust fund, and had nothing to do with me.

"Did you ever give that account number to anyone?"

"Marvin Plockman. I saw him in the lobby one day and he said he was ready to send your reimbursement, could I have you call him with an account number. I said I could give it to him right then and that one popped into my head so that's the one I gave him. He is a peculiar person. Every time he said, 're-imbursement,' he winked. Is he okay?"

"Not really. Did you tell me about that?"

"At dinner that night. We had fish, B.J. spilled his apple juice on Cici. She was crying. I cleaned up the kitchen, you gave the kids their baths, then we went to bed and read for six minutes, then you put your arm around me, and put your hand on my…" I grabbed the handset and turned the speaker off.

"Laurie, thanks. That's what I needed."

"Will you come see me tomorrow?"

"Yes."

34

MOORCLIFF VILLAGE IS AN ERRATIC ARRAY OF TUDOR-STYLE buildings set on a wooded hillside above the New Jersey Palisades. It's reminiscent of a Constable painting, idyllic and pastoral, perfect accommodations for reality-challenged rich people.

The receptionist at the main building was aloof but pleasant until I told her my name. She lifted the handset, pushed a button, spoke to someone. She hung up and asked me to have a seat.

I sat on the well-used leather sofa and opened an elastic file I had brought. In it were the pages I had salvaged from the Medora's financial records before they were stolen from my apartment. I never go anywhere to see anyone who goes by "doctor" without taking something to pass at least an hour's time.

It turned out I didn't need it. Before I had the pages out the of the envelope a cultured voice said, "Mr. Hall." It belonged to a slightly plump man with modern glasses, a red-and-blue bow tie and a gray half-tonsure that stood out on each side of his head like small wings.

His name was Dr. Rupert Wixon, and he was chief of staff and Laurie's personal doctor. He nodded to the receptionist and then led me to a substantial office that had the ordained precision of a magazine photo shoot. Even the smatterings of chaos looked planned. There was a seating area with upholstered chairs, but he sat behind his big oak desk and directed me to an armchair across from him. We exchanged pleasantries for a few seconds, then he sat back with his hands in front of his pursed lips, fingers spread, tips together, looking at me.

I said, "Doctor, what's your diagnosis?"

He shook his head. "I wish had one. I mean that literally. We've had half a dozen experts come in and we've got almost that many opinions. How many would you like?"

"However many it takes."

"Fine. ASD."

"What do you mean?"

"Autism Syndrome Disorder."

"I know what it is."

"Most people would get a little exercised about now."

"Most people haven't spent years with a wife with mental difficulties, and a daughter who also may have certain learning differences."

"Then you're aware autism is not a disease, as such, it's a syndrome, a collection of traits, and it ranges in severity from those who are low function, often non-verbal, who will never be able to live independently, to those who are savants, but have limitations, to those who are high function, seem normal, and may even be geniuses. Many think Einstein had a form of autism."

"I'm aware of that."

"We had two of the top autism specialists in the world eval-uate Laurie, and, not only could they not agree, they almost got into a fistfight. Your wife clearly presents with a number of characteristics consistent with autism, or Asperger's, such as giftedness in certain areas, but she manifests other traits that are the antithesis of any known ASD condition. For example, a common trait of the Aspergian is an inability, or limited ability, to read social cues in others. Laurie, on the other hand, seems to over read to the point that she almost experiences the feel-ings and reactions of others.

"Plus, many with ASD are often physically awkward, and again, as you know, Laurie is quite the opposite. Another sug-gestion was schizophrenia."

"I'll take the Asperger's."

He ignored that.

"One highly respected doctor suggested she had an allergy. Another possibility is something called dissociative fugue. Are you familiar with that?"

"I've read the DSM cover-to-cover so I know the term. But that's all."

"You've probably seen stories of someone going missing for weeks or months and finally showing up in another place with no idea who they are or what they've been doing since they left home."

I nodded.

"That is dissociative amnesia. Dissociative fugue describes a milder presentation, possibly a preliminary one. Dissociative disorders are not well understood. Often they seem to have no trigger, at least none that can be identified. But like all of Lau-rie's potential diagnoses, it doesn't quite fit. She hasn't exhibited memory loss."

I furrowed my brow. He said, "What?"

"What do you mean by memory loss?"

"Has there been?"

"A time or two," I said, "or maybe three. But it was always temporary. There were times she seemed not to know me, but it was like she knew she was supposed to and didn't want to hurt my feelings and worked around it. The day after the big event, the day I found her staring out the window, she looked into the playroom at our children and said, 'They're very cute. Whose are they?' But the next day she knew us again. Are you her therapist?"

"One of them. The main one, actually."

"To the best of your knowledge, was her dissociative episode, or whatever you want to call it, triggered by a particular event?"

He leaned back in his chair, looked at me, and kept looking at me. "Why do you ask?"

"Because I'd like to know what caused my wife to change from essentially normal, or at least Laurie's version of normal, to almost non-functional, literally, in one afternoon."

He nodded very slightly and looked at me some more.

"Doctor?"

"Mr. Hall, because you are her husband, I can share a lot with you, but there are certain things I can't share, such as the content of our therapy sessions. Even though she has told I'm free to share everything we've talked about, there are some things that shouldn't come from me. She will tell you when and if she feels like it."

In other words, the episode hadn't come from nowhere, as I had feared. There may have been—must have been—an event of monster proportions that triggered it. And I couldn't ask her about it without the risk of setting it off again, at least not now.

"Do you know? I'm not asking you to tell me, but do you know?"

He put his fingertips back together and looked at me some more. Because he wouldn't even tell me whether or not there was something, told me almost as much as if he had. There was a specific event that triggered Laurie's descent, and it was big.

"What else can you tell me, doctor?"

"She spends a lot of time reading." He swiveled and pointed to a shelf with maybe twenty books on it. "Those are hers. I keep them in here because if they're in her room she'll start reading and forget to sleep for a couple of days."

I walked to the bookcase. There were books on psychology, neurology, and mental illness. There was a copy of the current DSM, the *Diagnostic and Statistical Manual for Mental Disorders*, the basic reference book for psychologists and psychiatrists, and various books on specific conditions. There were several about logic, a couple on mathematics, and one on mathematical oddities and curiosities. There were several on psychopathy and psychopaths, including *The Executioner's Song*, Norman Mailer's hefty masterpiece about Gary Gilmore.

"What's with the interest in psychopaths? You don't think she's…"

"Of course not. If anything, she over empathizes, whereas psychopaths don't empathize at all."

"Then what?"

He looked at me and turned his hands out in a what-can-I-say gesture, as though there were more he would like to tell me, but couldn't. He looked at the bookshelf again, and at me. He seemed to want me to read his mind.

I sat back down. "Just tell me what yoou can."

"She's not like anyone we've ever encountered before. She has a very high IQ, and a comparable emotional sensitivity. She loves sports and craves physical activity, but hates to keep score. That's because she usually wins and then feels bad for her opponent.

"We have a physical activities coordinator, who was formerly responsible for both physical and psychological training for Army Special Forces. He's taken her to an archery range and a gun range and he said she was better at both than anyone he'd ever seen outside of world-class competitors. Something we all found particularly interesting is that Laurie doesn't transition."

"What do you mean?"

"Athletes, actors, a lawyer going to trial, a businessman going into an important meeting, a housewife picking up the kids from school, all of them transition from one mental and emotional situation to another. It's what people commonly call 'gearing up,' and what athletes mean when they say they're putting their *game face* on. And when you're finished with the activity, you 'wind down.' That can mean going to a bar, or sitting in your Barcalounger and watching a fishing show. But Laurie doesn't do that. She switches on-off-on-off, instantly."

I was used to that so I never thought much about it. Maybe I should have. Unlike all the other women I'd ever known, Laurie didn't need to be cajoled or seduced into sex. If she was in the kitchen and I walked up behind her and hugged her and kissed her on the back of her neck, half a minute later we were on the way to the bedroom. Or having sex in the kitchen.

I said, "She decides things quickly, and she decides only once. But, on the other hand, when something comes along that she can't make sense of..."

Dr. Wixon nodded slowly. "You come home and find her staring out the window. That's her loop. She's like a computer that never completes the problem. Step fifty is go back to step ten, an infinite loop."

We sat in silence for a few moments, until I said, "May I see her now?"

35

As we crossed the undulating lawn, the doctor pointed at a building a hundred yards from the others. It was long and low and on one side there was a buckboard fence. "That's our stable. Laurie has a horse here. We encourage residents to bring their pets, and we have horses of our own for them to ride if they choose, but she's the first to bring her own. She is quite the horsewoman." He shook his head. "I keep telling you things you obviously know."

"What's its name?"

"Rover."

I said, "Nice horse."

"They have a connection. Laurie will take a book and sit on a stool in the horse's stall and read to her for hours. The horse seems to enjoy it."

Rover was part thoroughbred and part quarter horse, sweet-tempered and gentle with the kids, but with Laurie in the saddle she was like a bottle rocket. I only rode her once and was glad to be able to get off of my own volition.

We entered the lobby of a long, Tudor-style building through double French doors, and headed toward a corridor on the left. In the lobby was a large fireplace and around the room were several seating areas. At the back of it, opposite the front door, was a desk where a receptionist sat, this one a thirty-year-old man in a pale green polo shirt and white slacks. He had close-cropped hair and his chest and arms stretched the fabric of his shirt. He stood when we entered, nodded, and sat back down. Dr. Wixon led me down a hall to Laurie's door and left.

I tapped once, twice, and waited. I was about to tap again when it opened slowly. Laurie was to the side, leaning against the jamb. Her head was down and her face half-concealed by her hair.

"Laurie." I lifted my hand toward her face but she raised her own and pulled mine down. Still not looking up, she placed my arm behind her and drew me close, nuzzling her head under my chin. I put both arms around her and we stood there, door open, half in the hallway for several minutes.

"Let's sit down," I said. She took my hand and led me to a loveseat.

"Laurie…"

"Let me say it first," she said, squeezing my hand.

"Say what?"

"You don't have to tell me, because I know, and it's all right. I want you both to be happy. I love you both."

"What are you talking about? Who do you love?"

"You and Jamie. That's why we had to finish the divorce, isn't it? I know you're together, I saw the pictures. Are you going to marry her? You should, she's wonderful."

I knew beforehand that I could not guess how our first conversation in three years would begin, but this not only wasn't in the ballpark of my expectations, it wasn't in the solar system.

She pressed closer. "I want you to be happy, sweetie."

Her voice was pleasant, interested, but not emotional, as though discussing the placement of furniture. Her eyes glistened with tears, but there was a soft smile on her lips. Then she saw something in my eyes.

"What?" she said. "What is it? Is Jamie living with you and the children? Are you already married?" She squinted. "Are we divorced? What is it, Porter? Tell me. Please."

"Why…where did you get the idea I wanted to marry Jamie?"

"I saw the pictures, you know, of the two of you. Together."

I got up and walked around the small room, stuck my hands in my pockets to stop the trembling. Those photos, the same ones Elizabeth Winslow, the prosecutor had, had to have come from Jack. Had he been there at that moment, I would have killed him. And that's not a figure of speech.

I leaned against the wall. Laurie walked over and stood in front of me, put her hands on my shoulders. I hung my head and closed my eyes. She touched the top of my head. "What happened to your head, sweetie? And your ear?"

I looked up. "Accident. Long story."

"Is that what's the matter? Because if you're worried about what I think of you and Jamie, you don't need to be. It's okay."

I took several short breaths, tried to relax my breathing. I was hyperventilating. "Let's sit down." We went back to the loveseat. Laurie sat with her knees resting on my lap and her left arm around my shoulders.

"What's wrong, Porter?" She was pleading.

"When did you find out about Jamie and me?"

"Daddy told me. That's when I told him I wanted to live someplace else for a while, and he found this place."

"Is that when you saw the pictures?"

"No, I saw those later, after I was here and Mother took me back to the house to get more clothes. When I was there, I told Daddy I'd changed my mind, that I wouldn't sign the divorce papers, because I wasn't sure you loved her. I told him I thought you still loved me and even if we weren't together, we didn't have to be divorced. That's when I found the pictures of the two of you." Laurie's voice wasn't much more than a whisper. "On the porch in the country, you know, when you took your clothes off."

"How did you get those?"

"They were on Daddy's desk. He told me to go in and wait for him, that he wanted to talk to me. They were there. I looked at them and then he came in and asked me to sign the papers. I said I still wanted to talk to you first, to make sure, but he said you didn't want to talk, you just wanted the divorce to be finished."

"Exactly when did you sign the divorce agreement?"

"Wednesday, 1:24 p.m. Daddy had a notary there."

Jamie's body had been found the preceding Sunday, I was arrested for her murder on Monday, and two days later Jack showed Laurie the pictures of Jamie and I that had been taken the previous summer to convince her I was in love with Jamie, who was already dead by then, to sign the divorce papers.

Jack could be cutthroat when he thought it was justified, but I'd never once known him to be cruel, and I never thought he was evil. This was both. And he'd done it to the one person he loved above all others. His own daughter.

Laurie was becoming agitated, confused by my lack of response, but I was stalling, desperately trying to think of a way out. There was none. The truth might crush her, but a lie would destroy her.

"Do you love her?" Her face was almost touching mine. "It's okay if you don't love me anymore. I left you, and I wasn't a good mother."

"I have never stopped loving you and will never stop loving you, and you were a wonderful mother. Except for a couple of days."

She smiled mechanically. "Anyway, it will be okay. I know J.T. loves you, and you love her. I love her too."

I removed Laurie's arm from my shoulder, put both of her hands in one of mine, and my arm around her.

I said, "Have you seen any newspapers lately?"

She laughed. "If by *lately* you mean in the last two and a half years, no."

"Did you know I was arrested?"

"Cici told me. Is that how your head got hurt?"

"No. When did you see Cici?"

"Last weekend when the kids were at the house, Mother brought them here for a while. I told you, it's okay about you and Jamie. The kids will love her."

I squeezed her hands hard. "Laurie, Jamie Trent, J.T., is dead."

After a moment of shock her eyes began to fill with tears. There were small movements around her mouth, followed by something in the shape of a smile.

"No, she's not. I saw the pictures."

"Those were taken last summer by a photographer probably hired by your father. Jamie was murdered last week. I was arrested for that, too."

Her chin began to tremble and she let out a wail, a keen, like nothing I'd ever heard. Her whole body became rigid and quivered like a tuning fork. After the long scream she went limp and looked at me. Her chest began heaving with sobs. There was pounding at the door.

"Mr. Hall, open the door please." It was the doctor.

Laurie's sobs turned to whimpering and she lay curled into a fetal position. He pounded again. I went to the door, and said, "Don't come in, please. You'll make it worse."

The door, which Laurie had locked, would have been accessible by master key anyway. I opened it slowly. Behind the doctor was the muscle-bound receptionist. The doctor looked past me at Laurie, and gave me a hard stare. "I'll be nearby. Please be careful with her."

When I turned back to the living room, Laurie was gone. I found her in the bedroom on the bed, lying on her side. I sat down. She moved closer and put her head in my lap. We stayed like that, not moving, not talking, for fifteen or twenty minutes while Laurie tried to process. I finally said, "I've got to go soon. I've already been here longer than the doctor wanted me to stay."

"I have a question," she said, turning onto her back and looking up. "Will you answer it?"

"If I can."

"You know how before the Big Bang all matter in the universe was very dense and all together?"

"Yes, and we've discussed this. We'll probably never know what created the spark that set the universe in motion."

"That's not my question. My question is where did the matter come from in the first place?" She waited for an answer.

"I'm sorry, sweetheart, but I don't know that either."

"Good-bye, Porter."

I kissed her on the cheek and stood up. I left her staring at the ceiling.

36

I SHUT HER DOOR BEHIND ME AND HAD ONLY GONE A FEW
feet when I realized I'd left the copies of the condominium documents in Laurie's apartment. I thought about going back, but
I could easily make other copies and I didn't want to risk upset-
ting her even more. I went to find Dr. Wixon.

Did he know what Jack had done? Why would Jack use
Jamie, who was already dead, to pressure Laurie into signing
the divorce papers? Jack had a reason for everything he did.
This smelled like desperation. As I neared the front desk I could
feel my anger rising.

At the moment I entered the reception area from the back, the
double French doors at the front were thrown open with such
force that lesser quality millwork would have shattered. Coming through them was a man in a black blazer, black slacks, and a
charcoal turtleneck. His cold blue eyes were blind with fury.

Hello, Jack.

We closed like uptown and downtown express trains on the same track. He failed to notice his own rage was pennies on the dollar compared to mine, and I didn't notice he came with backup. Neither would have mattered.

His hands went to my throat. I swung my arms up, blocking his hands, and shoved him in the chest. He gasped and staggered backwards, grabbing me as he fell. I landed on top of him. I grabbed his shirt and twisted. Someone put me in a headlock and threw me off him. I was on the floor on my back, someone was on my legs, someone else on my chest, a security guard from Jack's office, an albino bodybuilder named Sven. His eyes had a pinkish cast, his neck was covered with acne, and he smelled worse than he looked.

I said, "Get off." He didn't move. I lifted my face toward him and yelled, "Get off me you bloodless sissy pervert."

He backhanded me and I could taste blood. I said, "How tough are you without your friends, you squeaky-voiced Nazi weirdo?" I spat blood at him.

He raised his fist above his thick shoulder and started it downward. Fortunately for my face, a delicate, firm hand grabbed his arm. His fist paused as he turned to see who it was. When he saw Katherine, the tension in his body drained as though his main hydraulic line had been cut. She made a slight motion with her eyes and the albino and the other man got off.

"Doing this to Laurie, Porter," she shook her head, "was despicable."

I lifted myself to my elbows. "Compared to you and your husband I'm bush league. You two have set a low that a pack of hyenas couldn't match."

"What are you talking about?"

"I'm talking about using year-old pictures of me and Jamie, who is dead, who was a friend of Laurie's, and who Laurie didn't know was dead, to badger her into signing the divorce agreement."

Katherine looked from me to Jack. He was resting on one elbow, breathing heavily. His color was beginning to return. Jack looked at Katherine, then at the floor.

"Jack?" Katherine said.

With the help of someone behind him, Jack moved from his elbow to a seating position. A pair of hands tried to help him stand, but he slapped them off. His arms were wrapped around his knees, his head hanging between them.

I said, "And as long as we're talking about new lows, which of you told Laurie I wanted the divorce, and who told her I didn't love her?"

Katherine's eyes were as full of sparks as an electric mosquito zapper just hit by a swarm. You could almost smell the wings melting. I lifted myself, waited until my head cleared, and stood up. Jack was standing, head inclined, his right hand holding his left shoulder.

I said, "While we're here, Jack, do you want to tell us how you managed to get me harassed and arrested, repeatedly? Do you want to tell us why you did it? How did it make your life better to destroy mine and my children's and my wife's, your own daughter's? Why would you destroy your own family members?"

Two state troopers in their flat-brimmed hats came through the door. Jack looked at me and said in a tone as casual as if he were talking about which way a putt would break, "Arrest this man. He assaulted me." He turned to me. "I'm not saying..." He stopped and looked past me, past Katherine, in the direction from which I had come. His face turned as pale as the albino's. Katherine and I looked over. Laurie stood silently, staring blankly. In her hand were the pages from the financial reports. She let them fall to the floor and then, as in a trance, she crossed the lobby to the front door and walked out.

A trooper cuffed my hands behind me. I turned to the other one. "Officer, I want you to arrest that man." I nodded toward Jack. "He assaulted me."

"You can want all day, Hall," Jack said, chuckling, "but it's not going to happen. I've got witnesses. You don't."

Laurie had disappeared out the front door. Katherine had started after her, but she stopped and looked at the trooper. "I saw the whole thing, officer. Arrest them both."

"Katherine," I called after her, "the sitter leaves at five." She nodded over her shoulder. That was a relief. I hated having to use my one call to arrange a babysitter.

37

AN HOUR LATER, JACK AND I WERE IN SITTING IN SEPARATE cells in a picture-postcard jail in a quaint town called Redding. There are dozens of such towns in that part of New Jersey and they all look like the set for *It's a Wonderful Life*.

We both got a phone call, though it did neither of us any good since a judge would not be available until morning. I suspect Katherine made sure of that. About seven, the door to the detention area opened, and she entered escorted by a guard. She stopped in front of my cell. "Are you all right?"

"Been worse. How are the kids, and Laurie?"

Her eyes, which had the largest vocabulary of any I had ever met, were empty and flat, unreflective as chalk. She said, "The kids are used to this, I'm sorry to say. Cici asked if they should make you and Granddad get-out-of-jail-free cards."

She walked to Jack's cell. He stood and went to the door and waited. "Open it," he said to the guard. "Open it."

Katherine said, breezily, "But if he opened it, dear, you could get out." She turned and said something to the guard.

He stepped over to Jack's cell, and said, "Stand against the back wall and stay there."

Jack complied and the guard opened his cell door. Then he opened mine. "Step out," he said to me. Jack watched from the back of his cell. The deputy directed me to Jack's cell. "Step in." I did.

As the door clanged shut behind me, Jack, who seldom raised his voice, shouted, "Get him out of here, dammit. This isn't funny."

Katherine looked perplexed. "Are you talking to me? Well, first, my name's not *dammit*, and second, why are you under the impression this is supposed to be funny?"

She crossed her arms and looked at us. "The two of you may, one, work out the issues between you; or, two, one of you may kill the other; or, three, you may both kill each other. All of those outcomes are acceptable. If none of those happen, there is a good chance that Laurie or one of the children will end up dead or injured, which is not an acceptable outcome." She walked toward the door, stopped, looked back.

"You wanted to know how Laurie is, Porter? As bad as I've ever seen her. And three days ago she seemed almost normal. If either of you cared as much about her or the children as you do about this little war you've been running since the day you met, we would all have decent lives, and the two of you wouldn't be sharing a cell. Goodnight, gentlemen."

38

THE CELL WAS SMALL AND HAD NARROW COTS OPPOSITE EACH other, both with metal springs and thin lumpy mattresses. If you sat on one you could extend your leg and touch the other. I don't remember sleeping that night and I don't know if Jack did. I know we were both awake before the morning's cool light came in angled slats through the bars of our single window. When sunrays broke the shadows, Jack went to the window and tried to see out. He couldn't and sat back down. I sat up and leaned against the bars behind me that separated the two cells. We hadn't spoken since Katherine left.

"You sure got old Sven going good," Jack said, referring to his albino security guard. "You really think he's queer?"

"Excuse me, Jack, you Neoanderthal. I didn't call him *queer*. The civilized term is gay, or homosexual."

"You called him a 'sissy pervert.' Is that a politically correct term I should become aware of?"

"He's homophobic. I was trying to punch his hot button."

"Great strategy. You've got a muscle-bound moron sitting on your chest looking for an excuse to bash your face in, and you spit on him and call him names. I never would have thought of that."

"One question, Jack. Why did you drag this divorce out for over three years? Why not just get it over with?"

"You're an idiot, Hall. I was trying to save your family."

That statement made so little sense I didn't know how to argue with it. "Another question. Why did you claim to be me and transfer $20,000 out of the Western Jersey account?"

"I didn't. That was a clerical error, but it was a drain on your resources, which was fine with me."

I nodded, as though that made sense. "So the tape of you claiming to be me was a clerical error? Sounded more like a felony." I was only guessing that tape existed, but Jack seemed to buy it. "Maybe you should say you were misquoted. Why are you doing this to me?"

"I don't know what you're talking about."

"*How* are you doing this to me? I must say, it's amazing."

He lay down and looked at the ceiling.

Later he said, "I don't get it. They're angels." He swung his feet to the floor and sat up.

"Who?"

"Your children. How the hell can you be their father?"

I laughed. "They're not angels. They're children. They try to make us think they're angels, mainly at Christmas, but they're children."

I stood and walked to the cell door. As I leaned against it the outer door clicked and a deputy entered, followed by four New Jersey State troopers. They led us out, cuffed us, and drove us in separate cars to Newark where we were presented to a judge named Townsend. Brian Tortolo from Hamilton's office was waiting for me, and one of Jack's attorney's for him. Katherine sat in the courtroom several rows back.

"Mr. Hall." The judge looked briefly at me. "Mr. MacNeil." He looked at Jack for several seconds longer, like he knew him and wished he didn't. "You are wasting my time, and the court's. From what I can deduce, this entire squabble of yours is stupid and self-indulgent. Resolve it. If you are ever in front of me again, you won't care for the outcome. I guarantee it." He lifted his gavel and held it. "And if either of you ever again causes me to have to come in on a Saturday morning, you will more than regret it. That's a damn promise. Now get out of here." He slammed his gavel and left.

As we were leaving Katherine pulled me aside. She didn't say anything, but I knew her question. I shook my head. "Only Jack knows what this is about, unless you do." She shook her head. I said, "Let's talk."

She nodded. "The apartment, 12:30, Monday."

BRIAN TORTOLO DROVE me back to my truck at the restorative center. Something had been bothering me since my visit to Laurie, but I couldn't quite get to it. On the way back to the city, as I dipped into the grungy entrance of the grungy Holland Tunnel, it came.

What I believed about Jack's inability to tell the truth wasn't exactly true. In fact, Jack always told the truth, at least in his mind. The problem was that to Jack truth was completely detachable from fact. It was like something a McGovern spokesman said in 1972 about legendary "gonzo" journalist, Hunter

S. Thompson. He said of all the reporting about the campaign, Thompson's was probably the least factual and the most truthful. That was Jack.

In the tangled tapestry that was Jack's heart and soul, he always acted honorably and always in the cause of justice. He was very ethical in his own self-centric, distorted way.

I had no idea what was driving Jack, but whatever it was had taken over my life and was threatening to destroy it.

39

Monday, at 11:20 a.m., as I was leaving my apartment to meet my mother-in-law for lunch, the doorman handed me a large envelope. I stopped outside and opened it. It contained Jamie's crumpled note, and another, on ecru paper, embossed with the initials, "EVW." The writing was in black ink from a fountain pen.

Dear Porter

As this is no longer required for evidence, I wanted to return it. I also wanted to address other issues you previously raised.

The investigation is ongoing but we will be unable to take advantage of your offer to assist. Also, since we are not going to be trying you in this matter, we will be unable to take you up on your offer to help with your own prosecution. It appears that such an arrangement would not be permitted in any case.

However, if the offer still stands, I would like to be your friend.
Elizabeth

Also in the envelope were the DVDs from the security camera with a sticky note saying the DA's office had kept copies, and my keys with the tag number 611.

Because I needed gas and wanted to go through the car wash, I drove instead of taking the subway. As I pulled out of the garage I noticed a truck, a black Ford F350 duellie, sitting by a fire hydrant across the street. Its engine was running. As I pulled out of the ramp from the basement garage onto Twenty-second, the truck followed me. It was still behind me when I reached the East River and got on the FDR Drive northbound. On the shoulder of FDR near Thirty-fourth Street sat an NYPD patrol car. It's often there but never does anything, and I had always suspected it was either a prop or a good place to take a nap. As soon as I passed, its lights and siren came on and it pulled into traffic behind the black truck. I was assumed it was after me and pulled to the shoulder. The black truck kept going and passed me, and so did the cop car. It stayed on the tail of the truck until it pulled over. I merged back into traffic. The driver of the truck eyed me as I went by.

Around Sixtieth Street both lanes came to a dead stop. I switched from the classical station, WQXR, to 1010 WINS, "All news, all the time." The traffic reporter noted a minor collision near the Triboro was backing up northbound traffic all the way down to Midtown. After a few minutes we started to creep forward, but I no longer had enough time to get gas and go through the car wash.

On Sixty-eighth Street near Lexington, I lucked into a legitimate, unmetered space. I parked, looked up, and gave thanks to the god of parking, the most powerful in the New York City pantheon. I got to Katherine's early and was shown in by Big Stella. Katherine appeared at exactly 12:30, wearing a fashionable olive ensemble and an expression that told me nothing. She was cordial. We ate lunch, and talked about the children. Stella cleared the dishes and brought coffee.

"What's going on, Katherine?"

"What do you mean?"

"Your family is disintegrating before your eyes. If I go forty-eight hours without getting arrested or harassed, the Guinness people start calling to update the record book. That doesn't strike you as unusual?"

Her eyes were on her coffee, which she swirled gently around her cup. She quit swirling and let the coffee come to rest. She looked at me, but didn't speak.

"Why would he do it? What's the benefit to him? Why he doesn't just kill me? It'd be quicker and easier."

She set her cup down. "I asked him last night. He says he's not involved, and if you don't like what you have on your shoes, you should watch where you're stepping."

Jack probably phrased it differently.

"You're not paying attention, Katherine. My problems started three hours after I found out the divorce terms had been agreed to. Is that coincidence?"

She crossed her arms. What her eyes were saying was completely different than what came out of her mouth. Her eyes acknowledged there was something else going on, but that she didn't understand it herself, not yet. In the meantime, she was holding to the party line. She was about to say something when my phone rang. The ringtone told me it was school and, more specifically, the nurse.

"Is everything all right?" Katherine asked when I got off.

"B.J. was in the nurse's office. He said he felt dizzy, but went back to class. I've got to go by there to sign some release forms for a field trip the kids were supposed to bring home, but never did. I'll check on him when I get there."

Katherine gave me an odd look, got up, and left the table. She returned carrying six sheets of paper, two blue, two orange, two white. "For the Transit Museum?" She handed them to me.

I thumbed through them. "Thanks for passing these along on a timely basis." She gave me one of the stinging, split-second looks that might have hurt my feelings, once. "I've got to go. If they don't have these before two, the kids can't go."

"They'll enjoy it. A friend of Jack's is on the board. We went to a fundraiser there a few years ago. I've never ridden the subway, but it was nonetheless enchanting."

She walked me to the door, opened it, and followed me to the elevator.

I turned to her. "Jack is doing this, and you know it." Her eyes were strangely non-conversant. "And something else. If you don't stop him, you're as much to blame as he is."

"I'll talk to him again."

40

At Coldfield Academie, on East Eighty-eighth Street, I pulled into the no parking zone at the front door and got out. Inside I gave the forms to reception and went to the nurse's office.

The nurse was on the phone, and B.J. was on a cot, as pale and quiet as new snow. His eyes were closed and he had a washcloth on his forehead. I sat down beside him and touched his face. He opened his eyes.

I said, "Hey, buddy. Want to go home?"

He nodded and took hold of my arm. The nurse looked over. "He threw up in class. He has to go home."

Thank you, Nurse Ratched.

"Of course. Could you ask his teacher to send any assignments home with Cici?" She nodded.

We walked out and I put B.J. in the back seat. I strapped him in with the middle belt, took off my jacket, rolled it into a pillow, and laid his head on it.

As I CROSSED Ninety-second on the way to FDR, I once more saw the black truck in my mirror. The burly arm of the driver rested on the window, and his head poked out. He followed me to the FDR.

As I turned into the southbound feeder lane, I gunned the Rover, which is like going pedal-to-the-medal in a loaded cement truck. I barely hit fifty by the time I merged into traffic. I'd kept the old Rover mostly because Jack hated it. A few years ago, as a bonus for work I'd done, he'd given me a new Mercedes. I donated it to a charity auction. I felt a stiff bump from the truck behind me. At that moment I genuinely regretted being so generous and so stubborn.

When I passed the Seventy-first Street exit, I had gotten the Rover to seventy, and the truck was still on my bumper. I looked at the gas gauge. It read empty.

The truck thumped me from behind again, and the Rover started to wobble. I floored it and pulled away a few feet, but the truck quickly caught up. As we emerged from the underpass by the U.N., my engine began to sputter. I was out of gas. I moved to the right lane, shifted into neutral, and coasted. The black truck pulled even on my left then drifted toward me. At the last possible second I jerked the wheel to the right and cut into the exit lane for Thirty-fourth Street, just missing the raised curb divider. The truck didn't. It hit the divider, went over the top, bounced, came down, and slammed me from the side. The Rover tilted onto its right wheels. I tried to adjust but started to roll. The truck swerved to the left, back toward the

FDR. That was last I saw of it. It was the last I saw of anything for a while.

WHEN I OPENED my eyes, I was hanging upside down in my seat as the passenger compartment filled with smoke. As I tried to release my belt, I heard something crashing against the windshield. The glass splintered into a crystal web and bulged inward, held by the membrane. There was a second blow and a third, and shards of glass flew toward me. The hooked claw of a wrecking bar came through the window and jerked back, tearing the glass away. If this was the guy from the truck, I was dead.

Two thick arms reached in and a man said, "Release your belt." I found the latch, pulled and started to drop head first, but the hands slowed my fall and twisted me so I landed on my side. The man pulled me through the windshield and dragged me away from the car. I tried to talk, couldn't, tried to get up, but was held down. I looked at the Rover, which was full of smoke, and pointed.

He said, "Is there someone else, a passenger?" I nodded. The man, who was wearing a navy T-shirt, and looked like an ex-linebacker-turned-soap-star, left. Two others stayed with me.

"Let me up, please." After a few moments they let me sit, but held me. Twenty feet away B.J. was lying on the pavement on a blanket, not moving. The man in the navy T-shirt began administering CPR, paused, and said something to another man who went away. He came back with a small metal canister that had a mask attached to it and handed it to the other. He placed the mask over B.J.'s face and turned a knob.

The men who'd been holding me back released me and I went to B.J., knelt beside him, and picked up his hand.

"He's breathing, barely," the man said. "An ambulance is on the way."

At that moment two NYPD cars pulled up and an EMS bus followed. Two paramedics got out, pulled a stretcher from the rear, and came to B.J. A police officer said, "St. Vincent's."

I grabbed his shirt. "What did you say?"

"Saint Vincent's." He knocked my hand away.

"That's twenty minutes, you idiot, maybe more. NYU Hospital is two blocks."

"They're dispatched out of Saint Vincent's, and they're going to Saint Vincent's," said the officer. "It's my call."

"And it's my son, and that makes it my call, asshole." I turned and ran toward the stretcher. Two uniforms blocked me and put me on the ground.

One of those holding me said, "Sir, if you interfere, you will be arrested." They pulled me to my feet.

"And if my son dies, your life won't be worth living." I jerked my arm free and returned to the officer in charge.

He jabbed a finger at me. "One more word and you're under arrest." He looked toward the medics and repeated, "St. Vincent's." An inch from his mouth appeared a black plastic box the size of a Snickers. Holding it was Cat Marten.

She said, "Sergeant Apodaca, please help me explain to my readers why you give a higher priority to EMS dispatch instructions than a child's life. Is that official policy, or is it your own? Are you getting kickbacks from the dispatcher?"

He held her gaze for several seconds, and his cheeks turned red. "Hello, Miss Marten." Finally, he shook his head. "I think we've had a miscommunication." He turned to the EMS driver: "NYU."

They released me and I hugged Cat, held her until she pushed me away. She said, "Come on, let's go to the hospital. Check yourself in and I'll find B.J."

I took her arm. "First, come over here. I want you to meet someone." I found the man in the navy T-shirt arranging things in the back of a green Subaru wagon. I held out my hand. "I don't know your name, but you saved my son's life."

He took my hand and the day went dark.

41

I heard my name and opened my eyes. Cat was looking down on me. Déjà vu all over again.

"You were mumbling," she said.

Around us was the muffled clatter of an ER, and we were enclosed within a dull white privacy curtain. I tried to speak but nothing came out.

"You're on oxygen."

My mouth felt like it was full of cotton balls, and not the drugstore variety, but the kind you pick up in the red-dirt fields of West Texas still in the husk. I could feel the weight of several blankets but was shivering, almost uncontrollably.

"No concussion this time, but you were, and are, in shock. You had smoke inhalation, and your body temperature was down."

She leaned over and kissed me on the forehead. Before I could ask, she said, "B.J.'s in ICU. That's all I know. And there's a sitter with Cici. She'll stay until I get there. I'll stay with her tonight, if that's okay."

Like she knew my thought, she put a Styrofoam cup with a straw to my mouth and let me sip water. I spoke in a whisper. "That's better than okay. You're, you know..." My shivering had stopped.

"A good reporter?"

"A real good reporter. Why were you there? Just walking onto FDR against traffic and saw me?"

"I was about to catch the subway at Thirty-third and Park and someone from the city desk called. He'd been listening to the police band and told me there was a wreck on FDR involving a black truck and a Land Rover with camo paint. He thought it might be you."

"How did he know?"

"You should read the papers once in awhile. Your truck is almost as well known as you are. I ran from Park. I was real glad it was downhill."

"You know the officer?"

"Apodaca used to be at the Thirteenth, used to ask me out."

"Did you go?"

"He's married, with four kids, and he's a pig. What do you think?"

The curtain moved and the metal hangers scraped along the track. A young man with square-rimmed, tortoise-shell glasses stepped in. "I'm Dr. Kranz, B.J.'s doctor. How are you?"

"Fine. How's he?"

He nodded to Cat, leaned close, and studied me. "You and I may have a different definition of fine. As for your son, he has a collapsed lung and a subdural hematoma, but his vitals are strong. He was unconscious when he came in, and he's sedated now. We want him as still as possible. We did a scan and there was some fluid buildup. We drained it. We had to drill a small hole and put in a tube, which sounds worse than it actually is. Because we got to it quickly it's relatively minor. Untreated for much longer and it could have been deadly."

A shiver ran through me, and, I could tell, through Cat. "He has a hairline fracture in his right tibia. Smoke inhalation is less severe than it might have been had he been fully conscious immediately after the incident. Everything could have been worse, much worse. It appears you had a guardian angel today."

I said, "Who gave permission to work on B.J.?"

"You signed a release when you came in. You don't remember?" I shook my head. "You were a little incoherent, but you were able to answer a few questions and sign forms. Is there a problem?"

"Not at all."

For a moment I was afraid they'd called Laurie.

About seven they put me in my own room, semi-private, but the other bed was empty. At seven-thirty, as Cat was about to leave, I said, "Where have you been?"

"What do you mean?"

"The last couple of days. I haven't seen you, haven't talked to you. You didn't answer my emails. Did I do something?"

"I've been busy. That's all."

"With what?"

"My job. Two days ago when I checked my voice mail, I had three calls from reporters at other papers wanting to interview me, *interview me*, about my story. My editor's not happy with me right now. He says I'm too close to the story, and he's right. You can't cover the news if you are the news. I promised I'd start acting like a journalist, not a participant."

I reached for her hand, squeezed. "But you did it again today, and you heard the doctor. If you hadn't been there, if you hadn't made Apodaca…"

She put a finger on my lips and shook her head.

"What'll your editor say now?"

"I…" She forced a smile, shook her head. "I don't know. I can't worry about it."

"So what's your latest scoop that doesn't involve me?"

"It does involve you, sort of. Plockman may be dead."

"Marvin?" I felt an obligation to have at least a twinge of remorse, but my first thought was how his death would affect my own case. "What happened?"

"They found his car in the Hudson up near Albany."

"Suicide?"

"That's the theory. He left a note, but there's no body, not yet."

"There won't be. He's not the type. Too stubborn."

"Really? And you know what the type is?"

"I'm from Wyoming. From junior high through college one or two people I knew killed themselves every year. My dentist, a couple of teachers, some classmates."

"Cheery place."

"Boring place. What else have you found?"

"The first law," she said. "But I've got to go." She kissed my head and walked away.

"Newton's?" I called out to her back. "A body in motion…?"

"No, Birdie's," she said, as she went through the door.

"Who's Birdie?"

She poked her head back. "My mother."

USING A DIAGRAM a nurse made for me, I went in search of B.J.'s room. Without a map or good directions or GPS, looking for a specific location in one of the large New York City hospitals is like trying to find an abandoned gold mine that's "up in Alaska somewhere." Mt. Sinai, New York Hospital,

Sloan-Kettering, Columbia Presbyterian, NYU, are like mini-cities. In Bellevue you could wander forever.

I found Pediatric ICU and introduced myself at the nurse's station. The woman behind it looked at my hospital clothes for a moment and said, "Follow me."

Even though I knew what to expect, the actual sight of B.J. in bed, wan and lifeless, was a fist to the throat. In the dim room, with its faint green glow from the machine displays, I felt like I'd stepped into another world, one in which spirits moved freely and conversed with the unconscious. I went to the bed and touched his cheek, reached down and took his hand. It was cool and unresponsive.

I got a chair, pulled it close, and sat silently. Nothing flowed out, nothing in. Energy had been stilled, caught in a transverse where time is frozen and matter is an illusion. I was weak with grief and fear and too exhausted to cry. I fell asleep in the chair.

A nurse woke me. "It's ten-thirty. Doctor says you have to leave."

I sat up and tried to appear awake and in control. "I won't be in the way. I promise."

"Not his doctor, Mr. Hall. Your doctor. Your son needs you well."

I returned to my room and sat in the chair. After a minute I picked up the phone and pushed in numbers. Jack, who was probably sitting in bed with Katherine waiting for the news to come on, greeted me warmly. "You? What do you want?" I could hear a television in the background.

"There was a major traffic jam on FDR today, the result of a minor accident near the Triboro."

Jack said, "That has something to do with me, I suppose."

"Because of the backup on the drive, I wasn't able to get gas before having lunch with Katherine. Then, after lunch, as I was driving home, I was chased and rammed by a three-ton truck. The Rover was totaled."

"There's a big loss. One less ugly vehicle on the road." There was a shuffling of papers, and someone on the TV was about to talk to us live, from Bensonhurst, the scene of a triple homicide.

"B.J. was with me." The shuffling stopped, and the TV went silent. "He's in ICU, unconscious. If I had gotten to the gas station as I intended, if I'd had a full tank of gas, the Rover would be a burned-out shell, and you would no longer have a grandson."

The silence was so complete the line might have been dead.

"But it almost didn't matter, Jack, because B.J. had a concussion and the responding officer refused to allow the bus to take him anywhere but Saint Vincent's. Pressure was increasing inside his skull, and if the cop hadn't backed off and let him go to NYU, two blocks away, he might have died. By a complete fluke, Cat Marten, the *Journal* reporter who's been covering this, was nearby and got there in time to get the officer to change the order. If not for her, we'd probably be talking about funeral plans right now. If you ever meet her, you may want to say thanks.

"So back to your very reasonable question. Does this have anything to do with you? You tell me." Thirty seconds of silence followed. "By the way, tell Katherine that since you set me up, you're an accomplice. With grandparents like you a kid's set for life, right? Not a long life, necessarily, but just the same. Enjoy the rest of your evening."

42

THE NEXT MORNING MY DOCTOR CAME IN AND TOLD ME I was free to go. I dressed and found my way back to B.J.'s room. His doctor was just leaving. "He's awake. We're going to take him for an MRI later."

B.J. was drowsy, had a headache, his arm was in a soft cast, and he wanted to go to school because parts were being given out for a play. I called home and we both talked to Cici, who said she would tell the teacher what part he wanted. I talked to Cat, who said everything was fine, but was clearly upset about something. She sent Cici to get dressed.

"What's the matter? What's happening?"

"I'll tell you when I get it worked out."

"Does it have to do with Jamie, or the condo issues?"

After a moment she said, "Maybe."

"Which?"

"Jamie's note said she wanted to talk to you about something important. Do you have any idea what that was?"

"No." I had a suspicion it may have been related to the West Thirty-first Street apartment where Waneeta Perkins lived, but it could have been anything. "What have you found out?"

"Good-bye, Porter."

A Filipina nurse walked in and handed me the Metro section of the *Journal*, open to page three. It was a story about a high-speed truck chase down FDR. The write-up made it sound exciting. I just remembered being scared. One thing I did learn was that the black truck, after hitting me, lost control and was rammed by a wrecker on its way to an accident. Both drivers were taken to Bellevue in undetermined condition. FDR southbound was closed for an hour. There was a related story: "New York's Bravest Work 24/7," byline, Cat Marten, Staff Writer. It was about a man named Sam Brady, a thirty-two-year-old firefighter from Queens, father of three, whose Subaru wagon is outfitted like an EMS van. He carries tools, blankets, first aid equipment, a fire extinguisher, and a small oxygen tank. He had just gone off duty after a seventy-two hour shift, and was on his way to visit his father, a retired firefighter, who lives in Stuyvesant Town.

My phone rang, ID blocked.

"Porter."

"Elizabeth?"

"How are you feeling?"

"Not bad, all things considered."

"Good, because you're about to be arrested and charged with reckless driving, endangering the welfare of a minor, and vehicular homicide."

"Homicide? Who did I kill?"

"The driver of the truck. He died about 3 a.m."

"He chased me three miles, rammed me, and flipped me over. And I'm being charged?"

"They wanted me to handle it. I refused. Someone around here is scared as hell. And the reason Webster and Fenton dropped you, in case you didn't figure it out, is because their firm does twenty million a year in work for the city."

"So they had to choose between my business and the city's business."

She said, "According to Webster it wasn't a choice. It was an order. Not that they wouldn't have anyway, but it wasn't presented as an option. And the driver of the truck that chased you was Anthony Zinetti from Rego Park. His sister is married to a Columbo family captain so now the mafia is involved. You should probably call Hamilton. Good luck."

I called Clancy on his cell and told him about my impending arrest.

"We're already on it," he said.

"How did you know?"

"Sources. See you there."

I LEFT WHEN they took B.J. for his MRI. When the elevator finally came and the door opened, Katherine stepped out. I took a step back and we stood looking at each other. She was put together as always, but tired.

"Did Jack send you to finish the job?"

"He doesn't know I'm here. I'm sorry, Porter."

"Why? Because B.J. got hurt when it was supposed to be only me? Thanks."

She was holding a bouquet of Mylar balloons and a shopping bag. She cleared her throat and faced me. "I'm sorry. I didn't believe you. Jack called the apartment after lunch and I told him you'd been there and were on your way to the school. He's the only one I talked to. He must have set you up. After you called last night I told him that all of this, whatever it is, is finished now."

"What did he say?"

"Nothing. He got up, dressed and left. It sounded like he almost wrecked his Porsche getting out of the driveway. He hasn't been home since."

"Well, it's not over. They're about to charge me with murder. I'm glad you're here. I may be gone awhile."

I hit the call button. It lit up and something else did too. I visualized the poster board diagram that hung in my den. More lines were being drawn, and more connections being made. The city, or more accurately, as Elizabeth had called it, the machine that called itself a city was behind the nightmare that had become my life. This mammoth monster had been around, I was sure, since Manhattan was nothing more than a few hundred people at the southern tip of the island, but as always, in the beginning and throughout eternity, there had to be someone, a human, pulling levers and punching buttons. The machine didn't run itself. And it wasn't a man behind a curtain with a microphone. It had to be someone with the control of a dictator and the resources of a king. I couldn't even imagine what this person must look like, must be like, to manipulate and intimidate in the ways I'd seen.

Whoever it was, that person, that monster was my *force majeure*. I knew only two things about this creature. It had a connection to Jack, though Jack wasn't in control. And it was after me.

THE ELEVATOR CAME, but I didn't get on. I went back to B.J.'s room where Katherine sat reading a magazine. She looked up.

"Does Jack know someone who is well connected in the city, in the government, behind the scenes at the highest levels?"

She stared at me. Her eyes went completely blank. Seeing those high-capacity units totally shut down told me the question shocked her, woke her to something she hadn't thought about before, but probably should have.

She twisted her head and looked at the gray sky through the gaps in the half-open Venetian blinds. "A very good question, Porter."

I was about to follow up when my phone buzzed, a text from Clancy.

Outside. 34 st entrance. 3 min.

"Excuse me, but I've got to go get myself arrested again. We'll finish this later."

Her voice said, "Good luck, Porter," but her eyes said she was confused, and worried.

There was a small crowd outside the Thirty-fourth Street entrance to NYU Hospital, and homicide lieutenants Marsh and Erskine were among them.

Marsh didn't move toward me so I went to him and offered my wrists. He stood there, completely miserable. Erskine walked off and turned his attention to some gulls above the East River a couple of hundred yards away. Marsh kept his hands in his pockets.

I said, "Porter Hall, you're under arrest for…what is it this time, Marsh? Come on."

Marsh looked at Erskine who was looking at the clouds.

"Oliver, this is your chance." Several long lenses were pointed in our direction. "You can be famous."

He said grimly, "Porter Hall, you're under arrest for reckless driving, child endangerment, and the murder of Antonio Zinetti."

"Murder, Oliver? Not vehicular homicide?"

"Second degree."

"Last time it was first. Which is better?"

He said, "Don't do this, please."

"Reckless driving? If this makes my insurance go up, I'll have your badge. Put the cuffs on and tell me I have the right to remain silent. That anything I say can and will…"

As he reached for his cuffs, his phone rang. He took it out and listened and looked over his shoulder while I continued the Miranda. "…will be used against me in a court of law. But my attorney is already here so can I skip that part?"

Marsh turned back to me and dropped his phone in his pocket. "We're done here. So long, pal. It's been really, really real." He turned and went toward his car at just less than a trot. Erskine hurried after him.

I called across the street, "Aw, come on Marsh. Was it something I said?" He kept going. "Let's do lunch. Next Thursday? Oliver, did you hear me? My treat." As he got into his car he waved good-bye to me with one finger.

"Great," I said. "One o'clock it is."

"WHAT WAS THAT about?" I asked Clancy, when we were in the back of his car on the way to my apartment. "There must have been twenty reporters and photographers. Where'd they come from?"

"I called them. I believe in sharing the spotlight. If we're going to be headline news, so are they."

My phone buzzed. It was a text from Fred Althorn. He had finally tracked down the source of my bail money. Someone with deep pockets had used two bank letters of credit to cover the twenty million required. There was not a guarantee that the same person had both posted my bail and engaged Clancy Hamilton to represent me, but the probability was high enough for it to be a reasonable assumption. And, by coincidence, that person was sitting across from me.

"Why are you doing this?"

Clancy looked over. "Doing what?"

"Defending me for free."

"I said you had an angel."

"I do, and it's you. You posted my bail." He didn't deny it or ask how I knew. "I appreciate it more than I can tell you. I just don't understand it."

"The publicity. It's been great," he said.

"Not that great. Plus you can get on any news show anytime you want. Is it Mallory? Is she my angel?"

He shook his head. "If you must know, she's not your angel, you're her angel. In a way, I guess, you're your own angel."

"I don't follow."

"The day I met you I was in Austin to see her."

"You were speaking at the LBJ School, as I recall."

"Cooked up, last minute. I needed an excuse. She would have taken off if she knew I was there for her. It didn't go well. And I know what happened after that."

"What do you mean?"

"You saved her life."

I looked out the window for a minute. Two tugs seemed to be racing up the Hudson. "Oh, that?"

"Do you want to tell me what happened?" he said.

"Not really."

"Fine," he said, "I'll tell you what I heard. Correct me if I'm wrong."

I nodded.

"It was a Friday afternoon and she was supposed to meet you—for what, I'm not sure."

"To go over the topic for her term paper."

He continued, "And, when she didn't show, you went to her apartment, knocked, and she didn't answer. You went to her next door neighbor, who'd seen her earlier and who said she was sure Mallory was going to meet you. You broke the lock on her door, the two of you went in, and her friend found her."

"Janet, was that her name?"

"Janice," Clancy said, "Janice Colson. Janice found her in the tub, water up to her chin. It was tepid, like she'd been in the tub a long time. She was unconscious. Janice thought she was dead. You came in, found a pulse, pulled the plug, turned the shower on cold, and started filling it again. Janice called 9-1-1, you got ice cubes from her freezer and started rubbing them on her. Mallory started to shiver, you got her out of the tub, put a robe on her, took her outside and the two of you walked her around until EMS got there. It took about fifteen minutes for them to arrive, Janice said."

I said, "Janice and I together got her out of the tub. I couldn't have done it by myself." Mallory is six feet, maybe six-one, and athletic, and weighed a hundred forty, maybe more. Even with Janice's help I almost couldn't lift her. She was slippery wet, and we were lifting dead, floppy weight out of a bathtub.

I said, "I don't know how long the ambulance took. It seemed like an hour. Janice told you all this?" He nodded. "How do you know her?"

"One of those flukes. I've always told my kids it's better to fess up because you're going to get caught eventually anyway. Three years later we were at Beaver Creek and Janice was there with her family. Mallory hooked up with her, but wouldn't introduce her, except to say that she knew her in Austin. That was unlike Mallory. My wife invited Janice and her family to our place for dinner, which Mallory was unhappy about, also not typical. My wife got Janice alone. Janice thought she was just filling in the details. We had no idea. You saved her life."

"I did what anyone would have done."

Clancy gave me one of the incredulous looks he often directed at a hostile witness. "You were supposed to meet her at a beer place near campus, right? She didn't show, you went looking for her. Most professors…"

"Instructor. I was an instructor."

"Most would have gone home, and she'd be dead."

I shrugged, held up my hands, palms out. "Fine. So try to keep me out of jail if you want to."

Clancy narrowed both eyes, his don't-you-dare-lie-to-me look. "One more question and I'll let it go. What was the last thing she said to you when they put her in the ambulance?"

I smiled. "She said, 'Please don't tell my father.'"

43

WHEN I GOT BACK TO THE HOSPITAL A FEW HOURS LATER, I heard laughter and voices coming from B.J.'s room. I wasn't surprised to see Katherine and Laurie there, and I wasn't surprised to see Cat there, but seeing them all in the same room almost made my heart run backwards. Laurie was laughing and talking and Cat was smiling and miserable. B.J.'s bed was upright. Everyone stopped talking when I walked in. Laurie came over and hugged me, tight. Cat walked out.

B.J. seemed a little groggy, but close to normal, full of questions about his sister and school.

"How long are you staying?" I said to Katherine.

"Until they make us leave."

I looked around. "Where'd Laurie go?"

"Out in the hall, maybe, I don't know."

With Cat? Was that safe?

I went out, didn't see either, and went to a waiting area where I saw Cat talking on her cell phone. Laurie was leaning against a vending machine four feet from her, but Cat didn't seem to know she was there. Cat has having an intense discussion with the party on the other end of the line. Laurie smiled when she saw me, but seemed focused on Cat's conversation.

Cat said, "By the river? No way." She listened. "At Thirty-fifth, near the tunnel entrance? I know it. When?" She glanced at her watch. "In twenty-five. Three-forty. Okay."

Cat closed her phone for a second and stared at it for a moment, then opened it, and made a call. She said what sounded like "Elizabeth." I couldn't make out what she was saying though I suspected Laurie could.

I said to Laurie, "What's going on?" Cat flipped her phone shut and stared out the window for a minute. Laurie smiled at me with her whole face, shrugged, kissed me on the cheek. When Laurie needed to lie, that was how she did it. She couldn't outright lie, but she could withhold information as well as a mobster pleading the Fifth. Cat turned toward us as Laurie was kissing me.

Cat said, "I've got to get my jacket," and brushed past.

When Laurie and I got back to B.J.'s room, Cat was by his bed holding his hand. She kissed him on the forehead, told Katherine good-bye, and headed out the door without looking back. I followed her onto the elevator. She looked nice, silver earrings with some sort of stone and a matching necklace.

"Are you okay?" I said. She ignored me the way you ignore strangers on an elevator. We reached the ground floor and she walked brusquely toward the entrance. Outside she faced me.

"Why did you divorce her?"

"I didn't. She divorced me."

"She's perfect."

"What do you mean?"

"She's smart, witty, charming, tall, blond, gorgeous, and maybe the nicest person I ever met."

"You left out intermittently psychotic and obsessive-compulsive. And that she sometimes forgets everyone's name, including her own."

"You're never going to get over her, are you?"

I tried to think of an insightful response, or at least an artful dodge, but couldn't. A taxi pulled in and an older couple got out. I held the cab door for them and when they were out I held it for Cat to get in. She didn't.

"She acts like she's still married to you, and you let her." She looked at the cab. "I'm walking."

I closed the door. "I'll go with you."

"Stay." She pointed to the ground and I stopped.

"Cat…"

"Don't lie, Porter, don't pretend."

"I wasn't going to."

"I know. You won't even do that for me."

WHEN I GOT back up to the room, Katherine was reading to B.J. from *Tom Sawyer*. Laurie was looking out the window and had a large envelope in her hand. I went to B.J. and he took my hand. Katherine kept reading. After a moment, Laurie came over with the envelope.

"You left these when you came to see me that day."

I had completely forgotten. Those were the pages she had in her hand when she found Jack and me fighting in the lobby. Maybe that's why she followed me that day.

"I want to show you something." She pulled out the pages and spread them across B.J.'s bed. On many of the pages numbers were circled and there were notes.

"What is it?"

"These are from the condo, right?"

"Yes. Financial reports, copies of bills."

"The bills are okay."

"And the others?"

"The numbers aren't real. They're made up."

"How do you know?"

"The frequency of the digits is wrong. Too many nines, not enough ones, and the others too. Either too many or not enough."

"I don't understand."

"It's called Benford's Law, and it has to do with the distribution of numbers in data sets. If the data set is genuine, '1' appears about thirty percent of the time, and '9' less than five percent. The numbers in between scale down proportionately as they move toward nine. If the ratio is ever off by more than a little, it means the data was made up. All of these are made up."

I FELT LIKE I'd been kicked. I knew immediately what the fabricated numbers meant. They meant that the half million that was missing from double billings was probably miniscule compared to what was really missing. I walked over to a chair and sat down.

After the initial shock had worn off, and after my brain had a moment to put this latest event in rank order of significance as it related to the other problems in my life, I brushed it aside.

It was just one more thing. Since I was now sure everything was connected, it might actually be useful in getting to the bottom of it all. The Medora normally maintained a reserve fund of seven to ten million dollars. I had a hunch a big chunk of that, if not all, was probably missing. The more money that was missing the easier it would be to find, because the greater the sum the harder it is to conceal. It would also make it easier to find out who the real force behind everything was. It never could have been Marvin. He wasn't that smart. I started to say something to Laurie, and realized she wasn't in the room.

"Where's Laurie?"

Katherine shook her head. B.J. said, "She left."

"When?"

"A minute ago. She took her jacket."

The clock by B.J.'s bed said it was three thirty-seven. I remembered Cat saying she was going to meet someone at Thirty-fifth Street at three-forty. Laurie heard it, too.

I made a quick check of the floor, didn't see her, ran to the elevator, hit the button. When it wasn't there in ten seconds, I ran to the stairwell and down. At the Thirty-fourth Street entrance I found a security guard and asked if he noticed a five-eight blonde leave in the last few minutes. He let out a phlegmatic chuckle.

"Did I notice *that*? You kidding?"

"Which way did she go?"

"Same as that cute one, that dark-haired one you was talking to before. Know any others 'bout my age?"

I ran toward First Avenue and crossed Thirty-fourth Street in the middle of the block. I looked up toward the park that's bounded by First and Second Avenues and Thirty-fifth Street, just south of an entrance to the Midtown Tunnel. A beat-up burgundy van with lettering that had been sloppily sprayed over with primer pulled away, almost hitting a northbound taxi. I looked around and saw no one. My gut told me the van had taken Cat and Laurie.

I ran after it and tried to read the license plate, but it was too far away. As I neared the spot where the van had been I saw a large pool of blood on the sidewalk. It was fresh and bright. From the puddle it ran in an uneven stream of blobs and spatters into the street, where it abruptly stopped at the place the van had been. I started again to run in the direction it had gone, but something caught my eye. To my left, by a bush, against a wrought iron fence, was a woman with blonde hair. With her was a smaller woman with dark hair. Neither was moving.

I went to them. Laurie's arms were tight around Cat, who was in a fetal position, shaking.

I put my hand on Laurie's shoulder, shook her gently, pushed the hair from her eyes. She didn't respond. I touched Cat. She looked up. "Cat? What happened? Are you okay?"

Cat began to shake harder. Laurie looked up, gave me a fractured smile, and said, "Hi, sweetie." I called 9-1-1.

FOUR COPS AND two ambulances arrived within three minutes. The cops wanted to question Laurie and Cat about the blood on the sidewalk, mainly whose it was, since it didn't appear to have come from either of them. Neither would talk.

The police cordoned the area, waited for the techs, and stood around looking confused. It was a weird crime scene if that's even what it was. The buses took Laurie and Cat to ER at NYU

Hospital two blocks away. I ran and got there as they pulled up. A doctor who had been on duty the day before looked at me rolled his eyes, said something about a family plan and volume discounts.

Laurie had minor abrasions on her hands, but nothing else was wrong with either of them. After half an hour they were released. The police tried again for statements. As her husband I refused them permission to speak with Laurie, although she wasn't talking anyway. I figured it would take them a while to figure out whether I was her husband or her ex-husband, since I didn't know myself. I also tried to stop them from questioning Cat.

"What's she to you?" said the cop.

I stammered. "Uh…my girlfriend."

Cat looked at me like I'd just told a joke she didn't get. The cop looked at Cat, at Laurie, spoke to his partner.

"Kev, you know that song goes 'some guys have all the luck'? This is the guy."

Laurie left with Katherine, and I took Cat to her place.

On the way I said, "What happened?"

"A woman called and said she had information."

"About what?"

"About Jamie. Of course I'm going to meet her. It's a woman, we're meeting on the street during the day, and I'm not worried she'll hurt me. But this…I've never seen anything like this, have never been part of anything like this. It was terrifying."

The taxi let us out in front of a sadly nondescript apartment building in an area called Turtle Bay, a complex of apartments on the East River in the Thirties. On the well-worn lawn stood an empty bench. We sat there and looked at the flat sky and listened to the distant sound of water birds. A helicopter descended on a nearby heliport and drowned all the other sounds of the city for a moment.

"Of course it was frightening. Someone tried to kidnap you."

"Not that. Worse."

"Than someone trying to kidnap you. What's worse than that?"

"Laurie killed a man."

44

I PUT MY ARMS AROUND HER SHOULDER AND WE WENT UP TO her apartment.

It was on the seventh floor and was small. She was right about my living room being bigger. Much bigger. She hadn't done much decorating since there wasn't much to decorate, but she'd made the most of what she had. There was a living-dining area, and a small table covered by a tablecloth with printed flowers on it. There was a small blue sofa that was probably a foldout, coffee and end tables, probably from Ikea, and a door that opened to a bedroom. There would be a bathroom off the bedroom. She told me to sit on the sofa and she went into the bedroom and closed the door.

She came back a few minutes later wearing a large T-shirt that had the Abbey Road album cover on it and sat next to me. She had removed her make-up, her hair was pulled back, and she was barefoot. She curled up close to me and put her feet on my lap.

"What should I do?" She lifted her face. "I witnessed a murder."

"Are you sure the man was dead?"

"Oh my, God. Yes."

"Why were you even there?"

"Last night I got a call from a woman who said she knew what happened to Jamie, wanted to meet me, and would call back with a time and place. She called back when I was at the hospital and wanted me to meet me over on the River Walk. That's too isolated. I should have known right then it was a setup. I told her I'd meet her by the park, middle of the day, busy street, I wasn't worried. I guess I should have been. That was so stupid."

"It's your job."

"I know. But you don't go alone, especially if you're a woman. Unless someone is watching."

"Someone was."

She pulled away and looked at me. "I know. How did she know? Why did she…and she wasn't even afraid. If Laurie hadn't followed me, I'd be dead now. I know that."

"What happened?"

"The van pulled up and stopped, and a guy with a hoodie over his head got out of the passenger side, walked over near me, lit a cigarette, and looked at me. I recognized him. It was the skanky guy I saw on the subway.

"I started to run and got three or four steps before he caught me. He wrapped his arms around me and was pulling me toward the van. I was screaming and kicking and trying to hit him, but I couldn't. He was really strong.

"When we were almost to the street, the rear doors of the van flew open and there was another man inside. He was yelling at the one who had me, telling him to hurry up. I heard a thump and the guy holding me fell onto the sidewalk. I landed on top of him. His arms opened and I rolled off. Laurie was above us. She pulled me away and went back and kicked him in the ribs and head.

"He rolled over, got to his feet, and started toward the van. Then he stopped and said, 'No bitch doing that shit to me,' and went back to her. He took a swing and missed. She kicked him in the balls and punched him in the throat. She grabbed his arm and hammered down on the back of his elbow with her fist. There was a loud crack. His mouth was open but no sound was coming out. She hit him in the face with her elbow, put her heel behind his foot and shoved him. Everything happened so slowly. It was like watching a movie frame-by-frame.

"His head hit the ground so hard it sounded like a paper bag popping. Blood started gushing everywhere. He convulsed for a few seconds then stopped. The man in the van jumped out to get him and Laurie went after him too. I yelled at her to stop and she did. The second man picked up the first, carried him to the van and slung him in like he was a sack of flour. He drove off. Laurie helped me over to the fence and we both sat down. And then you came."

"Who was it, Cat? You know, don't you?"

"Not for sure." She sighed and closed her eyes. She opened them. "How big is Mark Henberg?"

"Five-nine, I'd guess, one sixty-five. Was he the other man?"

"No."

"Why did they come after you? Did you do something, something related to Jamie?"

She looked at me for several moments. "I've got to lie down. I'm exhausted."

"Do you want me to stay? I can sleep on the couch, or you can come to my apartment. You can have the guest room. I won't bother you, and you can sleep as long as you want."

"I'll be okay. I'll talk to you later." We both stood, and she nodded at her door eight feet away. "Can you find your way out?" She forced a tired smile.

IN MY APARTMENT, the sitter the agency had sent was cleaning up the kitchen. She said Cici had eaten and was watching TV. The sitter left and I started toward the den, but the landline rang. Katherine calling. I went to the kitchen, checked the ID and answered. It had to be Katherine because she was the only person I knew who still called people on their home phones.

"How's Cat?" she said.

"Numb. She's at her place, trying to sleep. How about Laurie?"

"She's on the sofa. She won't go to bed."

"Did she talk about what happened?"

"No. But she asked if Cici could come stay here."

"I'll talk to her and call you back."

Cici was watching a show on the Discovery Channel about sloths. I sat down and she came and got in my lap. We exchanged our news of the day. I left out the part about the man trying to kidnap Cat and her mother killing him. I told her Laurie wanted her to stay with her at her grandparents' apartment. She asked if Cat was coming back for another sleepover. I told her no.

While she packed, I called Katherine to tell her Cici was coming and said if it was all right, she and B.J., when he got out of the hospital, would stay with them until, I cleared my throat and tried to think of a palatable phrase. "Until, well…"

"All of this blows over."

WHEN I GOT back from delivering Cici, I took out a beer and sat in a chair and watched the sun sink behind the Jersey sky-line. I was hoping all of this would just "blow over," but I was more optimistic the Easter bunny would come with a basket of golden eggs and season tickets to the Giants. I dozed off think-ing about the bunny.

When I woke, the day was gone and my beer was warm and flat and I had a lot more questions. I found the marked-up poster board, which was nicer than I left it because Cici had decorated it with flowers and geometrics and bands of color. I got a clean piece of board and took it and the old one and a handful of markers to the kitchen.

On the right side of the new board I drew a circle and la-beled it FM, *force majeure*. On the left side I made two col-umns, labeled one "JACK," and the other "?".

I divided the Jack-column into a plus and a minus, good traits and bad traits. In the plus column I wrote "Integrity." Jack may be crazy, but he's incorruptible. In the negative column I wrote, "Lies, deceives, manipulates." He would do those things, but only in service of those he cares about. He would kill, and I was sure he had. He flew helicopters in Korea and went from the Marines to the State Department, as he calls it, or, as every-one else calls it, the CIA. But there was one attribute that sub-sumed everything. I wrote PRAGMATIC. He is pragmatic. Always.

I remembered Cat's mention of 'the first law.' I went to the computer and started searching. A lot of laws float around cyberspace, none of them called Birdie's. There was Newton's first law of motion, Kepler's first law of planetary motion, and the first law of thermodynamics. Finally, I found Barry Commoner's Four Laws. Commoner was an environmental activist. His laws were about man's effect on nature. That made sense because Cat had once said her mother was an unreformed hippie.

His first law stated *Everything is connected to everything else.* That was followed by *Everything must go somewhere, Nature knows best,* and *There is no such thing as a free lunch.*

Next time I saw Cat I would ask if that was it. Given the state she was in when I left her, however, I didn't expect that to be anytime soon.

I picked up the markers and poster board and went to the living room, put it all on the coffee table and was about to sit when my doorbell gonged.

That was unusual, and it wasn't good. When you live in a highrise, gongs are preceded by a buzz from the house intercom and the doorman asking if it's all right if someone comes up and gongs you. Even people who live in your building will call down to the doorman and ask if they can gong you before doing so. But I was curious. I went to the door with an ice-cold bottle of Duvel as my only weapon.

I looked out the peephole and saw the top of a head I knew. I opened the door. The person reached out, took my beer, and said, "Thanks." She walked toward the living room. When she was halfway there, I said, "Hi, Cat, would you like to come in? Can I get you a beer?"

45

SHE HAD ON HER BROWN LEATHER JACKET, A WHITE SHIRT with the tails hanging out, faded jeans, and a pair of roughout cowboy boots worn almost to a patina. Slung over her shoulder was a large quilted bag. I went to the kitchen, got another beer, and went back to the living room. Cat was sitting in a chair, cross-legged, boots off, her jacket on top of her quilted bag next to the chair.

"Are you okay?" I sat on the sofa.

She nodded, said, "I'm fine." She seemed different, as though an odd calm had come to her. She pointed the top of her bottle in my direction as a toast. I did the same.

"How are you?" she said.

I shrugged. "Would you like a glass, for your beer?"

She lifted the bottle and looked at the label. "I'm okay."

"I want a glass," I said. "It's Duvel. It's made by Trappist monks and they don't like it if you drink out of the bottle. You should use a glass."

I went to the kitchen and came back with two stemmed glasses that were tall and tulip-shaped. They said Duvel on them. *Devil.*

As I poured, she watched. She picked up the glass and sipped the foam and nodded at the poster board and markers. "Craft project?"

I spread them out so she could see both and explained what they were.

She said, "Any big surprises?"

"The kids are more connected than I realized."

Her face said *Duh.*

"Did I tell you about the custody hearing?"

"No."

"It's next week. I have to prove why my kids shouldn't be taken away given my recent legal issues. It proves Jack's behind some of it."

"But not all of it?" she said.

"No. He would never let strangers touch his grandchildren. And I'm sure he doesn't want me dead, if only for the effect it would have on the kids. If he did, I'd be long gone.

"Then there's the way he manipulated Laurie into signing the divorce papers. He worships her, but using the pictures of Jamie and me half-undressed *after* Jamie was dead is borderline cruel."

"No," Cat said, as she drained her beer, "that was over-the-line cruel."

"Which means something powerful is driving him."

She set the glass down and rested her elbows on her knees. "Can I have another one?"

I started to point out that Belgian beer has two to three times the alcohol content of most American beer, but what came out was, "Sure." I finished mine and went to the kitchen.

When I got back, Cat had moved to the sofa and was studying the first diagram. After a moment she looked up and said, "Hmm."

I poured the new beers and sat next to her. "What?"

"Just thinking."

I said, "How is the notion that everything is connected to everything relevant to what's going on?"

"You figured out what the law was. How?"

"Google and a guess. What's it got to do with Jamie?"

She faced me, folded one leg so a knee was resting on my thigh, and put an arm on the back of the sofa. She said, "This story has been getting crazier and crazier and I've just been getting more and more lost, so I decided to make some assumptions. My first was that Jamie's death is not a separate event, but one that's connected to everything. Second, and this was something the best investigative reporter I ever knew taught me, if you can't untangle a story from the back end, make your best guess where it started and go from there. After you talked about Waneeta Perkins' building, and Mark Henberg, I decided to treat that as the start point. If that was where Jamie started, then maybe I could retrace her footsteps."

"And you did," I said, "and the same thing almost happened to you as happened to Jamie."

"Except I had a guardian angel. Laurie."

"And Jamie had a guardian angle named Porter. Bad choice."

"No." She reached over and squeezed my knee. "She had a friend named Porter, and he'd gotten caught up in something, too, maybe the same thing she was."

"What was it?"

She stared into her beer for several moments, then looked at me. She said, "I started asking questions about Marvin Plockman."

"Is he dead, or not?"

She said, "I don't know. What matters is what he was involved in, and who's behind it. He's definitely part of what Jamie was looking into, and probably what she wanted to talk to you about at lunch. I went to see Herb Schneider, and he let me see all of Jamie's closed contracts for the last six months. Then I went through the contracts that were signed but didn't close. You would know this, Porter, but I didn't. If you've got an escrow contract for a co-op or condo, one of the first things your lawyer does is pull the building's financials. Herb keeps a file of those documents. Ten minutes in, I found a file of Jamie's that had everything I was looking for. You and Herb missed it because it was in the office's file, not Jamie's."

"And Plockman was involved."

"Yes," she said, "with every single building she looked into. And Jamie noticed something else. What's the name of the security company that installed and services this building's video security system?"

"Highrise Eye. Why?"

"How many companies in the city do that?"

"Dozens. We went with Highrise because they offered a comparable system for a lot less."

"Well, every one of those buildings had the same security system from the same company."

"What does it mean?" I said.

"I don't know, but I think Jamie did. I'd made several calls about Plockman and the security company when, out of the blue, I got this call from a woman named Zoe Kelner, who said she could tell me what happened to Jamie."

"Who owns the company?"

She said, "I don't know. That one's going to take some time, maybe an FOI request."

"The paper's attorneys must do that all the time."

She picked up her beer and took a long drink. She set the glass down, put her hand over mine and squeezed, as though she were trying to comfort me. She said, "I'm sure they could, Porter, but here's the thing. I don't work at that paper any more. They fired me."

46

"Fired you? When? *Why?*"

"After you left my apartment, my editor called and asked me to come in. Short version, the managing editor got tired of seeing me in the news. I've been mentioned in other papers, online, and been on TV twice. That part was new to me since I don't own a TV. He'd heard about the kidnap attempt too.

"The clincher was the call the editor got from a representative of the Police Benevolent Association wanting me and the paper to apologize to Apodaca for embarrassing him in front of his men."

"Because you forced him to send B.J.'s bus to NYU? Did you mention that 'disrespect' saved my son's life?"

"He said it didn't matter, we do our job, and the police and EMS do theirs."

We both picked up our glasses and finished our beers. "Another?" I reached for her glass.

She said, "I'll get them."

As she headed to the kitchen, the home phone rang. I picked up an extension near the front door. I said, "Hi, Katherine. How's Cici?"

"It's me, Dad. Grandmother dialed."

"Okay, same question?"

"I'm okay. I'm going to bed. Mom wants me to sleep with her."

"How is she?"

"She's kind of quiet, but she's talking a little bit, and she knows who I am."

"That's good." B.J. and Cici had been dealing with their mother's peculiarities for so long they weren't fazed when she lost touch. "Is your grandmother around?"

Katherine came on and confirmed what Cici had said, that Laurie was subdued, but functional. She asked if I'd talked to Cat.

"I have. She's fine, considering she got fired."

"What on earth for?"

I explained.

"In other words," Katherine said, "she got fired for saving my grandson's life."

"That's about it."

She let out a snort. "I'll talk to you tomorrow."

CAT WAS BACK on the sofa and there were new beers in new glasses that said Chimay and were the shape of bowls. I narrowed my eyes. "Duvel in a Chimay glass?"

"Trappist monks don't scare me." She wasn't slurring quite, but her normally taut diction had lost its crispness, like a high-performance sports car with bad struts.

I sat next to her. "Are you all right?"

"What do you mean?"

"I'd have guessed you'd be more upset about getting fired."

She nodded her head up and down in long strokes. "And I'd've said you'd've been right about that. Coupla days ago I'd've been frantic." She touched her fingers to my face, left them there for a moment, and smiled. "After someone tries to kidnap you and you watch the nicest person you've ever met kill someone, it kind of knocks a hole in your silo."

She held up a finger. "One minute later, Porter, if Laurie'd gotten there one single minute later, I'd've been gone. And…" She shuddered. "After something like that, a job is just a job. The guy who fired me is an asshole, and he's the one who should be fired but I'm not upset. There are other jobs. But dead is dead. Know what I mean?" She took a long drink of her beer and set the glass solidly on the table. "You know what else, Porter, one other thing?"

"Tell me."

She lifted herself up, swung a leg over mine, and sat straddling my lap. She put her arms around my neck and kissed me hard and long. "Remember how you invited me to spend the night? Here I am." She kissed me again, harder. "But I'm not sleeping in the guest room." She tilted her head back, almost closing one eye. "Unless that's where you're sleeping because I'm sleeping where you're sleeping. That work?" She had a slightly crooked smile, and the eye that was open had a twinkle.

"Yeah."

She kissed me again and began to unbutton my shirt as I began to unbutton hers. When her top two buttons were undone, she reached down, lifted her shirt by the tails, and slid it off over her head. Then she did the same to mine. I put my arms around her waist and stood. Her arms were around my neck, and her legs were tight around my waist. I carried her across the living room and down the long hall as she continued to undress us both.

47

When I opened my eyes, the well-lit numerals of the Met Life clock across the street indicated it was one-thirty. The blinds were open and silver moonlight filled the room. Cat's dark hair was splayed over the white pillowcase like spilled silk. I watched her sleep for a few minutes, then went to the kitchen for water. As I started back, I heard a distant chirp, my phone telling me I had a message.

I found it in the living room sofa between two cushions. I had a text from Sue Dershon at Clancy's office, sent about the time I carried Cat to bed. It told me to check my email for a video clip she wanted me to look at. I went to my office and opened it.

A note that was attached explained the video clip was taken outside the hospital during my aborted arrest. Sue told me to pay attention to Lt. Marsh when he got the call as he was about to arrest me, and special attention to a black limo about thirty feet behind him.

I found the segment and watched as Marsh reached into his pocket to get his cuffs, stopped, took his phone out, and answered. After three or four seconds he looked over his right shoulder toward the street at the long black car. A rear window went halfway down. I couldn't make out the face. Marsh listened, hung up, turned back to me, and told me I wasn't going to be arrested. Behind him the window of the limo went up.

I stopped the video, extracted a frame, put it in my photo editor and enlarged it. I could see a hand holding a phone, and a set of eyes, but there wasn't enough detail to recognize the person behind the glass. I adjusted the contrast, the saturation and color, and finally made out one other thing. He was wearing a hat, a bowler.

Bowlers, the hats worn by the likes of Charlie Chaplin and Hercules Poirot, the kind you'd expect to find on the cover of an E.B. White novel, are uncommon these days. The only one I'd seen recently had been on the head of my neighbor in 28A. I didn't know his name. I went to the intercom and buzzed the doorman. The one who answered was a man named Rafael, who had been there since the building opened.

"Raffie, who lives in 28A?"

"Mr. V."

"Full name?"

"I don't know, sir. That's all we've ever called him."

"Does he get mail, packages?"

"No mail, but if he gets a delivery it says Mr. V."

"Check the owner roster. See what it says."

I heard rummaging as he looked for the book kept at the doorman's station that had a presumably up-to-date list of every owner and, if rented, the name of the tenant, for every apartment in the building.

"It says G-A-S-L-L-P, all caps."

"Thanks."

G.A.S. LLP indicated the owner of record was a limited liability partnership. I wondered what G.A.S. stood for. I knew who would know, and by a stroke of good fortune, he would be awake because, if it was dark outside, Fred Althorn was awake.

I called Fred, told him about GAS LLP, and asked if he could access the database of the Secretary of State's office.

He said, "New York or federal?"

"State. Does it matter?"

"I'm on probation. I can't touch federal without permission."

I still wasn't sure the man in the car was my neighbor. At that moment Cat walked in. She studied the screen for a minute and said, "That's 28A."

"How can you tell?"

"I don't know, I just can. What's his name?"

"Fred's trying to find out."

"Where does he get those silly hats?"

I kissed her on the cheek. "Thanks."

"For what?"

"For asking where the hat came from." I went to my desk, found a school directory from two years ago, and looked up Tomas Severio.

JORGE HAD GIVEN 28A a box from Severio's the day the process server caught me. I buy my hats at Severio's. It's one of only two traditional hat stores left in Manhattan, since John Kennedy had largely killed the business by his refusal to wear one.

Tomas Severio, manager of the store and son of the owner, was a friend, and owed me a favor because I helped get his kids into the premier downtown nursery school. That improved their chances of getting into a respected K-12 school, which increased their chances of getting into Harvard, which increased their chances of getting jobs on Wall Street, and, when convicted of market manipulation, it improved their chances of being sent to a white-collar prison instead of Sing-Sing. Tomas owed me big.

He still didn't like being called in the middle of the night. "What the hell, man?"

"Sorry, Tomas, but I'm trying to find out the name of a man who's one of your customers."

"At...at...what? One in the morning?"

"Two. It's important."

"Must be." Behind him a woman's voice wanted to know what was going on. "What customer you need?"

"He buys bowlers from you."

"We don't call them bowlers. We call them derbies."

"Okay, derbies. He lives in my building, small, impeccable dresser."

"Vane."

"Obviously."

"No, that's his name. Vane. Abel Vane. He buys two or three Borsalinos a year, in brown, gray, or black. If there's even a tiny flaw, he returns it. I sent him a charcoal about a week ago. Abel Vane. Can I go back to sleep now?"

As I put away the directory I noticed a small FedEx package that had been opened. I looked inside and saw a dozen or so sets of keys, but nothing explaining what they were.

"Sorry," Cat said. She was standing in the door. She had on a cream-colored robe that came almost to her ankles. It was Laurie's, although on Laurie it came to mid-calf.

"Those came the night I stayed with Cici. I forgot to tell you. There was a letter, too." She walked over, opened a drawer and pulled it out. "I read it. You were in the hospital and I thought it might have something to do with Jamie."

It did. According to the letter, I, Porter Hall, had just inherited eleven apartments, though they technically weren't mine. I was holding them in trust for their current residents, having been ceded that responsibility in Jamie Trent's will.

The building, owned by a partnership controlled by Mark Henberg, had been converted to condominiums under an eviction plan, meaning the units could be sold and the new owners could evict the current tenants and take the apartments for their own use. However, the units were first offered to residents at discounted "insider" prices. Since the occupants were poor, and few, if any, could afford even the discounted price. That meant they would be out on the street. Jamie worked out financing, took title, and was holding them in trust until the tenants were ready to sell, or able to arrange their own financing. One man was moving out of town so Jamie paid him a fair price for his right to purchase and then bought it herself. That one would go to her mother and sister.

"Do you think this got her killed?" I said.

"Not that itself. Apparently Henberg wasn't happy about Jamie's interference because he could have sold those units to outsiders at higher prices, which is why he made the earlier attempt to drive them out. But he didn't want to take on Jamie again, along with the state attorney general, so he let it go. And for the record, Henberg was out of town for a month prior to Jamie's murder and had literally just gotten back the day you saw him. His girlfriend really does live on the Upper East Side. I met her for coffee at, guess where, Starbucks.

"So Henberg, himself," she said with finality, "is clear. However, the super was a guy named Antonio Griffin and he has a two-megabyte rap sheet that includes assault and battery, sexual assault, drugs, grand larceny, you name it. I'm almost positive he was the one I saw on the subway and that he was the one who tried to get me into the van."

"The one Laurie killed. What else?"

"Plockman was the building's account exec."

I felt nauseated. Once Jamie asked me if I could recommend a management company. I put her in touch with Plockman. That's how she met him.

"Marvin was doing the same sort of skimming on West Thirty-first Street as he was at the Medora and every other building he managed. She also realized they had the same video security system from the same company, based on the timing. That's probably what she wanted to talk to you about at lunch."

"Was Marvin the other person in the van?"

"Maybe. I don't know him."

"Laurie does."

She said, "I knew she would, and I asked her."

"Whatever she told you was the truth. What'd she say?"

"She said, 'Don't worry about it. It will all be fine.'"

"Who was the woman who called to set up the meeting?"

"Zoe Kelman."

"And who is that?"

"No one, but I back-traced the number she called from and it turns out Zoe Kelman is actually Zora Kalber. I back-traced her phone number. She was dumb enough to call me from home."

"Okay, so who is Zora Kalber?"

She smiled. "Mrs. Marvin Plockman."

"It is a small world, after all."

"Yes, it is," she said.

Cat left the room. As I started to close my laptop, a new email came in. It was from Fred. I clicked it open as my phone rang, also Fred.

He said, "Got to give you credit, Porter."

"For what?"

"You know how to pick your enemies."

"How do you figure?"

"The guy who owns GAS LLP is a man named Abel…"

"Vane."

"You're psychic now. So I guess you also know what he does."

"No."

"From what I can deduce, for all intents and purposes, he runs the city."

I stared at the screen until Fred said, "Porter, are you still there?"

"Yes."

"There's one more thing you might find interesting."

"What?"

"G-A-S stands for Governmental Advisory Services and LLP means it's a partnership. Want to guess the name of the partner?"

"Not really."

"Come on. One guess. I'll give you a hint."

"Fine. What's the hint?"

"Your children call him 'Granddad.'"

48

I READ THE FILE ON THE INCREDIBLE MR. VANE.

He first came to view as assistant corporation counsel, reporting to the main legal advisor to the mayor under Robert Wagner, and later had advisory posts under Lindsay, Beame, and Koch. He was mentioned in labor negotiations with any number of unions, contractors, carters, and concrete suppliers. If the mafia had an outlet center, those would be the anchors. There was enough in what Fred sent to start a grand jury investigation into the man, if not send him to prison. Yet he clearly had enough juice to control the prosecutors since he had to be the one who put the fear of God into Russ Lewsky, Elizabeth's boss. I wondered what he had on Lewsky.

It was almost three when I finished. I went to the kitchen, put the oven on pre-heat, found cupcake mix, mixed it up, spooned the batter into a cupcake pan and put it in the oven. I summarized the report, printed three copies, included instructions, put them in envelopes, and addressed them to three people I trusted in various parts of the country. I added postage, and emailed copies to Fred and Cat.

By then the cupcakes were finished. I set them out to cool and took a shower. After I dressed, I iced them and put on rainbow sprinkles. I set aside two for Cat, put the rest on a plastic serving tray, and covered them with red-tinted Saran Wrap. It was 4 a.m.

I called the front desk, told the doorman to find the night porter and have him come up. When he arrived, I gave him the envelopes and a tip and told him to take the envelopes to the mail drop on the corner at once.

I took the cupcakes and walked down the hall to pay an overdue visit to my neighbor. I rang the doorbell of 28A and listened as a chime played the opening notes of Pachebel's Canon in D. I was about to ring again when I heard a faint shuffle and the soft scrape of the peephole-cover being opened and closed. A few seconds later there was the sound of a security chain being removed, followed by the solid click of a deadbolt opening, a second deadbolt, a third, and finally a slip-bolt being undone at the top and again at the bottom. A moment later there was a series of beeps as an intrusion alarm was disabled. The door opened slowly.

"Yes," the man said, in a tone that was curious, and neither hostile nor warm. He wore a burgundy silk robe with a fringed sash tied at the waist, white silk pajamas in a jacquard weave with stripes, and brown leather scuffs. What hair he had was neat and damp, apparently combed before he answered the door. The right side of his face was red and puffy.

"Mr. Vane," I said, bowing slightly, "I wish to offer my apologies for taking so long to welcome you to the building. My manners are awful. You won't say anything, I hope."

He looked at me and the cupcakes. Finally, with a slight conspiratorial nod, he said, "Our secret." He took the tray and stepped aside for me to enter.

Except for the floor-to-ceiling windows, the apartment did not look like a modern high rise, but a Park Avenue pre-war. The original floor tile, an adhesive–back parquet, had been replaced by three-inch oak planks, stained to a dark, glossy walnut and covered with antique Kilims and Bokharas. There were elaborate crown and base moldings, chair rail, and wainscoting. Old Master prints hung alongside three small impressionist oils. All looked to be originals. On one wall were two objects that were, in my mind, out of character. In a velvet-lined shadow box was a silver six-shooter with a pearl handle. Mounted next to it was an ornate Samurai sword.

There was a small Chippendale table in very fine condition, except that one of its legs was broken off and lay on the floor beside it. A cut-off yellow broom handle held in place by duct tape kept the table from toppling.

"What happened to your table?"

He turned slowly and looked at it as though he had no idea what table I was talking about. He looked at me and said, "You don't know?" as though I should have.

"No."

"It got broken."

He said, "Excuse me," and went to the kitchen. A moment later he returned with a half dozen on a small China plate. He set them on a lamp table between two red and gold brocade chairs. "I put on water for tea. Have you a preference?"

"No." I extended my hand. "By the way, I'm Porter Hall." We shook. His hand was soft and fleshy though his grip was firm. "But perhaps you knew that."

"Perhaps I did know that." He shook his head. "I told him you would come. He said you wouldn't. I said you would." A whistle came from the kitchen. He excused himself and returned in less than a minute with a silver tray bearing two small teapots, cups, saucers, sugar, milk, lemon and a selection of teas in foil bags. When we were seated he said, "So your visit is…"

"A not totally unexpected pleasure," I said.

"I might have chosen different words."

He arranged his silk robe so it draped properly over his legs. "Do you expect to kill me tonight, Mr. Hall?"

"Please, call me Porter. Not planning on it. And you?"

"No." He lifted his cup toward me. "And do call me Abie."

"Okay, Abie, for the record, I have sent out packets containing summaries of everything I know and most of what I suspect about you and your operations to be opened in case of my death or disappearance."

He selected an Earl Grey and dropped it into the pot near him. "Of course you have. You are so much like…" He let the thought trail away like distant smoke pushed over a mountain by a breeze. "Where shall we begin? You choose."

His fingertips grazed the pocket of his dressing gown as though checking for something. I grabbed his fingers, bent them back and reached into the pocket. He yelped. I removed a small digital recorder.

I said, "Hello," and a light on the end lit, as did one in my head.

"Do you always carry this?"

"In my business," he said, choosing his words, "it is often useful to have an accurate record of who says what. You know, memory being what it is."

I did know. I hit the rewind button and played it. It was men talking. I hit it again, same thing, and again. Abie watched with some anxiety. Then I found it. The voices had a reverb to them as though recorded in an enclosed space, like an elevator cab. "…what time is it, and the other person says, brillig, then we say, 'Did the professor…"

Another voice cut in, "No, we say 'Did you and the professor find Ginger's shoe?'"

"Oh, that's right," said Cici, who then recited the entire routine to perfection. Which is where the woman who took them from the school had to have learned it.

"Abie, what I said about not killing you tonight…" His face was calm but there was a small tremor in his hand. "I'm having second thoughts." I dropped the recorder in my pocket.

"Where were we? Oh, yes. How do you know Jack MacNeil and why you would commit several felonies, including murder, for him?" I unwrapped an Irish Breakfast and placed it in the pot.

"Not murder," he said.

"Zinetti tried to kill me."

"He wasn't supposed to." He poured tea into his cup. The rising steam smelled like perfume.

"Well, I was there. He tried to kill me and my son."

"Stop that." He gave me a peevish look to let me know I was being entirely unreasonable. "We didn't know your son was with you and, as I told you, John doesn't want you dead. For some reason that doesn't work for him. Honestly, I don't get it."

"It doesn't work very well for me either."

"Whatever his thinking, it made it much more difficult. Death is easy and quick. Injury, embarrassment, incapacitation, those are more of a challenge."

He picked up a cupcake, lifted it to eye level, studied it. "Excuse me. What are these multi-colored items on top?"

"Rainbow sprinkles. According to my kids they aren't cupcakes if they don't have sprinkles."

"Interesting." He took a bite.

"What was the purpose of first arrest?"

"Making you look like a bad father. When you don't meet your children's bus because you've been arrested and are sitting in a police station, that doesn't play too well…" He let the thought slide, frowned and took a sip of his tea.

"At a child custody hearing."

He shrugged. "Anywhere."

"And how do you get the police commissioner involved in something like that?"

He flopped a hand dismissively. "It was nothing, really." He leaned forward and narrowed his eyes. "If I asked, the man would pick up my cleaning and polish my shoes.

"John gave me two instructions. Make you look like a bad father, and don't kill you. If your kids are found at a coffee shop, unattended, by someone from child services, that's a bad father."

"The condo fraud charges, Jamie Trent's murder. What about those?"

"Mere windfalls of which I took maximum advantage. You play the hand you're dealt. John Pershing MacNeil taught me that. Though he did say he would like you to be charged with a felony or two."

"Two? By my account it's pushing twenty."

He leaned back and twisted his lips into a smirk. "Under promise, over deliver. That's my philosophy."

"What do you owe Jack that you would do this for him?"

He put both feet flat on the floor and rested his hands on his lap. "My life."

49

"Explain."

He lifted his cup and held it in his small hands. "Jack was a Marine helicopter pilot in Korea. He was nineteen and had just finished his second year at Princeton. He joined the Marines, went to Officer Training School, got his commission. I was a signal corps corporal, Army infantry." He snorted and curled his lip. "That was all they thought I was good for. When you weigh a hundred and thirty pounds they're reluctant to send you into combat with fifty pounds of gear. But I was quite good at my job, good at relaying messages, coordinating, staying on top of things.

"My platoon walked into an ambush. It was horrid. The survivors left me, which they should have. I was dying. At dusk I heard a chopper and for a minute my spirits lifted. I thought it might be one of the big Sikorsky transports, but a second later

I knew it was small, a Bell 47." He lifted his eyes. "You know those?"

I shook my head.

"You've seen them. There's one in the opening scene of M.A.S.H., the TV show. They were like a big glass bubble with an open tail. Room for a pilot and two passengers, supposedly. They weren't hard to fly, but their missions were dangerous. Recon, laying communications cable through the jungle, evacuation. Only the best pilots flew them, and John was the best of the best.

"Korea was the first helicopter war, you know, whirlybirds, we called them. They came into use at the end of World War Two, but it was Korea where they really found their place. That country is so mountainous and there's so much jungle, I don't know what would have happened without the rotaries. I really don't." His eyes were wide and a little glazed. "I've got a book here somewhere..." He looked slowly around the room. "No, wait." He lifted a finger.

"Abie." I grabbed his arm and squeezed. "Abie, stop."

"John was the best at everything. Always. He saved my life."

"Right. You were on patrol, there was a firefight, they left you for dead. Go on."

He sipped tea and went back to his story.

"There were North Korean stragglers not two hundred yards away, and I was afraid if they found me they'd do a lot worse than just kill me. I was trying to get out my weapon to kill myself when I felt a hand on my shoulder. This rough voice said, 'Let's go, soldier. I don't intend to miss chow for you.'" Abie tried to mimic Jack's voice. "This man, a man like I had never seen, carried me back, put me in the chopper, and went back for two others who were still alive. It was so tight he could hardly fly. One died on the way back. The other is now a United States Senator."

"Why is Jack a partner in your consulting firm?"

He made a quick blink like he'd been squirted in the face with lemon juice. "He helped me start it."

"What does he do?"

"Nothing. He's too good to do the kind of work I do. But he still takes half."

"That doesn't seem fair."

"It does to him." Vane reached for another cupcake. "And again in Europe."

"Excuse me."

"He saved my life in Eastern Europe during the Cold War. I was sent to Poland to do counterintelligence and disinformation, to disrupt Soviet operations. But my cover was mysteriously blown. It turned out it was Kim Philby, of course, as everyone later found out. The damn Brits didn't get onto him and Burgess and MacClean and the other communists until Sixty-three. Although it wasn't just Jack who saved me, it was Jesus, too."

"Now, you've got my attention. Jesus saved you in Eastern Europe."

He laughed loudly and swallowed half a cupcake in a single bite. He smacked his lips and wiped the back of his hand across his mouth. "Technically, it was *Jesus,*" he said, giving it the Spanish pronunciation. "James Jesus Angleton, head of American counterintelligence for the CIA from the Fifties to the Seventies. James was onto Philby in the Forties, even reported him, but no one would listen. Not coincidentally, Angleton's father and John's father served together under Pershing in World War I. Angleton was acquainted with John and John knew me, which is why Angleton asked John to…" He cleared his throat.

"To what?"

"To make sure I wasn't going to become an asset to the opposition."

I smiled. "He sent Jack in to kill you."

His mouth tightened and his eyes puckered. "That was perhaps the preferred option. At great risk to himself, Jack chose to get me out."

"Why is Jack doing this to me?"

"I don't know. He didn't tell me. I always thought he rather liked you, the way he would talk." He sighed. "But apparently not. Not that I saw him much, after…"

"After what?"

"Time, that's all. It gets away."

"Why do you have an apartment in my building on my floor? That can't be a coincidence."

"I was here first, years before you. The fact that there were two units you could combine into a nice, family-size apartment, and that they happened to be on my floor, no, that was not coincidence."

"Then you should have brought me cupcakes."

He nodded absently. "This apartment and three others, including one of the ones you now own, were my fee for a certain project I undertook. About a year ago, at John's urging, I moved in here so I could keep an eye on you."

"Your fee for what?"

"I'm an expediter. A facilitator. I deal with community boards, landmarks, zoning, regulators, unions, suppliers. I make the city work."

"You promote graft and corruption and help organized crime stay in business."

He waved off the insinuation. "If someone wants to take them out, more power to them, but as long as they're there, someone has to deal with them. Do you know how many strikes and walkouts I've stopped, how many projects I've saved, including this one? Thirty-two buildings. Thousands of jobs. I keep the peace."

I looked at the wall again. "Got it. The Colt .45. The Peacemaker."

"It's a Series One, quite rare. Do you know firearms?"

"Some. What's with the sword?"

"You figure it out."

I walked to the wall and took it down. I thought about taking the Colt, too, but didn't. I don't trust myself with guns. I looked at Abie sitting there, prim and pompous.

It was almost five. I started toward the door, the sword in my hand.

"That," he said, "is mine and it is special. Put it down."

I walked over and leaned down until my nose was almost touching his. "I could take everything in here, little man, and we still wouldn't be close to even."

When I got to the door, I stopped and looked back. He hadn't moved. His face was stone and his eyes were drilling into me. He said, "Don't call me little."

I stepped into the hall and pulled the door shut. Just before it closed, he said, "No one touches Yo…" The door cut off the sentence. I tried to open it because I wanted to hear the rest, but the handle was locked. A moment later, like the proverbial doors closing after the proverbial cattle are out of the proverbial barn, Abie's deadbolts slid into place, one, two, three.

MY OWN DOOR was locked and I didn't have anything to shim it with. I tapped lightly, waited, and was about to go downstairs to get a key when it opened. Cat stood there with a piece of cupcake in her hand wearing one of Laurie's robes. She took the last bite and licked her fingertips.

She looked at me and the sword. "This is where you tell me there's a reasonable explanation for all this."

"There isn't."

She stuck one finger in her mouth, closed her lips around it, and pulled it out slowly. She turned and started toward the bedroom. After two steps the robe fell from her shoulders onto the floor. I set the sword down, stepped over the robe, and followed her down the dim hall.

IT WAS NOT quite light when I woke. Cat's head was by my shoulder, and she breathed in a slow and dreamless rhythm. Her hair was a dark effluvial over her pillow. I kissed her forehead and got out of bed. As I reached for my phone, it buzzed and slid sideways. I looked at the ID and picked it up.

I said, "Hello, Jack."

50

Jack said, "What the hell do you think you're doing, Hall?"

"Trying to stay alive, things like that. And you?"

"Vane called," he said.

I got up and went into the hallway to keep from waking Cat. I said, "Did he mention we ran into each other?"

"He wants his sword back and intends to have you killed. He said a relative of Zinetti, the one who died in the truck, has offered to do it for free."

"You started this, Jack. You stop it."

"Damn it, Hall. There are three types of people you never want to take on. Crazy people, cowards, and those with nothing to lose. Vane, now that you've backed him into a corner, is all three. And he's also the most vindictive person I've ever known. Just out of curiosity, do you have a plan?"

"I do. I'm going to have coffee. And you can tell him he can have the sword back on one condition."

"What?"

"He uses it for hara-kiri."

I DRESSED, WENT down to the street and around the corner for my usual bagel and coffee, the same for Cat. I had to order because the girl behind the counter had a different smile, different hair and a different shirt. Different girl. "Where's Mira?" I asked the new one.

"Gave up on acting and moved back to Houston."

I went to a newsstand to get the papers I don't subscribe to and went back up stairs. In the kitchen I found a note on the table from Cat apologizing for leaving abruptly. Someone from the paper called and she had to go to the office, but she'd call later. That struck me as odd since she no longer worked for the paper and had no office to go to.

I took my coffee to the living room, stared out the window and tried to come up with a plan. After twenty minutes I went to the kitchen and re-heated my coffee in the microwave. While I was waiting, I went to the foyer and got Abie's sword. I pulled it from its scabbard and studied it.

It had detailed scrollwork and inlays of pearl, ivory and gold on the handle. It was clearly ceremonial, unlike the purely functional sword used by—

I looked at my reflection in the blade.

Yojimbo.

Was that what Abie was about to say? Don't mess with Yojimbo? In the Kurosawa movie, he was a traveling samurai, with a strict code of conduct but no loyalties. He sold his services to the highest bidder.

I doubted I could get away with killing Abie even if I'd wanted to. But something had to be done because, like a serial killer with a few bodies under his belt, he seemed to be escalating.

Then, like the toy hidden in a cereal box that spills into your bowl, a plan came to me. It might not have been the best plan ever, but it was a plan.

I went to my computer and printed out the version of the Vane story I'd sent out. It was two pages, and even though it only contained about half of what I suspected, it was probably enough to end his career and maybe trigger an investigation that would lead to charges. I wanted to visit Vane, but I was sure he wouldn't let me in a second time.

I went to the medicine cabinet and found a plastic bottle with several Co-Tylenol left over from two years earlier when I broke my hand rollerblading. They were past their expiration date but I didn't care. Next, I found a shoebox, took one of Cici's six plaster dogs, a "takeaway" from a popular grade-school birthday party venue, put it inside the box for heft, and enclosed the incriminating summary. I addressed it to "Abel Vane, 28A." As a return address I put "JPM, One Carlton Road, Short Hills, NJ." In bold letters I printed, HAND DELIVERY, and took it down to the front desk. I told the doorman it had been accidentally delivered to me, that he needed to call Vane and ask if he wanted Bobby to bring it up. I waited.

Vane asked what it was and whom it was from. The doorman described it, said it was heavy, and read him the initials and return address. Abie mulled for a moment and decided, perhaps, that it was a peace offering from Jack.

Bobby and I rode up together, went to Vane's door. Bobby banged three times. From inside a voice screamed. "Enough." I prodded Bobby and he banged again. "Stop. I'm coming. You don't have to break it down, damn it."

The door swung open and Abie faced us, still in his pajamas and robe. He looked at Bobby, at me, said, "What the…"

"A gift."

He tried to slam the door but Bobby put his hand on it. "Someone sent you a package Mr. V. show him Porter."

I ripped open the box, removed the summary and handed it to Vane. I gave the box with the plaster dog to Bobby and told him to throw it down the compactor chute.

Bobby looked at the plaster animal. "Can I keep it Porter it's nice?"

"Sure, but come back in fifteen minutes and wait by the door."

I followed Abie in and closed the door, making sure it was unlocked. Vane backed into the room, staring at the paper.

"What is this shit?" He was less cordial than before.

"A synopsis of your life. I may try to get a book deal with it. Where's your liquor?"

He flipped from one page to the next, and the next. "Drinking this early in the day is symptomatic of alcoholism, you sot."

"It's not for me, Abie, it's for you."

He stiffened.

I said, "Would you rather I found it myself?"

He pointed to a hutch. I removed a bottle of The Macallan single-malt Scotch and a bottle of Armagnac, each about a third full. From the upper cabinet I took a brandy snifter. I took the codeine-laced tablets from my pocket and dropped four into each bottle. I'm not an anesthesiologist, but I didn't figure it would kill him. And if I was wrong, oh, well. I set the liquor bottles on his dining table, and told him to sit. I poured two fingers of Scotch into the snifter.

He finished the story, tore the sheet into small pieces, and sprinkled them over the floor.

"Drink, Abie."

"I don't drink alone and I won't drink with you, puissant."
He looked at the glass and wrinkled his lip. "And furthermore,
you Idaho hick, you put The Macallan in a brandy glass."

"Wyoming."

"Oh, right. Wyoming, the cultural epicenter of the universe."

"Wrong glass?" I looked at it, tilted my head, lay my hand
against my chest. "Oh, pardon mois, monsieur Vane." I reached
over, picked up the snifter and threw the Scotch in his face. He
remained strangely composed as the liquor ran down his face
and dripped onto his robe, but his eyes held enough fury to run
the fires of hell for several months.

I poured two fingers of Armagnac into the rounded glass and
swirled it.

"That's better, I hope." I pushed it toward him.

He sipped. "Why are you doing this?"

"So you will never bother me or anyone else again."

"This is going to do that?" He sipped again.

I said, "Drink, faster. This is taking too long."

"And if I don't?"

"You'll be dead before I leave this room."

He looked at me for a few seconds and took another drink,
sneered.

"Would you *really* do that?"

"I don't know, which means you don't either. Shall we find
out?"

He took one sip, then another. As the minutes passed, his
face began to sag. He looked old.

"Okay, Abie, say, 'Plain pickled pigs feet are probably more
plentiful than flat fat platters of fleet fickle fish.'"

He stared at me.

"Drink." He finished the drink and I refilled it. "Abie, name
all of the mayors of New York City since 1960."

"Wagner, Bean." He squinted. "Lindley. Or was Lindy first?"

"Stand up."

He did, slowly. I threw the rest of the drink on his chest.

"What'd you do that for?"

"Good measure. Come here, Abie." I helped him stand and guided him by the arm to the sliding door of his terrace. "You need some fresh air."

Abie's personal outdoor space was a five-by-nine slab of concrete with a metal railing a little over three feet high. There was a small table, an outdoor chair, and a footrest. In each corner was a planter with a sizeable evergreen.

He started to step out, looked at me, and tried to step back in. I pushed him further out. "Fresh air will make you feel better. I promise."

"No, no, no. Don't do this. Please, Porter." He stiffened and pushed back against me. "I won't bother you anymore. I won't. I promise. I don't like high places. I'm sick."

I grabbed the long silk sash and looped it several times around my wrist, and made it tight around his waist. I turned him so he was facing away from me, put an arm around his neck and grabbed a handful of silk robe. I pushed him against the rail and lifted him a couple of inches.

My expectation was that Abie would scream and people would come out onto their own terraces. I would yell that he was trying to jump, and tell someone to call 911. That was the plan.

Abie didn't panic, he became hysterical. He started flailing and kicking, and somehow got one foot on top of one of the planters and the other on the table. He was grabbing at my head and we got further tangled up in his robe and sash. One of his kicks caused a leg to go over the railing. I yelled at him told him to stop. Doors opened and people stepped onto their balconies in various stages of dress. I tried to pull him inside, but one of his feet was stuck in the railing and he clutched me in a death-grip. I tripped on a chair and fell forward. Abie's lower half and my upper half hung over the rail. He was about to pull us both over. It was a three-hundred foot drop to the courtyard. I shouted, "Bobby. Help."

The door opened and Bobby's heavy steps thumped toward us. "Get him in, Bobby. He's trying to jump."

Bobby wrapped his huge arms around us and pulled us backward into the living room. We all fell in a heap.

From beneath us Bobby said, "Are you okay Porter you scared me I thought you were falling you okay?" Vane rolled off of me onto all fours and threw up on a very fine Kilim.

EMS ARRIVED IN ten minutes. They strapped Vane to a stretcher and wheeled him to the elevator. I made sure they understood he was drunk, delusional, and suicidal.

I then searched Abie's apartment. On the wall beneath the oils stood a small, gilded chest, a commode, I believe the French would call it, an original from one of the Louis kings, maybe, or a very fine reproduction. The cabinet was locked. It would have been easy to pop it, but that wasn't necessary because beneath the base of a tasseled lamp on top of it was the key. Inside the cabinet were thirteen journals and an expansion file. I took them all.

As I walked into my apartment my phone rang. Cat said, "I got my job back, sort of."

"What happened? What do you mean, sort of?"

"I'll tell you later."

"I've got a story for you." She didn't respond. "If you want it, I mean."

She sighed. "What the hell. Give it to me."

After I gave her my spin of Abie's apparent suicide attempt, I called Jack and told him Vane was taken care of. He listened as I explained but didn't say anything for a while.

Finally, a long, low hiss came from the phone. "Do you know what you just did, Hall? You humiliated an obsessive, vengeful little monster, but he's still alive, and he still knows everyone he knew two days ago. He'll get even if it's the last thing he does. You should have thrown him off the damn balcony and walked away."

"And you should have left him in the rice paddy in Korea?"

"First," Jack said with a long sigh, "it wasn't a rice paddy. Second, if I'd known he was going to get tangled up with my idiot son-in-law, I would have shot him."

Son-in-law?

51

Cat's story of Vane's misdeeds ran on page one of the Metro section and detailed his mob connections, abuse of authority, misuse of public resources, and kickbacks. It also gave an account of the time Vane and a seventeen-year-old boy named Guillermo were denied admission to an Atlantic City casino.

The sidebar of Vane's attempted suicide carried a picture of Abie with his legs dangling over the rail, taken by one of our neighbors. There was an inset of Bobby, who was presented as the hero, and who really was the hero, wearing a grin the size of a toaster. Vane, according to the write-up, found out about the upcoming exposé, started drinking and decided to jump off his balcony. This was confirmed by the fact that he reeked of liquor and had a blood alcohol level of .23.

Jack's skepticism notwithstanding, I was convinced Abie's powerbase would be neutralized. I thought. I hoped. I prayed.

AT ELEVEN, KATHERINE called and summoned me into executive session at their apartment.

An hour later Jack and I were in opposing armchairs and Katherine was on an adjacent loveseat.

Jack said, "Thanks to you, Porter, we have a serious problem."

"Do you have Alzheimer's? Thanks to *you* we have a problem."

Jack gave me an acid look, but before he could speak Katherine said, in a voice so soft you knew she was at the end of her rope, "Stop." She leaned back and spoke. "I will tell you what the two of you are going to do." We looked at each other then her. "Nothing."

Jack and I opened our mouths, but she gave us each a look and we shut them.

"You will do nothing because I am going to take care of it myself. I called Abie at the hospital, expressed my concern, and invited him to lunch Monday. He should be recovered by then. In the meantime, you are both to stay away from him. Understood?"

Jack turned to Katherine and in a tone perilously close to that bottomless pit called patronization, said, "Dear, I don't think…"

"I know that. Neither of you do, but you both think you think and that's dangerous for everyone. Show him your hand, Jack."

Jack's left arm was across his chest and his hand was covered by his right arm. He pulled it out. The middle and index fingers were taped together and his thumb was in a splint.

"What happened?"

"Jack's feeble attempt to straighten out a mess. After you called from the hospital that night and told us about the incident on the FDR, he went to see Abie."

I looked at Jack. "So that's how the Chippendale got broken."

"What Chippendale?" said Kathrine. Jack stood, walked over to the bar, and made a drink. Katherine went to the dining room.

"Come in here, Porter," she called. "You, too, Jack."

On the table were several file folders. From one she removed a small black-and-white photo and handed it to me.

It was a figure of a woman in a flowing, sheer dress leaning on an early Forties coupe, a Buick, or maybe an Oldsmobile, one foot resting on the running board. No, an Olds because Buick's signature portholes were missing. "Is this Laurie? She looks...different." I held it close. "When was this taken?"

Jack was studying his thumb.

"Jack. Tell him."

"1946."

"But...who is this?"

"Jack's mother."

I looked closer. The resemblance to Laurie was so strong it was harder to find differences than similarities. "What happened to her?"

"Three days after this was taken she drove that car into the Delaware River."

"Accident?"

"They called it that, but it wasn't. She was sweet, kind, quirky, very bright. But she couldn't handle stress of any kind. Remind you of anyone?"

Kathrine pulled out another photo, one of a man with a long, gaunt face and deep expressionless eyes. Even in the photo there was something more than hardness.

"Who's he?"

"My grandfather," said Jack, "on my father's side."

Katherine said, "The last three years of your life, the last three weeks, this is the story. These two people."

"I don't get it."

"Until two nights ago, neither did I. Fill in the blanks, Jack."

He went for more Scotch and came back with two. He offered me one and I took it. We all sat.

Jack said, "When Laurie started having problems, I knew where it was going. I didn't want to get her away from you, Porter, I wanted to get her away from the kids. Children are as stressful as anything in life. I didn't want...I'd rather your kids had a mother two weekends a month than not at all."

"And your grandfather?"

"The orneriest son-of-a-bitch I ever met, just plain mean. My father said he wasn't always like that. He built a small fortune and almost lost it. At the end of the war my father came home to try to save it. It was difficult. My grandfather had legal control, but his mind was gone. Most people had never heard of Alzheimer's, and it was long before the courts began to recognize it as a basis for having someone declared incompetent."

Katherine reached for an inch-thick folder and pushed it toward me.

"What's this?"

"Leisure-time reading. Every relevant document relating to the MacNeil Family Trust. It directly affects Laurie and your children. And us. And you."

"Why me, other than whatever passive interest I have because of the kids?"

"Your interest is hardly passive. As of January 1st, seven weeks from now, you will be legally in charge of the trust in its entirety."

I took a long drink of the Scotch, and began coughing. I set my drink down and wiped tears from my eyes. "You will be well-compensated, of course."

"This is crazy. I don't want to be in charge of a trust."

"And Jack doesn't want you to be, but you are. It's Jack's father's response to a wife and father who both lost their minds. George, Jack's father, saved his father's business and then built a decent estate himself. He didn't want Jack or Jack's children to go through what he did, which, given the mental issues on both sides of the family, he thought was highly probable. He set up a sum-of-the-ages formula that's a bit complicated, but as each generation comes of age, control is passed automatically to the younger generation. As of the first of the year, B.J. and Cici will have twenty percent voting control, which is controlled by you since you have sole custody, Laurie will have thirty-five and Jack forty-five. When Laurie married you, she designated you as her representative. She didn't want the stress. She wants it even less now, and she made it clear she's not changing her proxy from you, whether you're married or not."

I said, "That's what the custody fight was about." Jack seemed suddenly fascinated by his drink. "And it explains the timing."

Pieces of a puzzle were being laid down one at a time and a picture was forming. Jack looked at me to see if I had figured it out. I nodded.

He lifted his head and twisted it, as though he had a kink in his neck. "There's one exception. If the person to whom control has passed is unable or unwilling to perform those duties, it reverts to the previous party for up to three years, or until a successor can be arranged. I just wanted some minor legal matters to tangle you up for a while. And since there's not a nook or cranny in the city where Abie doesn't have influence, I figured he could take care of it. He was thrilled to help, to show me how powerful he is, to finally show me he was worthy of my friendship."

"Minor legal things? Rape, kidnapping, murder, extortion, bank fraud. What would constitute major?"

Jack took a deep breath but didn't look away. Katherine was glaring at him. I thought she was going to speak, but she didn't.

"But no matter what Abie did," Jack said, "you found a way around it. You meet Cat Marten at the precinct and she gets to your apartment in time to meet the kids' bus. You're set up to be charged with more than a dozen felonies, your bail is twenty million, and Clancy Hamilton shows up to post your bail and defend you. Abie was furious.

"He got his first job with the city because I made some introductions and some sizeable campaign donations. Twice I saved the little bastard's life, and when he finally gets a chance to pay me back, you wreck it for him.

"On top of that, he thinks when Laurie married you, I moved him to 'the back row of my life.' His words. Then the kids came along, and, the way he saw it, he was out on the street. He blames you for all of that. He's jealous. He wants you out of the way."

Katherine leaned forward and rested her head in her hands. She mumbled, "Hell hath no fury..." She leaned back and crossed her arms.

I said, "What?"

She shook her head. "Nothing."

I turned back to Jack. "Abie said you take half his profits."

Jack poked his dislocated fingers toward me. "I've never taken a nickel from him, and never will, not the way he makes money."

"You've created a golem you can't control, because, of course, there was no other way you could have dealt with all this," I said. "Was there?" Jack had an innocent look. "Well?"

He shook his head. "Not that I can think of."

I looked at the ceiling. "Let me think here, uh, how about just asking? How about coming to me and saying 'Laurie has some problems, like my mother did, and there are these issues with the estate. Let's work this out.' Did you ever think of that?"

"Tip my hand." He jerked his chin up. "You're kidding, right? Haven't I taught you a damn thing?"

I shook my head. "I guess not. And apparently I didn't teach you a damn thing either."

"Like what?"

"There's this thing called the direct approach. If you go up to the front of the house and knock, about ninety percent of the time someone opens the door. You don't always have to start by breaking in a back window."

"Unbelievable," said Katherine. She stood up. "You two are playing poker and Laurie and the kids are the pot."

She walked out of the room and Jack looked at me. "Want another drink?"

I shook my head, but he ignored me, went to the liquor cabinet, removed a bottle, set it on the cabinet.

"The Macallan," he said, using the article as though not to was sacrilege. "Fifty Year. A gift from Abie."

We'd been drinking eighteen-year, which was smooth as liquid velvet. Fifty-year would be like warm butter.

"No, thanks."

He pushed the bottle aside. "Listen, Porter, that thing with the bank. The transfer…"

"You mean the two or three felonies you're looking at for trying to keep me away from money I didn't know I had and

didn't want? How does it feel to face time?" He wanted to leave
the question as rhetorical, let it drop, but I waited.

"Not so good."

"Then compare that to fifteen or sixteen felonies that add up
to three life sentences for things I didn't do. At least your crimes
you committed."

"I was wrong. I'm sorry. What are you going to tell them?"

"First, the money you and Laurie gave away belonged to the
condo, not me, so all of it has to be repaid with interest. Second, the way I remember it right now is that I asked you to
transfer some funds and there was some confusion about it.

"You've got another year before the statute of limitations runs
out, but any more dirty tricks between now and then and my
recollection will get a lot better."

It wasn't the get-out-of-jail-free card he wanted, but after a
moment he said, "That works," and walked toward the door.

"Jack." He stopped and looked back. "Did you have anything
to do with Watergate?"

He looked at me for a few seconds then left the room, grinning as he turned away.

WHEN I GOT home, I had an email from Fred with info on Zoe
Kelman-slash-Zora Kalber-slash-Mrs. Marvin Plockman. She
lived on East Seventy-seventh Street. For a moment I felt odd,
even sad, that in all the years I'd known Marvin I never knew
he was married and never knew where he lived.

In any case, I was obviously overdue in paying Marvin's
widow a shiva visit. Perhaps I should have called one of my Jewish friends to see if they could tell me protocol for calling on
the mourning wife when there was no body, no funeral, and
probably no actual death. I knew that suicides in the Jewish

faith were treated with such disdain that the deceased might be exiled to the far reaches of the cemetery. But what about fake suicides? I doubted they would know any more than I did.

THE BUILDING WAS dismal orange brick with casement windows, an unstately, ten-story, post-war with an even less stately doorman. There were probably doormen in my building who lived in better places than Marvin did.

I entered the small vestibule and told the man, who was Hispanic, overweight, and indifferent to my presence, to tell Ms. Kalber someone was here to see her. On the wall behind him was a roster with names and buttons. Like a lot of third-tier rental buildings of that age, it was set up for a part-time doorman with a buzzer system for visitors when no one was on duty. A piece of brittle label tape said, "Plockman/Kalber."

The doorman said, "Name."

"Kalber or Plockman."

He looked at me with loathing. "No, your name."

"Antonio Griffin."

He narrowed his eyes, then spoke into the handset. "She'll be down."

"I'll be at the corner."

I was beginning to think she wasn't coming when the door opened and a woman with a narrow face and soupy brown hair pulled into a tight ponytail walked out. She was wrapped in a dated, camel-colored, wool coat, and was short, with thick legs. She had sallow skin and colorless eyes and an unpleasantness that said life had failed to give her what she deserved and she was mad as hell about it.

She scanned the street, saw me, and came at me like she was laser-locked.

"You cruel bastard," she said, when she was a foot away. "What do you want?"

"Mrs. Plockman, it is so nice to finally meet you. In all the years I knew Marvin he never said anything about you that wasn't glowing praise."

Her head yanked a little and I thought she was going to speak but she just looked at me. I could have added that he never said anything about her at all, and I never even knew he was married because everywhere I ever went with him he was hitting on everything that resembled female.

"What do you want?"

I studied her face until she turned away. "You know what I want."

"If you want to betray him again, you're too late."

"I want Marvin to turn himself in. He killed Jamie Trent, or helped, and tried to kidnap Cat Marten."

She turned away, but I grabbed her coat sleeve and turned her back toward me. She struck at me with her free hand and I grabbed that wrist and pulled her close to me.

She sneered up at me. "He's dead. Isn't that enough?" She had her story, and even if she didn't believe it she seemed convinced I would.

"You set Cat up for Marvin to kidnap the same way he did Jamie Trent." I released her arm.

She stepped away, but didn't leave. Her eyes widened. "Who…" She let the thought trail away as she connected some dots for the first time. In that one word she had acknowledged her involvement in the scheme to kidnap Cat, but had shown she didn't know about Jamie.

"Listen, Zora, I know you're only trying to help your husband, but you're in as much trouble as he is. In the future don't use your own phone."

Her face softened for a moment but immediately turned hard again. She backed away a couple of steps, put her palm toward me as a warning, and glanced at the doorman to see if he was coming to her aid. He was leaning against the wall with his eyes shut.

"Marvin is dead because of you." She turned and hurried into her building, clasping the front of her coat against the cold.

I waited a few minutes, went to a pay phone, and called her home number. When she answered, I said, "Have him call me. He's got my number."

52

FRIDAY, AFTER SCHOOL, THE KIDS AND I HEADED UP THAT historically rich but tarnished landscape known as the Lower Hudson Valley. It is full of history and ghosts and stories. Cooper and Irving, George Washington and Benedict Arnold. A major portion of early American history was written along the path of the New York State Thruway, and some of it is inscribed on plaques at rest stops.

The kids were strangely quiet, not complaining of boredom, not arguing, just sitting or sleeping. We stopped at Cooper Lake above Woodstock and watched the sun quickly set as it does in the mountains, all mountains, even hills that only think they are mountains. We had grilled cheese sandwiches for dinner and played Texas hold 'em until bedtime.

The kids decided to put up their canvas teepee and camp in the guest room, a room that, except for the occasional camping trip, was almost never used. They packed bagels for breakfast and B.J. took his Swiss Army knife in case he saw a bear. Cici took her bow and a quiver of arrows in case she had to kill a few wild Indians. I was about to explain that we call them Native Americans, and we don't kill them, merely go to their casinos and lose back some of the money we made on the land we stole from them. I decided to save it for another time.

After the kids were camped, I got Cognac, plugged my iPod into the stereo, and pulled up a playlist labeled HOME. It started with Judy Collins singing about a young man she knew from Southern Colorado, while behind her Buddy Emmons played pedal steel the way it will be played in heaven, if there is such a place, and if you're fortunate enough to make it there. I fell asleep and woke about twenty songs later. I turned off the music and went upstairs. I cracked the window a little because the night was mild and the air smelled like country. I got into bed feeling more content than I had in a long while. My children were healthy and happy and safe in their teepee twenty feet down the hall. That was all I could ask for, maybe all there was to ask for. Things were good. For the moment, things were good.

ON THE OTHER hand, when you're awakened in the middle of the night by a shrill blast that sounds like a banshee in a 'roid rage, things are not good. My head felt like it had a tomahawk in it, but all I wanted was to go back to sleep. That told me all I needed to know. It was not the smoke alarm shrieking, but the carbon monoxide detector. I knew if I didn't get up and do something, we could all die. I still didn't move. If I could sleep a few more minutes, then I would get up. I closed my eyes.

A moment later, in the greatest act of sheer will in my entire life, I rolled out of bed and onto the floor. The jolt woke me enough that I was able to force myself to crawl to the window and open it further. It was stuck. It occurred to me the first thing I should do was turn off the furnace. The thermostat was outside my door. I stood, staggered to the door and opened it.

In the hallway I saw what looked like a very large insect jumping up and down and swinging a claw hammer at a shrieking piece of plastic.

The insect saw me and stopped. It made one more leap and planted a chop in the middle of the grill. The device shattered, the battery flew out, and there was a spray of shrapnel. The alarm went silent. The insect turned to me and in a distorted voice said, "Hello, Porter."

I nodded slowly. "Hello, Marvin."

He faced me and relaxed, the hammer in one hand, a .22 semi-automatic U.S Army service pistol in the other. A black molded mask, some kind of aerator, covered the lower part of his face. I recognized both the pistol and the aerator. The aerator I used when I was sanding or cutting wood and the pistol, which I kept hidden in a crevice behind the furnace, had belonged to my father.

"Downstairs," he said. I went first.

Marvin sat in a chair near the wall, holding the gun on me, and I sat on the sofa.

"What's going on, Marvin?"

The reply, barely intelligible through the breathing apparatus, was, "Carbon monoxide."

"I figured. How?"

"I rigged the furnace."

I was drowsy, though not as much as I had been in the bed-room. I started to ask him to let my kids go outside then de-cided not to. My thinking was muddled and I wasn't sure why I didn't mention them, but I knew there was a reason. I was thankful for their ability to sleep though almost anything.

"Marvin."

"What?"

"I don't know. I'm tired."

"Of course you are. This is a good way to die. At least I've heard that." He laughed, but through the mask but it sounded like hee-haw. "Beats drowning in a river." *Hee-haw, hee-haw.*

"I'll let you know about that. Why are you doing this?"

"You made me. You should have left my wife alone, let me disappear like I wanted to."

"Did you kill Jamie?"

His head weaved slowly back-and-forth like that of some-one riding in a horse drawn wagon. He didn't speak for about a minute.

"Porter…"

"What?"

"That wasn't supposed to happen. Just wanted to talk, ex plain, she had to back off. She wouldn't listen."

"You thought she would?"

"It wasn't an option. She needed to understand who she was dealing with."

"She was dealing with you. You were skimming from the Me-dora and West Thirty-first Street and a lot of others."

He lifted his head and pulled the mask away from his face. He looked at me for a long time. "You…" he took a couple of deep breaths. "You don't have a clue, do you? You really don't." His shoulders sagged. "I thought you knew. I really thought you knew. He did too."

"Knew what? Who's *he*?"

"She said you didn't, but I didn't believe her. I just wanted to know how much she told you. Not everything. That was what lunch was for, wasn't it?"

"Not anything. And how would I know what lunch was for? You killed her before I found out. Remember?"

"She was one stubborn bitch. You know that?"

"Why kill her?"

"It was…in the back of the van…" Marvin's speech was slowing. "…Griffin…was there and…she tried to get out, he grabbed her and…you know."

"Then you took her and dumped her off the road? Was that your idea?"

"What?" he looked out the window and squinted as though he could see the place a half-mile away where her body was found.

"Was it your idea to bring her up here?"

"No. No, that was…someone else. I wasn't with Griffin. He thought she was dead. She wasn't. So he finishes it. Anyway, that's what he said. But he's totally freaked by that point and can't read the map I drew. He was supposed to put her behind your house somewhere, cover her with dirt and leaves, like it was you who did it, see. But not too good, like you were in a hurry. It was a good plan. Idiot panicked. He goes and dumps her on the wrong side of the damn road."

"Her name was Jamie."

"But right up till then it was just about perfect. You got picked up by the cops at just the right time, I mean just right, down to the minute." He moved the mask back to cover his face.

He started with his hee-haw again, but his head slumped to the side. He shook it. "What is it with these women of yours? Trent…she fights with us and gets herself killed, and then that wacko wife of yours kills Griffin and wants to kill me. They're animals."

"Speaking of wives, how come you never brought yours to any of the holiday parties? Or mentioned she existed."

"Yeah, that. Would you have wanted that hanging on your arm? She's such a…" He pulled the mask away from his mouth. "You saw where I lived, you saw my wife. And then there's you, you lucky, rotten, unappreciative bastard. You live in a palace, at least compared to me, and that wife of yours. Give me a piece of that…but you couldn't even keep her. You're so pathetic." He put the mask back on.

"Your wife is going to end up doing time because of you. I should never have helped you get that building. Jamie would be alive now."

"What are you talking about? You never got me anything." His head bobbed. "Got any coffee?"

"I introduced you to Jamie." His chin dropped, jerked up. "No, I don't have coffee." I nodded toward a breakfront. "I've got Cognac, Scotch."

"You're so full of yourself. I manage thirty-one buildings. I think it's thirty-one. Or thirty-two. Did you get me all those? I'll take Scotch."

"You can get it. It's over there." I pointed.

He looked toward the cabinet then turned back to me.

I said, "Were you skimming all of them?"

He nodded very slowly. "Yeah, but it wasn't about the skim. You wouldn't believe who owns apartments in some of those."

"What's that got to do with it?"

"It's the security system. Why do you think we put it in?"

"I don't know, Marvin. To improve security."

"HAW HEE HEE HEE HAW HAW." That got the biggest laugh of the night.

"And what was with the phony financial statements? What are those about?"

"What phony financial statements?"

"From the accountants. All of the reports, the audits, the reconciliations, are all made up."

"You're really out of it now." He pulled the mask away from his face for a moment and squinted at me, like he was wondering if I knew something he didn't. "I don't know what you're talking about."

"Yes, you do. I called and asked about the double billings."

"Come on, Porter, it's just us here. You were squeezing me for more money." He put the mask back on his face.

I said, "No, I wasn't. Benford's Law."

He leaned back in his chair. "I don't know who that is. Why don't you just shut up and die? I'm kind of tired myself."

"Why did you have the financial records cleaned out of my apartment?" That was a guess although I figured it was a good one.

He titled his head as though trying to remember. "Orders."

"Did the same person tell you to attack me in the basement?" Another guess.

"Hell, no. You think I can't do anything on my own? I do some of my own initiatives."

"You could have killed me."

"I should have killed you. Would make this all a lot easier now."

"Who are you afraid of, Marvin?"

"Not you. Used to be, not any more. Now shut up and go to sleep, Porter. Go to sleep while you can."

"That doesn't make sense. Where's Griffin?"

Marvin's head was bobbng. "Griffin? Maine, Florida. Who knows? Depends on the currents, I guess."

"Where was all the money going?"

He lifted his head and his eyes got big, enhancing the bug effect. "You don't know? You really don't know?"

"I really don't."

"Jamie knew. She was going to tell you. That's why I had to talk to her. Do you have any Tylenol?"

Marvin's head drifted down, jerked up, lowered slowly. It stopped when the mask was resting his chest. He was out.

All I had to do was get up, walk over and take the gun. Instead, I went to sleep.

THERE WAS A shriek, loud enough to wake me, not the banshee again, but close. Cici.

She and B.J. were behind the second floor railing looking down at Marvin, who sat unmoving. The gun was on his lap pointing at me. Cici had loaded a rubber-tipped arrow into her bow and was aiming. I tried to tell her to stop but my voice was a whisper.

B.J. yelled, "Drop it, mister."

Cici told B.J. to shut up and there was a thwang followed by a crash as Cici's the arrow hit a shelf a foot from Marvin and knocked a glass candy dish to the floor. Marvin didn't move. Cici said, "Did I kill him, Dad?"

B.J. called 911, spoke with the operator and brought me his phone. Within ten minutes a policeman arrived along with an officer from the Ulster County sheriff's department and two ambulances. Half an hour later the medical examiner arrived.

The EMS crew gave me oxygen. The kids hadn't been affected. They had opened the window a couple of inches to make it feel like they were outside, and because the room was seldom used the vents were closed.

The M.E. suspected that Marvin had succumbed to carbon monoxide asphyxia. His theory as to why Marvin died and I didn't had to do with the respirator he was wearing. It was for particulates, not gases, and Marvin probably figured a respirator is a respirator.

"Guy was stupid," he said. "It probably concentrated the fumes, plus he was sitting on top of a vent. You could make everyone sick, but this house is so old and drafty you'd have to run the furnace for days to get enough concentration to kill anyone. Unless you're wearing that mask and sitting over a duct."

Marvin. Died of being a klutz.

53

When Monday came, for some reason I couldn't figure out, I felt compelled to oversee Katherine's lunch with Abie. The problem was I wasn't invited, wasn't welcome, and didn't know where it was. I called six restaurants before I found the location. The Four Seasons. It wasn't one of Katherine's favorite places, so it must have been one of Abie's.

"I wish to confirm Mrs. Katherine MacNeil's reservation for lunch," I said, in my version of the voice of a prissy personal assistant. "One o'clock, that's right, the Grill Room…? The Pool Room, this time, oh, yes, a table near the window? Perfect. Thank you so much."

Interesting that Katherine chose the Pool Room, with its soft colors and gurgling fountain. She generally preferred the darker, power-lunch setting of the Grill Room, because she was less likely to run into her dearest friends, most of whom she couldn't stand.

I hit redial to make a reservation, but hung up. Getting a reservation for lunch this late would be iffy unless you were a regular. If your name was Porter Hall, it went from iffy to nada. I needed a ticket. I made a call.

"It's Porter. Is Clancy in?"

"I was about to call you," he said when he came on. "Care to tell me about the picture of you and Abel Vane looking like you're about to go off a balcony three hundred feet above the ground? I suspect there's a story and that it isn't the one in the paper."

"It never is. Meet me for lunch at the Four Seasons and I'll tell you about it. My treat, but you have to book it. As far from the window as possible, Pool Room. One o'clock."

"Pool Room? I've never eaten in there. Let me guess. Another story."

JUST BEFORE ONE, I watched Clancy enter the restaurant as I skulked behind a delivery van across the street. He was accompanied by his red-haired associate, Carol Flannery. A minute later the MacNeils' Town Car pulled up. Ike, their driver, got out and opened the back door. Katherine, followed by Vane, entered the Seagram Building, a Mies van der Rohe, land-marked skyscraper, with its restaurant jewel, designed by Philip Johnson.

I waited two minutes and went in. I slipstreamed the hostess, hoping to go unnoticed, but halfway to the table my internal sensor told me I was on someone's screen. I glanced toward the windows and saw Katherine. Her eyes were on me, locked and loaded. They said, *Porter Hall, what the hell are you doing here? You've already put your entire family in jeopardy. What now?* My eyes responded, *What a coincidence.* Hers didn't buy it. I glanced at the room to say, *The Pool Room?* She replied, *His choice.* Vane was studying the menu. I told her to have a nice lunch. She said, *Fat chance.* I continued to my table, where Clancy looked up at me, then over at Katherine. Something passed between them though I couldn't imagine what.

I took Carol's hand. "Nice of you to join us."

"Thank you for having me."

Clancy said, "There was no way I was having lunch with you in the Pool Room without a female to ascribe the choice to."

I said, "You know my mother-in-law?"

He raised a brow. "I've met her," which could cover everything from I spoke with her at a party to we have a love child together. She wouldn't have told me that much.

Clancy said, "She's why we're here, obviously. And what a coincidence she's with a man you appeared to be throwing off a building a couple of days ago."

"I was saving him. The story said so."

"I read the story. Explain."

I told him. Clancy listened with resignation. Carol enjoyed it. She said, "Do you want to update us on the news we got this morning about Marvin Plockman being found dead in your living room, or save that for another time?"

"Not much to tell. Plockman broke into my house, tried to kill me with carbon monoxide, ended up killing himself."

A couple of waiters set appetizers in front of us. Clancy studied his like it was the engine of a car he was thinking about buying, looking at it from multiple angles, checking to see if it was going to do anything. He picked up his fork and said, "For the record, you're the first client I ever had that someone who was already dead came back to try to kill."

Katherine and Vane were half of a course ahead of us, and shortly after our entrees arrived, theirs were cleared. Vane was doing the talking, animated, agitated, while Katherine listened, motionless, expressionless. She was leaning back, he was bent forward. He seemed to be lecturing her, once even poking a finger towards her. Not something I would do, or recommend.

Vane had desert, something with red berries, and Katherine went straight to coffee. He continued talking, occasionally sipping at some drink with froth on it. As he talked, Katherine reached into her bag, removed a micro-cassette and laid it on the table. Vane froze, stared at it. He pushed his plate away, reached for the tape and stuck it into his pocket. He leaned in and spoke emphatically, face red, chin pushed out.

The three of us dropped any pretense of doing anything but watching. Katherine leaned forward. An ironic smile came to her lips. It went away at the same time her right hand flashed across the table and raked down Vane's left cheek. She picked up her bag and started toward the door. She stopped, said something to the hostess, and glanced at me.

Vane remained at the table, stunned, his hand covering the left side of his face. After a moment he took it away and looked. Three lines striped his cheek and blood ran down his neck. His open hand was the color of his desert.

A few minutes later Vane left. He seemed disoriented, holding the arm of the maitre d' with one hand, and a napkin to his face with the other.

I got our waiter and offered him my credit card. He said, "It's taken care of, sir," and nodded toward Hamilton.

I said, "Thank you, Clancy."

"The show was worth it."

I was about to put my card away when the waiter cleared his throat. "However, Mrs. MacNeil said you would take care of this." He handed me the bill for her and Vane.

54

I had a voicemail from Katherine, angry and firm. "Apartment, four o'clock."

When I got there, Jack was reading a golf magazine and Katherine was staring at the nails of her right hand. She stood, went to the bar, and made a martini from a bottle of Kerel One.

I said, "That worked well."

Katherine didn't reply.

"What's Plan B? Or Plan C? Or whatever we're on. What happened?"

She swallowed about half of her dink in one gulp. "I invited him to lunch him so we could work things out, yet somehow I ended up spending the entire meal listening to him tell me everything that was wrong with you. Like I hadn't heard it all before. Then he set forth criteria that would allow us to peacefully coexist."

"Which were?"

"Leave him alone, stay out of his business, apologize, and one other."

I looked at her.

"He said you needed to be dead."

"And you said…?"

"I told him I had a problem with that. It was civil to that point. He said I had no choice. I told him I did."

I said, "Is that when you gave him the cassette?"

Jack looked at her. "Cassette?"

There was a grim smirk on her face. "The Abie Double-doodle tape."

"What?" Jack mouthed it almost silently. "How do you know about that?"

She looked at me. "The phone in Jack's office is taped on microcassette. There's also one on the answering machine. That's the one I gave Abie."

"You still use microcassettes?"

Katherine said, "Guess who suggested to Nixon he put a recorder on the Oval Office line."

I looked at Jack with admiration. He shrugged.

"What's the *Abie Double-doodle*?"

Jack said, "You have to understand Abie's business model. He's a mediator, a dealmaker, a go-between, and sometimes a peacemaker.

"When one party can't, or won't sit down with the other, or can't be seen sitting down with the other, he bridges the gap. The mayor of New York can't sit down with the head of a crime family or a union boss with mob ties, but there's a need for communication. Abie fills it. Sometimes he gets paid as a consultant, sometimes he gets paid with favors, sometimes both.

"One night years ago he called me, middle of the night, drunk. I wasn't there and he talked to the machine. He said…"

Katherine said, "I thought you might want to listen." She got a micro-cassette player from a cabinet, slipped in the tape, hit play.

"John, John, John, my dear old friend," Vane said, slurring his words. "I wish you were here. I've got a bottle of Chianti and we could talk about old times. I've had the best day. You know the Bonano under-bosses who hate each other and each thinks the other is out to get him? Let me tell you what I did."

The tape lasted six minutes. Abie had resolved a disagreement between the two, but it was one of his own making. Each party paid him fifty grand to fix something that wasn't broken. At the end he said, "And that's what will become known as the Abie Double-doodle. Both sides of the fence. I am Yojimbo." Then he started singing The Sidewalks of New York.

"The next morning he called, hysterical. He said I had to get rid of that tape. I told him not to worry."

"But you kept it."

"I just left it in the machine." He looked at Katherine. "How did you get it?"

"The travel agent leaves messages on Jack's line. I heard it when I was listening to one of those and thought it was worth keeping. I hate that worm. I switched tapes."

"So you gave him a copy at the restaurant. Then what?"

"First, he said it was embarrassingly rude behavior that anyone would betray a confidence like that."

"That's like Jack the Ripper criticizing someone for using the wrong fork."

Katherine continued: "He said I had made it impossible for him to enjoy his raspberry compote cheesecake." She took a couple of deep breaths to compose her self, looked at Jack, at me, at her nails.

"Then Abel said, very calmly, 'Katherine, my dear. Do you think I am more afraid of that tape being disseminated, or that you are more afraid of something horrid happening to your grandchildren?' That's when I tried to rip his face off."

She leaned back and let out a sigh that seemed to drain her anger and energy. "He won't really harm the children, will he, Jack?" She was pleading. "Would he really hurt them?"

Jack stared into his drink. "First chance he gets."

Katherine normally held up to emotional adversity about the same as Pike's Peak holds up to snow, but she was beginning to melt. She raised her eyes over my shoulder and froze. Laurie was in the doorway. She looked at me for a moment and went away.

I checked several rooms before I finally found her in her father's den. She was standing at his desk and in front of her was a clip from a semi-automatic pistol and a box of shells. In her hand was a .9mm Glock, which she was checking out with the deft movements of an expert. She checked the chamber, racked the slide, pulled the trigger, and laid it down. She loaded cartridges into the magazine, slid it into the handle, and engaged the safety.

I sat on a leather sofa and she came and sat beside me, gun in hand. She smiled. "Hi, sweetie."

"Hi, Laurie. What are you going to do with the gun?"

"Kill Uncle Abie."

"Why?"

"So he doesn't hurt our children."

"Is that the only option?"

"Of course not. But it's the most predictable, and the safest."

"Laurie."

"What?"

"You could go to prison for a very long time."

"I know. But if I don't stop him, he'll hurt our children. Would you rather do it?"

As irrational as such discussions with her tended to be the seemingly rational side of the argument never came out ahead. Fortunately, Jack appeared at the door and said, "It's taken care of." We both looked at him.

"What?"

"Vane. I gave the tape to Ike." He was the MacNeil's driver. "He'll take it to my secretary. She'll send it to all the media outlets."

"I think it would be better to kill him."

Jack walked over and stood in front of her. "We'll keep them out of sight until this is resolved. You don't need to do anything, angel." He held his hand out and Laurie put the gun in it.

She said, "I understand." That sent a chill up my spine, because Laurie was invariably literal. *I understand* meant she understood Jack's logic and point of view. It didn't mean she agreed or would adhere to it or that she was promising not to kill Vane. All it meant was that she wasn't going to kill him with the Glock, at least not at that moment. If she were set on killing him, it would be very hard to stop her. She left the room.

When she was gone, I said, "Where'd she get that gun? Please tell me it wasn't in your desk drawer where the kids could find it."

Jack nodded at a door at one end of the room, and I followed him. I had always assumed it was a closet. It was, but it was the size of a small bedroom. In front of us stood a rack of rifles with heavy cable running through the trigger guards, locked on the end. On our left was a cabinet with archery equipment, several long bows, two compounds, and a couple of crossbows. There were feathered shafts and a box with various, lethal-looking heads. A cabinet on the right had handguns, revolvers and semi-automatics, ranging from a two-shot Derringer, to a Taurus Raging Bull, a Brazilian-made revolver that loads .454 Casull cartridges. It could bring down a Humvee, rip apart its engine block, at two hundred yards. You didn't want to think about what it could do to a human.

One space was empty. Jack put the Glock back in the slot from which Laurie had taken it.

I said, "Jesus, Jack."

"What?"

"You expecting an alien invasion or something?"

He closed the doors to the handgun cabinet and clicked a combination lock into place on a hasp that held a metal bar over the doors. He gave me a deadly serious look. "It happened once. It can happen again."

"That was Grover's Mills, New Jersey, not Manhattan."

He shook his head as though he felt sorry for someone so ignorant. "And you think those space ships won't come into the city next time because, what, they left their EZ Pass at home?"

55

When we got back to the kitchen, Katherine was there with a glass of water about to take a pill of some kind. She said, "What will they do to Abel after they hear the tape?"

"It's not *what*," Jack said, "it's *when*. He ripped them off, ridiculed them, and bragged about it. They won't let that stand. They can't. If they do, they appear weak, and someone comes after them."

"Okay, when?"

"I'm already thinking about his memorial service."

I said, "Won't he run?"

"No. He's a coward, but he thinks he's indispensable."

The only real difference between 6:00 p.m. on the Upper Eastside of Manhattan and midnight in a Kansas farm town is that in a small town in Kansas you could probably find more fun. Carnegie Hill, as the neighborhood is known, has one of its pedicured feet and half its exfoliated body in the box by the time the sun goes down. You would never know that a mile away is Times Square, where nights are as bright as day, and that a couple of miles further south is Greenwich Village, where life rises and falls and beats its way through negro streets till dawn.

When I got back to the Medora, I found Abie in a chair in the lobby reading *The New Yorker*. He didn't look up.

He was dressed formally, but not in a standard tux like I wear a few times a year. His pants were black and his jacket gray satin. He wore a gray long tie with a silk vest, and suede slippers with gold medallions. His overall sartorial splendor was diminished by his head, which looked like a cast that was running out of room for members of my family to sign, the bandage on the left courtesy of Katherine, the swelling on the right courtesy of Jack, and the red, chafed chin that traced to his encounter with me. On his knees sat a black derby.

"Nice hat."

His nostrils flared.

"Stitches," I said.

"Seventeen."

"No, I meant you had the rest of us in stitches, at lunch."

He turned a page and without taking his eyes from the magazine, said, "This is almost over. You are aware of that."

"The sooner the better."

"Really?" he said. "We must be anticipating different outcomes."

"That's possible."

The doorman said, "Mr. V, your car is here."

Vane stood, dropped the magazine onto a table, put his hat on his head, and moved in small, quick steps toward the door. As he passed me I said, "Double-doodle. Has a ring."

He stopped. "Double children. That has a ring, too." Then he went into the night to spend it with those who might still think him an important man.

56

THE MAN WHO MAKES THE CITY WORK WAS THE TITLE OF the article on the front page of the *Journal*. Those were Vane's words. The Daily News called him "Double-Doodle Man," but the Newsday headline hit nothing but net: "Making the Mob Pay for Protection—from Itself."

When I finished reading Cat's story I called her. "Nice write up. Did you get your job back?"

"No, a different job. I'm not a staff reporter. I'm a feature writer with some reporting duties."

"Did the guy who fired you have an epiphany in the middle of the night, something about how one's responsibilities as a human being supersede her obligations as a reporter?"

She said, "All I know is I got a better cubicle, a new job description, and a significant raise. And the man who fired me, according to the grapevine, is on his way to take over the Bozeman bureau."

"Something happened," I said. "What?"

"I'm not sure," she said, "but I could make an educated guess based on other tidbits dropping from the grapevine. Someone on the masthead wasn't happy about a reporter getting fired for saving a kid's life."

"That's it?"

"That, and the fact that the kid's grandfather owns half a million shares of the holding company that owns the paper and is a golf buddy of the publisher."

It was a quarter till nine the next morning when I got back uptown to the MacNeils' apartment. Katherine and Laurie had just returned from taking B.J. and Cici to school. The three of us were sitting in the kitchen talking about the splash Abie had made in the media when my phone rang. I didn't recognize the number, but I answered.

"Porter," said Vane with pinched elegance. "Meet me at One Hundred Twenty-second Street and Riverside. Forty-five minutes. Inside, please. Are you familiar?"

"With Grant's Tomb?"

"Yes. I am so looking forward to this."

Laurie was at the window looking out at the blustery day. Katherine said, "Abie."

"He wants to meet."

"Why?" She pulled her lips in until they were almost gone.

"I have no idea, but it should be interesting."

"You're going?" she said, as Jack walked in.

His eyes were stone cold and distant. I looked at him. "You heard." He gave a small nod.

I went to the table and sat. Katherine was across from me and didn't look well. My phone rang. The ID said NYC

TRANSIT MUSEUM. Weird time for a museum to call, I thought. I killed it. The only reason museums ever call, in my experience, has to do with subscriptions, donations, and to get you to buy tickets to a fundraiser.

I laid the phone on the table and tried to think what Vane might want. I wasn't worried about my own safety since we were meeting at a national monument mid-morning on a weekday and there would be people around. My phone rang again. Again, the Transit Museum. But this time tumblers in my head started clicking into place, lining up, and a moment later the door to the vault I call my brain opened wide. But even before I could see inside I knew what was there, or at least part of it. My heart was close to stopping and I struggled to breathe. I looked at Katherine, who was looking at my phone. She was as white as the porcelain of her cup.

She said, "The field trip." Her hand was trembling.

I lifted the phone. "Jack's friend, the one on the board of the Transit Museum. What's his name?" I hit the answer button but kept my eyes on Katherine.

Her hands were shaking so hard she had to set her cup down to keep from spilling her coffee. "Abel Vane."

57

THE VOICE ON THE OTHER END WAS CHIRPY. "OH, GOOD morning, Mr. Hall, this is Jenna Paggi, one of B.J.'s and Cici's teachers. Sorry to bother you, but we're at the Transit Museum and, you know, I'm sure it's nothing, but, well, a little something has come up."

"What, Jenna?"

"It's nothing I'm sure but…have you been to the museum?"

"Why are you calling?"

"Well, we were watching this movie called *River of Steel*, very interesting…"

"My kids are missing."

"And…how did you know?"

"Call security, tell them to put the building in total lockdown, immediately. No one in, no one out. Then call 911."

"Mr. Hall, do you really think that's necessary?"

"Jenna. Now." I hung up.

Truthfully, I didn't think it was necessary. Truthfully, I thought it was too late.

The terror lasted only a moment for all of us. Except Laurie, who wasted no time on it at all.

Katherine stood. "I'll go to the museum."

Jack said, "Ike's back. Take the car."

"What about Porter?"

"I'll take a cab."

Katherine said, "You're still going to meet Abel, after this?"

"It's even more important now."

Katherine grabbed her bag, went to the elevator, and Jack called the museum to talk to security. I turned to Laurie but she wasn't there. She wasn't anywhere else in the apartment either.

Her purse, which usually sat on the dresser in her bedroom, was there and her phone was next to it. Bad sign. She left it so she couldn't be tracked. She would either go look for the children herself, or go after Vane, alone. I went to Jack's closet to inventory the guns. He was already there.

"Did she take one?" I said.

"No. They're all accounted for." He picked up a Beretta. "It's a three-and-a-half inch barrel so it fits your pocket. Take it."

I started to say something. He added, "If you have it and don't need it, fine. If you need it and don't have it, you're dead."

"You think he's going to shoot me in a public place?"

He pushed his jaw out. "I made a promise to Katherine I'd quit calling you an idiot. Don't make me break it." He held the gun. "9mm, manual safety, 10 plus one. Shoot him, not yourself." He handed me the pistol.

"What's Laurie doing?"

"I have no idea."

I said, "Well, at least she didn't take a gun."

He let out a grim chuckle. "Oh, yeah, that makes it all better."

"We're screwed, aren't we?"

"Yeah."

58

RIVERSIDE DRIVE IS ONE OF THE MOST BEAUTIFUL THOR-
oughfares in the city, snaking seventy blocks through tall trees
along the crest of a hill, the Hudson River below it on the west,
and, on the other side, stately pre-wars, once home to the likes
of Babe Ruth and William Randolph Hearst.

I spent most of the ride wondering what Laurie was planning
to do. The fact that she hadn't taken a gun, as Jack noted, meant
nothing. If she wanted a gun, she'd get one. If she wanted an ar-
mored personnel carrier, she'd get one of those. I couldn't control
Laurie, and I avoided thinking about B.J. and Cici. I needed a
clear head. I couldn't worry about what I couldn't control.

GRANT'S TOMB SITS on a pear-shaped parcel past Riverside
Church. The memorial has eight columns that support a dome

over an interior rotunda. I paid the cabbie, stuck the gun in the small of my back under my belt, and got out. I looked around, didn't see Laurie, which didn't mean she wasn't there. I went to find Vane.

Inside the monument, atop the high walls that supported the rotunda, were four mosaics. In the middle, protected by a granite railing , is an opening to the floor below, where the sarcophagi of President Grant and his wife reside. The monument is free, but it has few visitors, because there's not much to see.

The mosaic on the east wall depicted the surrender of Robert E. Lee to Grant at Appomattox Court House. Vane was looking up at it. My urge was to end it quickly, but that wouldn't get my children back. Abie had set this scene for drama, and I had to play it his way.

I circled the other direction, gazed briefly at the exhibits, peeked over the railing to the floor below where the Grant's lay, and made my way slowly around the circumference.

Vane was wearing a gray tweed topcoat with a black velvet collar, and a gray derby. His hands rested on the handle of a silver-tipped umbrella. He didn't look at me as I approached, but spoke upward to the mosaic. "One of the great moments in American history, I believe." He looked at me. "Who was the better general?"

"Where are my children?"

"Are we to dispense with all pretense of civility?"

"I'm being civil. Where the hell are they?"

He made a *harrumph* sound that could have come out of a Dickens character. "Well, Porter, for the moment, they're safe. As to what will happen later, that's entirely up to you. What else would you like to discuss?"

"Did you have Jamie killed?"

"Come, come, come. Must we be so insouciant?" His mouth turned into a small O, and his eyebrows formed a V, as though he simply could not comprehend how anyone could be so impolite. "Let's step outside." We walked together out the door and down the first flight of steps. On the landing between flights he stopped. "If it were anyone's fault, it was hers."

"Well, of course it was her fault. She got herself kidnapped."

"It was a pity," he said with mocking sincerity, "but I was able to use it. That's my gift. Whatever is given me, I use. If you give me dirt, I will pile it six-feet high and bury you. Give me information, why that's my *franca lingua,* worth more than gold. Why do you think we put that security system in?"

I gave him a blank look. I had heard Marvin's version, but I wanted to hear his.

He sighed, annoyed I wasn't holding up my end of the discussion. "Doormen are rather imperfect sources of information, Porter. A video record of an event, say an escort visiting a city councilman, now that is priceless. Or at least ten thousand dollars. And the resident doesn't even have to call the escort. Someone else can. On video it looks the same. It's a lot to explain to your husband, wife, constituents."

"Got it, " I said. "You're running the standard protection-slash-extortion racket, except you do it for the rich, famous, and powerful."

He poked me with his finger. "Exactly. You are a bright boy. Why shake down some bodega owner when you can shake down a Fortune 500 CEO. No wonder Jack likes you."

"And if a developer, for example, didn't pay you off, they'd be up to their water tanks in strikes and material shortages and hard-ass inspectors. Am I right?"

"Assuming they ever got their permits to start with. Many complain about bureaucracies, but from my point of view, the more burdensome, the better.

"Remember that building in the low Seventies, the one the developer completed and then the city made him take two stories off the top?"

"Yes."

He smiled. "One of my greatest successes. They were an hour away from a judge ordering them to take the whole building down."

"Ah, yes, judges. Which is why two of them, back-to-back, set my bail at ten million. It was a message that I was out of my league."

The smile went away. "I was livid you even got bail on the murder charge. Someone is still going to pay for that. Still, I thought twenty million would keep you there. And it would have except for that damn that Clancy Hamilton. I had no idea you even knew him, let alone that you had something on him to cause him to help you."

I laughed. "I didn't know him, and I didn't have *something on him*, as you say. I once helped someone he cares about."

He made a disgusted face, and brushed invisible lint from his sleeve.

"People do that, Abie. Jack helped you many times. Do you think it was because he thought someone as insignificant as you was ever going to help someone like him? Get real."

His cheeks turned bright red. "I am not..." He looked away to compose himself. "Jack..." His face sank. "John betrayed me. I thought we were so much more. He risked his life for me, twice. I just knew we were more. If you risk your life for someone..." He shook his head.

"Abie, one question, one thing I don't get. Why let Marvin run a penny-ante supply skim? That's high-risk. And to you it was chump change."

Now that the subject had shifted from Jack, he relaxed a little. "True, but it didn't just go to Marvin. It was spread around to people like you. Boards of large buildings, as you know, control tens of millions of dollars. They're like a taxing authority that can tax at will, no approval necessary. You wouldn't believe how many board members I have in my pocket." He shook his head as though deeply hurt again. "But you, Porter, you misled me, or perhaps Plockman did. I thought I had you. Once again, I was betrayed. And I hate betrayal. When I look at you, I think, *deceit*. You're a monster, you know."

I started to say, *No, you're the monster*, but there was no adult around to settle that argument.

He turned and I followed him across the plaza to a large tree and stood so close his left shoulder was brushing the massive trunk.

I said, "Do your remember what happened to Yojimbo?"

"I am quite certain you're going to tell me."

"He got beat to within an inch of his life."

"Yes, but in the end he won."

"Only because the people he helped risked their lives for him."

"Your point, if you have one?"

"Your friends want you dead. You don't even need enemies." I stepped closer so that we were inches apart. He took a half step back and glanced toward the monument.

"Get this over with. Abie. Why are we here?"

"I have a final offer." He glanced to his right, again, and focused on some bushes next to the front steps where there was a man who looked like a maintenance worker.

I said, "I'm listening."

"Leave. Now. Today. Go to Texas or South Dakota or Nebraska and I will leave you alone. Take your children, your wife, your girlfriend, your mother-in-law, whomever. Get the hell out of my city and don't come back."

"I would love to, Abie, but I can't. We're in the middle of a school year, and I've paid the full tuition. No refunds."

"You think this is funny?"

"Ironic," I said, "not funny. If I were in your slippers, I'd be the one hitting the road. Someone is going to kill you, Abie."

"So it would seem, Porter, but I took a page from your book. I have prepared a document for dissemination in the event of my demise. It contains information that would embarrass some people and put others in prison. I have spoken with those involved and everything, it seems, is copasetic. Any residual animosity will blow over in a few days. They need me." He straightened up, lifted his chin.

I raised one eyebrow. "The mob needs you?"

"Mobs," he said, drawing out the *s*. "Legal and illegal, from Wall Street to Midtown to Rego Park and Brighton Beach, this town is full of them. And the mayor needs me, and the city council, the unions, even the legislature. And they know it." He spoke in a low voice through clinched teeth. "Every damn one of them knows it, and they won't forget. I won't let them."

A sound came from his pocket. *Ding-dong-ding-dong.*

His eyes sparkled like a kid who'd just heard the music of the ice cream truck. "Excuse me."

He said, "Viko." He listened, nodded, smiled. "I understand, Viko. Calm down. Call me back in five minutes. I'll give you final instructions."

His eyes narrowed. "You're not going to ask about your little ones?" He dropped his phone into a small pocket in the front of his coat.

"Is it a coincidence they had a field trip to the Transit Museum today?"

He reached out and squeezed my arm. "Oh my. Are you one of those bumpkins who believes in coincidence? Santa Claus, too? You are too delicious."

"Where are they?"

"On a special tour of the city. According to their escort that girl of yours is something else, a real pistol. The boy, on the other hand, seems to be ill. He's in the back lying down."

"The back of what?"

"A small coach, a nice one. I borrowed it from a tour company."

There was a tell there, though Abie didn't know it. B.J. was prone to motion sickness, though not as badly as his sister, and knew better than to ride in the back of any large vehicle. If he was all the way in the back the bus, he was trying to make himself sick, or...I didn't know, but there was a reason. It suggested the kids understood their situation. Still, it was two six-year-olds against Abie's thugs.

"Aren't you going to demand their return, threaten me?"

I tried to slow my breathing. "What do you want, Abie, really?"

"I already told you. Leave. Move to a different time zone. Stay out of my way." He glanced at his watch.

"Done. Bring my children to me and we'll leave this afternoon."

"Oh, Porter." He put his hand on my arm and squeezed. "I liked it better when you were telling the truth. Lying is so common."

He glanced at the bushes again. "I can work with almost anyone. That's my job, and I'm superb at it. Unfortunately, you are an exception. Not only that, but you have come between John and me. I'm sorry. I really am."

Abie pulled his hand away, touched his hat and again looked toward the bushes.

My right hand went to the handle of the gun in my waistband. There was a rifle shot and a foot above my head a chunk of bark flew off the tree. We were both looking toward the monument and the man beside it. He suddenly dropped to the ground and fell face forward.

Abie's hand went to his pocket as mine came around. I was faster, but the tail of my jacket was between my hand and the handle of the gun. I lost my grip and the Beretta spun to the ground a few feet away.

Abie was holding a small, silver semi-automatic. He said, "It is so hard to find good help these days, don't you agree? But this is even better. You had a gun so it's clearly self-defense. And I get to kill you myself. You have no idea how happy that makes me."

As he raised his gun toward my chest there was a soft THUD. Abie fell sideways into the tree, and blood began to gush from his throat. An arrow was sticking out of his neck. His eyes bulged and his jaw dropped. A heartbeat later another arrow went through his ear. Others followed.

I took a step back and looked toward the bushes. A figure in a flowing green cloak ran away. A moment later, from behind the monument, a large black horse emerged at full gallop. The horse and rider ran onto Riverside Drive and followed it for a ways, the sleek animal's hooves clacking time on the asphalt. They cut between two cars and onto the turf of Sakura Park. the cloak surging and flapping with the hoof beats of the shining animal. They disappeared.

Then there were sirens, and Abie's phone began to ring, that same *ding-dong-ding-dong* as before. I grabbed at the pocket where he had put it, but he started to slide toward the ground, his dead weight too much for the arrow shafts. He flopped onto his back. His legs were buckled beneath him, and his eyes were open wide to the sky. He was soaked in blood. How could someone so small could have so much blood in him, I wondered.

The sirens were getting close, coming from every direction. I dropped to my knees and grabbed at the phone. As I pulled it from his pocket the sirens stopped.

I hit the button to answer. There were police officers, one barely out of arms reach, and others arriving. One told me to get face down on the ground and put my hands above me.

Some had nightsticks raised, others had guns drawn. One yelled, "Put it down, now."

I had to take that call. Had to.

I showed them the phone and slowly moved it to my ear. One was a young woman, very young, looked barely old enough to be out of high school. I looked her in the eye, nodded calmly, tried to create a bond.

Her eyes were full of fear. She would kill me because she didn't know what else to do. A voice said, "Vane, Mr. Vane. What we do? Keep, deliver, get rid of? What?"

To the officer five feet away, I said softly, "My children have been kidnapped. This is about them."

My hand was bloody and the phone was covered with blood. No matter what she had been taught in the academy, this was different. This was real. My eyes were begging her.

Finally, she nodded.

"Drive more," I said.

"Vane! Who is this?"

She glanced above and behind me, and nodded. I felt a sharp blow to my neck, my shoulder, my arm, my side, my legs. Another and another.

59

I DIDN'T LOSE CONSCIOUSNESS, BUT I WISH I HAD. ROUGHLY they put me in the back of a cruiser. I was in cuffs, and chained to the D-ring. They took me to a stationhouse I'd never been to and turned me over to some other cops who put me in a cell. After some time, a man dressed in an EMS uniform came into my cell and said, "Come with me, please." He extended his hand.

"Where?"

"Hospital."

I held out a hand. "I've got to go find my children."

I got halfway up and fell back. I felt like a jockey who'd fallen in the home stretch and been run over by the field.

I looked up. "I've got to look for my children."

He spoke to someone and in a couple of minutes a wheeled stretcher arrived and they took me away.

OUTSIDE, AN EMS bus waited. Watching, were two men in suits. Both had unhappy faces. One was Clancy Hamilton, and the other I didn't know.

Clancy said, "You've seen him. You can go now."

The man looked at Clancy, hesitated, started to leave then said, "Come on, Clancy, it was a misunderstanding, a couple of good people doing their job. A tough job, I might add."

"Try nine. Nine out of control people. They may have been dressed like cops, but they were a mob in uniform."

"But Clancy…"

"An unarmed citizen asks for help and their *tough job* is to beat him and arrest him? Send me a copy of that particular *tough job* description for my files."

"Listen, Clancy…"

"And while you're locating that one, Gene, find me the one where it says the staff at a city museum is to aid and abet a kidnapping. Of minors. Can you do that for me?"

They wheeled me out and Clancy walked alongside.

I said, "My kids."

Clancy looked down. "Everyone is looking, everyone. Police, FBI, your father-in-law, the *New York Journal*. The good news is there's no bad news."

"What time is it?"

"Two."

"Did I call you?"

"Cat Marten did. You know Vane's..."

"Yeah. I remember that part."

Clancy squeezed my forearm. I winced. He said, "I'll see you at the hospital."

AN HOUR LATER I was at Columbia Presbyterian. They had cleaned me up, put some stitches in my face, and moved me to a deluxe private room, the sort usually reserved for major donors and politicians and members of the Rolling Stones. Clancy appeared at the door.

"You look a little better," he said.

"It would've been hard to look worse."

"That's true."

"Who was that at the jail?"

"An old friend, or maybe an old ex-friend. He's the chief corporation counsel for the city. When this is over you may be rich. The cops lost it, and there are several videos. Along with what happened at the Transit Museum, you may never need to work again. The city is taking care of the hospital bills, and I haven't even threatened to sue them."

Clancy removed his phone from his pocket and listened.

"Excuse me for a moment, Porter." He stepped into the hall.

A few seconds later someone said, "Hey." Cat was in the doorway.

I searched her face for bad news or good news but there was no news in it at all. She walked in followed by Laurie.

Laurie came to one side. "Hi, sweetie."

Cat leaned against the bed on the other side.

"The kids?" I said.

Cat said, "What kids?" She looked at Laurie.

Laurie said, "These kids?" and looked toward the door.

60

B.J. RAN TO ME, AND CICI WALKED SLOWLY, HEAD TILTED down. B.J. jumped on the bed and hugged me. Cici stood next to it until Laurie lifted her. After a moment she laid her head on my chest. "Hi, Dad." I looked at Laurie and raised an eyebrow, wondering what the problem was.

Katherine came in a moment later. There were some glances and Katherine said, "Okay, kids, you heard the doctor. Your father needs rest. You can see him tomorrow." B.J. went reluctantly, and Cici was out the door before Katherine finished her sentence.

I said, "What's up with Cici? What happened? How did they get rescued?"

Cat said, "So far, this is the story. Vane had the help of an employee at the museum, who separated them from their class after they watched a movie. There was a van waiting with a man and a woman, a brother and sister from some Eastern block country, who worked for Vane. They drove around Long

Island for several hours, ate at a McDonald's, and the man kept trying to get ahold of Vane to find out what he was supposed to do with them. The kids realized they'd been kidnapped."

"How did they get found?"

Cat and Laurie looked at each other. Cat smiled. "Cici had her phone in her sock. Eventually, she told B.J. about it and gave it to him. He went to the back seat and called you. You were probably in jail by then. He tried Jack and Katherine and Laurie and finally me. I was at the office. He was speaking Spanish so the captors wouldn't understand if they heard him. I got someone to translate, told him to call 9-1-1 and hold, just keep the line open so they could track it. I called and told them B.J. was calling in and what was happening. They had them stopped in six minutes."

Laurie said, "So Cici thinks she's in trouble again because she didn't leaver her phone in her cubby. And B.J. was almost as upset as Cici because they ate at McDonald's and you never let them eat there. He said to tell you he only had a fish sand-wich and no fries."

61

A FEW WEEKS LATER ELIZABETH WINSLOW CALLED AND ASKED me to lunch. We reconstructed the events from Jamie's disappearance to my final confrontation with Vane. When the table had been cleared and we were sitting with coffee, she said, "Porter, I know."

"Know what?"

"Who killed Vane."

"That's great. Have you made an arrest?"

"Stop it."

"What?"

"Bullshitting me."

I sipped my coffee. "About what?"

"I know her, remember. And we found the horse. A former racehorse named Mr. Inside Trader."

"What did he say?"

"Unfortunately, it wasn't Mr. Ed, so he kept his mouth shut. And you don't have to say anything, but I know you know. too. I've known her since I played junior tennis against her at twelve. As soon as I heard what happened, I knew it was her." She sipped her coffee, set it down, continued.

"A woman, who keeps her horse in the stables in Central Park, had just come back from a ride. Another woman comes out, says she'll take the horse. The woman thinks it's someone who works there. She didn't get a look at the other woman because she stayed on the far side of the horse. Trader, as they call him, was missing for a little over an hour, right around the time of the incident at Grant's Tomb, and found tied up later in the parking lot. He was a little lathered, but fine. Probably the most fun that horse has had since he quit racing."

"Does anyone else know?"

She shook her head. "Not as far as I know."

"What are you going to do?"

"Nothing. By avoiding the prosecution of Vane and putting him in prison, I figure the city, state, and federal government saved millions. If it were up to me I'd give Laurel MacNeil Hall a tickertape parade. But that would blow her cover."

She extended her hand across the table. I took it and held it a moment. She said, "I need to get back to the office."

I said, "One more thing."

She pulled her hand back and her face hardened. "No, Porter, don't go there. Please."

Her battered woman defense system shot up like deflector shields.

"I wasn't going to."

"Then what?"

I pulled out a thumb drive and slid it across the table.

"I was in Vane's will."

Her head tilted forward and she stared at the small device.
"What?"

"During one of our conversations he told me he had put together a dead man's switch, a fail safe, and let his enemies know that if he died all of their secrets would be spilled. A couple of days before he died he amended his will and left certain things to me. This is one of them."

"Why you? He hated you."

"That was my reaction. But according to Jack's analysis, as much as Vane hated me, he respected me. He knew I was ethical since he spent years trying to bribe me and it didn't work."

"What are you going to do with all of it?"

"I don't know. We don't even know everything that's there, yet. It's coded and we only found the key a couple of days ago."

She looked at the black and green plastic housing that held eight gigs of data and videos.

"So what's this?"

"Files and videos on Russell Lewsky."

"My boss? Interesting. What do you want me to do with it?"

"It's up to you. But the next time he tries to prosecute someone you know is innocent, you've got leverage."

She smiled, dropped it in her pocket and slipped out of the booth. She started to leave, but after a few steps came back. "Porter, it's not that I don't want help with, you know…"

She couldn't even say *abuse*.

"I don't what to do, how to handle it. Right now, I'm hanging on, trying to survive. But thank you. I know I can call you.

Someday, I may. If and when that happens, you may wish I hadn't. Because when it gets to that point, it's not going to be easy."

She turned and was gone, slicing effortlessly through the surly lunch crowd, which parted before her. A minute later her profile passed outside the window with the establishment's name and year of founding written in two colors of paint, the message backwards, as in a mirror.

Epilogue

THANKSGIVING I TOOK THE KIDS TO NEW JERSEY. THERE were about a hundred people at dinner, many from Jack's office, and others who had no place else to go. In the late afternoon, after the guests were gone, Laurie and I were sitting on a stone bench in the backyard watching the kids play. Without looking she said, "Do you want to ask me?"

We both knew what she was talking about, but she added, "What happened? Why I left?"

"Yes."

"I'll tell you, if you want me to, but if I do, bad things will happen."

"To whom?"

She faced me. "All of us. It can't be fixed or changed and it's going to be bad because of what you will do."

"I won't have a choice?"

"Having a choice won't help, because you can't change who you are."

"Will I find out anyway, eventually?"

"Maybe. But the longer you don't know, the better it is for the kids, and me, and especially for you. And the more time that passes the more chance there is you'll never know, that you'll never have to know."

It was a conundrum. As badly as I wanted to know, I trusted Laurie's judgment more than my own. I had lived without knowing for more than three years.

"Then I won't ask."

"Thank you." Her smile was grateful and sad. "Thank you."

At that moment Cici ran up, and B.J. a few paces behind. She stopped in front of Laurie and said, "Mom, we're cold." Laurie touched her face, and I did the same to B.J.'s. I was an only child for most of my life and I never ceased to be amazed how my two were able to speak for each other. I wondered if other siblings were like that.

Laurie stood and each of them took one of her hands and they went inside. I sat for a few minutes and watched the darkness come down and settle itself on the horizon. When the day was completely gone, I followed them inside, leaving the hills and forest to fade into the winter and night.

About the Author

David Hansard has worked on a road crew in North Dakota, built snow fences in Wyoming, taught English, pumped diesel fuel, and been involved in real estate among other things, some of which he has forgotten. He is a native of Wyoming, or Texas, or both, but spent more years in New York City, where *One Minute Gone* is set. He now lives and writes in Colorado Springs. The second novel in the Porter Hall series, *Blue-Eyed Boy*, will be released in the fall of 2013.

Acknowledgements

When it comes to transforming thousands of words into a decent and readable form, writing is anything but solitary. This conversion would not have happened without many, but most critically, the following:

My critiqueros, the Greater Austin Mystery Writers: Julie Burns, Jerry Cavin, Heidi Johnson, Donna Snyder and Bill Woodburn, all fine writers and good friends. And, from the earliest drafts, Rachel Brady, who was an insightful and reassuring presence.

Sue Preston, for her precise and thorough editing.

Keith Snyder at Typeflow, who made the unformed manuscript look like a thing worth reading.

And, most importantly, my family, without whom it's just not worth it. You are my blessing.

David Hansard
Colorado Springs, September 2013

Printed in Great Britain
by Amazon.co.uk, Ltd.,
Marston Gate.